D0483802

Healing Hearts

Healing Hearts

PROPER ROMANCE

SARAH M. EDEN

SHADOW
MOUNTAIN

Library of Congress Cataloging-in-Publication Data
Names: Eden, Sarah M., author.
Title: Healing hearts / Sarah M. Eden.
Description: Salt Lake City, Utah : Shadow Mountain, [2019]
Identifiers: LCCN 2018016728 | ISBN 9781629724584 (paperbound)
Subjects: LCSH: Nurses—Fiction. | Physicians—Fiction. | Wyoming, setting.
   | Nineteenth century, setting.
Classification: LCC PS3605.D45365 H43 2019 | DDC 813/.6—dc23
LC record available at https://lccn.loc.gov/2018016728

Printed in Canada
Marquis Printing, Montreal, Quebec, Canada

10   9   8   7   6   5   4   3   2

To the hours of 1 to 3 a.m.
Without you, this book would have
taken far longer to complete.

Chapter 1

Savage Wells, Wyoming Territory, 1876

Miriam Bricks sat in the cramped and rancid interior of a rickety stagecoach and contemplated for the hundredth time how fortunate she was to be there. In many ways, being pressed between two passengers—one of whom clearly hadn't bathed in months, perhaps years, and neither of whom had stopped arguing since embarking that morning—was still an improvement over her previous circumstances.

The swaying of the coach had left her ill, her body had grown painfully stiff, her head pounded, and she was hungry and exhausted. But more than anything, she was grateful.

When a person had been confined to a cold, heartless mental institution, even the most uncomfortable, miserable moments spent in freedom were a welcome improvement.

Beyond her independence, she had a new job in a new town where no one had any idea about her past. She could make a fresh start. She could rebuild her life.

Yes. She was desperately grateful.

The stagecoach came to a rocking, jarring halt in Savage Wells, her new home. Miriam didn't waste a moment but opened the stagecoach door and clamored out, clutching tightly to her worn, leather-covered sketchbook. She pulled in a breath of blessedly fresh air. Her eyes scanned the tall, well-kept buildings and colorful storefronts and the crowd of people gathered at the stage stop.

The bureau only had a scant bit of information for her, none of which described Dr. MacNamara, the man who'd hired her to work as a nurse. She'd assumed he would be the only one to meet the stage, but an entire crowd stood there, watching her.

She'd heard the ratio of women to men was lopsided out West. That appeared to be entirely true. But which of the many men standing about watching her was the man she was looking for? And who were the others there to see?

She checked the stagecoach once more. The other passengers were filing into the nearby restaurant. The townspeople were all watching *her*, then. She was not generally shy, but this was overwhelming. She folded her arms around her sketchbook and pressed it to her heart like a shield.

"I'm—I'm looking for Dr. MacNamara," she said to all of them at once.

Chuckles and grins spread through the crowd. That was not reassuring. Miriam inched back toward the stagecoach.

An older lady, seventy years if she was a day, stepped forward, reaching out to take one of Miriam's hands in her own. "He wanted to meet the stage, but a patient came by. I'm certain with all of your nursing experience you know how unpredictable things can be."

She nodded. She was well aware of the chaotic nature of the medical profession.

The woman smiled warmly, almost maternally. "But that is why you're here, isn't it? To help our dear doctor."

"Yes. That is why I am here." It was the one reason she was willing to admit to.

"Gideon said he'll meet up with us as soon as he's able." The woman hooked her arm through Miriam's. "The entire town has gathered. We are all so happy for our doctor. He has needed someone for such a long time."

The crowd followed behind as Miriam was led up the street. "The town must be very fond of Dr. MacNamara."

The woman gave her an amused sideways glance. "I am certain you can call him Gideon."

Miriam had never called any of the doctors she'd worked for by their given names. She knew social niceties were often more lax in the West, but being that familiar would take a great deal of getting used to. And, yet, winning Dr. MacNamara's trust was crucial to her success in Savage Wells. As was, apparently, enduring the crowd of people keeping pace with her nameless guide.

"I hadn't expected such a welcome." She hadn't wanted one, truth be told.

"We are so happy you are here. Ever since Gideon told us, we've been beside ourselves trying to think of a way to welcome you properly, to support the both of you."

All of this over the arrival of a nurse? Either this was the most friendly town in all the world or the most ill.

They continued down the street at such a fast clip that Miriam hardly had time to register the buildings they passed. She would need to take time later to familiarize herself with the place, perhaps sketch the main street so she could commit it to memory. Growing accustomed to the horde of people would take a bit longer. She hoped they wouldn't follow her about on a daily basis. Secrets were far more easily kept from a distance.

"Does Dr. MacNamara see a lot of patients?"

"Oh, yes. He is the only doctor in a hundred miles, further in some directions. People come from all over to see him, and he travels all over to see them. He is sometimes gone for weeks at a time."

That was precisely what Miriam needed. Solitude. Quiet. Peace. The asylum had never been peaceful. Not ever. And every movement, every breath, every word it seemed, had been watched and controlled. In Savage Wells, she would finally be free again.

The older woman led Miriam toward a schoolhouse, one surrounded by wagons and buggies and horses tied to hitching posts. More people gathered around, adding to the crowd trickling up from behind her

"Oh, Mrs. Wilhite!" A woman older than Miriam but not nearly as old as Miriam's companion hurried up, hands clasped in front of her. "Is this Miriam?"

Mrs. Wilhite—it helped having a name for her guide—nodded enthusiastically. "Yes. And isn't she lovely? She seems nervous, though." She turned her gaze on Miriam. "Are you nervous, dear?"

Several dozen people were watching her, most of whom had followed her all the way from the stagecoach. "I am, a bit."

"Well, what woman in your situation wouldn't be?" Mrs. Wilhite patted Miriam's hand. "But we can assure you that Gideon is so kind and gentle and caring. He really is a wonderful person."

She was glad to hear it. Dr. Blackburn at the asylum had been nothing short of a monster.

Mrs. Wilhite still had one of Miriam's arms hooked through hers. The newly arrived woman claimed Miriam's other one. Together they pulled her toward the schoolhouse.

"Have you met Sheriff O'Brien yet?" the new woman asked.

"I have not even met *Dr. MacNamara* yet."

"He wouldn't miss this, I promise you." The two women laughed. Miriam wasn't sure what was so amusing.

They quickly took the three stairs up to the schoolhouse and stepped inside. Flowers filled the interior, and a shocking abundance of ribbon framed the windows, tied in bows along the rows of benches, and adorned the lectern at the front of the room as well as a nearby table that held a cake and punch bowl, along with piles of plates and cutlery. Savage Wells, it seemed, spared no effort in welcoming a new citizen.

Mrs. Wilhite remained at Miriam's side, though her other companion slipped away into the crowd. The townsfolk trickled in, filling in the rows of seats. She received smiles and hand squeezes and an unending supply of "Welcome to Savage Wells" and "So pleased to meet you."

She had accepted the job in Savage Wells in part because it was so isolated; she was unlikely to encounter anyone who knew her or her past. If the town reacted this way to new arrivals, perhaps it was even more isolated than she'd realized.

"Oh, there's Gideon!" Mrs. Wilhite actually bounced a little.

"Which one is he?" Miriam asked.

"He's standing up at the front, of course." Mrs. Wilhite swatted at her teasingly, quite as if Miriam ought to have been able to identify a man who was a stranger to her.

Three men stood near the lectern. One was older than the others and appeared to be a preacher. The tallest of the three sported a gun belt and wore a silver sheriff's badge pinned to his leather vest. Dr. MacNamara must have been the third man.

He was younger than she'd expected, likely not even thirty. His clothes were finely cut and fashionable. His tailcoat and red silk waistcoat would not have been out of place in even the finest drawing rooms back East. And he was handsome, with his nearly black hair and gray eyes. Not that any of those things truly mattered in an employer; they were simply the first things she noticed. That likely made her shallow, she chided herself, but she had nothing else to go on. She knew of him only through what the employment bureau had told her: his profession, a few details of his education to assure her he was a legitimate doctor, and his need for a nurse.

Mrs. Wilhite took Miriam up to the front. "Here she is, Gideon." She hugged him tightly. "Oh, I'm so happy for you." She looked from Gideon to Miriam, dabbed at her eyes with a handkerchief, then stepped away.

This town places a great deal of importance on their medical treatment.

"You are Miriam Bricks?" Dr. MacNamara asked.

She nodded.

"Welcome." His smile could have melted a glacier. It sent warmth straight to Miriam's cheeks. "I am sorry if the town has overwhelmed you with their enthusiasm. I lost control of all of this the moment I told them about you."

"They are very kind." At least she hoped they were.

"I don't want to rush you," he said, "but the children aren't likely to wait much longer without diving for the cake."

"Of course, Dr. MacNamara," she said.

"Gideon. Please."

She gave a tiny nod, though she knew adjusting to that request would take some doing.

He turned toward the sheriff and the preacher. "I think we're ready."

The sheriff thumped Gideon on the shoulder and moved away. The preacher stepped up to the lectern. A hush fell over the gathering.

What had caught their attention so immediately? No one had called for quiet. Was this some kind of meeting rather than a welcoming party? The presence of cake made that unlikely.

The preacher pulled out a Bible and set it, opened, on the lectern. He looked over the room serenely. "Dearly beloved."

Dearly beloved?

"We are gathered today in the sight of God—"

A horrifying sense of familiarity slid over her. She knew this beginning. Worse still, she knew where it ended.

"—to join this man and this woman—"

Goodness gracious.

"—in the bonds of holy matrimony."

Her eyes threatened to pop out of their sockets. These were not words she'd anticipated at all.

"This is a wedding," she whispered.

Gideon nodded. "Yes."

This was a wedding. Gideon and *the preacher* were standing at the front of the room. Only one person would be placed there with them, as she was, and it wasn't because she was the newly arrived town nurse.

"This is *our* wedding." The strangled words clawed their way out of her.

Gideon nodded, again, but slowly. "Of course."

"I didn't—This wasn't—" *Goodness gracious.*

She tried to breathe through the ever-thickening lump in her throat. She took a frantic step backward, holding to her sketchbook with a viselike grip. Everyone was watching her, all having come expecting her to marry a man she'd never met, one whom she'd only agreed to *work for*.

Absolutely not. She hadn't fled one form of undeserved imprisonment in order to blindly accept another.

She did the only thing a woman could reasonably be expected to do in her situation: run.

Chapter 2

Gideon MacNamara was a man of experience; he knew what it was to be jilted. He pushed out a heavy breath, eyeing the fleeing mop of curly, copper hair. Why was it his fiancées continually ran away from him? Literally, in this case. "I suppose I had best go discover what pressing appointment she just remembered."

"That'd be the logical next step," his best friend, Cade O'Brien, said.

He turned toward the startled townsfolk who were all watching him with a mixture of horror and confusion. "Pardon me," he said. "It seems I have misplaced . . . someone."

He hurried from the room. Arranging for a wife by way of an agency was supposed to have been easier—less dramatic, at least—than traditional methods. Yet, there he was, chasing after yet another woman who'd undertaken a very expressive matrimonial exit.

Gideon found his missing bride quickly. She stood at the edge of the street, looking frantically in both directions. She clung to her thick leather notebook the way one would to a lifeboat on a sinking ship.

"The stage depot is to the right," he said.

She spun about, staring at him wide-eyed. It was the same panicked expression she'd worn ever since Reverend Endecott had started speaking. She'd seemed fine up until that moment. Apparently, the phrase "Dearly beloved" was more frightening than he'd realized.

"The stage has already left, though." He watched her as he spoke, trying to piece together what had inspired her sudden objection to this arrangement. "The next one won't come through until Tuesday."

She took a step backward. Gideon could hear the hum of voices behind him. The wedding guests, it seemed, hadn't been content to wait.

He lowered his voice, not wishing to make his humiliation even more public than it already was. "There are a great many people, myself included, who are quite curious to know why you changed your mind. Were you hoping for someone . . . younger? Wealthier? Not as breathtakingly handsome?" Humor had always been his shield in tense and uncomfortable situations.

She looked over her shoulder toward the empty depot, though she didn't leave. "I'm a nurse."

"I know. That was one of my requirements." Marrying a woman with medical knowledge and experience had been crucial to the success of this arrangement. He needed someone who would understand the professional demands on his time, especially when it took him away from town, as well as someone who could tend to people who came by in his absence.

She paced, her fingers fussing with the leather strap wrapped around her notebook. "I came here for a job, and that"—she pointed at the schoolhouse-turned-chapel—"was a *wedding*."

The pieces fell quite suddenly into place. "You didn't know you were coming as a bride."

"I came here for a job," she repeated.

He'd been clear in his correspondence with the Western Women's Bureau. They'd obviously understood the requirement about her education and expertise. They couldn't possibly have misunderstood that he was looking for a wife. But why would an organization with a reputation to uphold mislead a client so monumentally?

"Are you certain you didn't misunderstand?" he asked Miriam.

"I am not a simpleton." It was a fiercer response than he'd expected.

"I didn't say that you were."

Mrs. Wilhite stepped away from the crowd of wedding guests and moved determinedly toward them.

"What a mess," Gideon muttered.

Miriam's eyes lowered. She hugged her notebook to herself, turning away from everyone.

Mrs. Wilhite stepped closer to her, worry warring with hope in her wrinkled face. "Gideon really is a wonderful person. We all love him."

"But *I* don't."

This day kept getting better and better. "I appreciate your efforts, Mrs. Wilhite, but I don't think this is the best way to address this difficulty."

"But this wouldn't be difficult if only she realized how remarkable you are." Mrs. Wilhite always had been a very vocal supporter of his. "She should consider herself lucky to have been chosen by someone of your caliber."

He tossed Miriam an amused glance. He was determined not

to let his frustration boil over. She, however, didn't even crack a smile.

"He did *choose* you, after all," Mrs. Wilhite added with emphasis.

Miriam shook her head. "I understand that. I do. But *I* didn't choose *him*."

"You're turning him down?" Mrs. Wilhite could not have sounded more shocked.

"She has every right to," Gideon said. "No one should be forced to marry another, even if that person is shockingly handsome and disarmingly charming, as I clearly am. I realize it is difficult to believe, Mrs. Wilhite, but even my claims to being 'wonderful' might not appeal to every young lady."

"But—but this was supposed to be such a happy day for you." The poor woman looked ready to weep. Meanwhile, Miriam looked ready to run. Again.

Gideon motioned his anxious advocate aside. "I appreciate your defense of me, I truly do. But if Miss Bricks is set against the idea of marrying me, compelling her to do so will likely only make the situation worse than it already is."

"Oh, Gideon." Mrs. Wilhite clasped his hands with hers. "This is so horrible. We weren't too sure of your idea to send for a wife, but everything you told us about her and how excited you were—" She sighed. "We want you to be happy."

He kissed her wrinkled cheek. "When have you ever known me to be anything but happy?" He had learned from his father the art of appearing as though everything was grand, even when absolutely nothing was.

Mrs. Wilhite offered a tremulous smile.

He squeezed her hands. "Go tell the townsfolk to enjoy the cake and punch. There is no point letting it go to waste."

"Oh, Gideon." She looked near to tears. "You poor, poor man."

He would likely hear that sentiment from everyone he encountered. *Joy.*

"I need to see that Miss Bricks has a place to stay and a way home," he said.

"You are a good man." Her eyes darted toward Miriam, who was pacing in tiny circles nearby. "Perhaps if I told her again—"

He shook his head firmly. "She has made her wishes clear. Go on back inside. And try not to worry."

"We'll find someone for you," she promised.

He waved his hands in protest. "Please, don't. I would prefer to leave this aspect of my life alone for a long while."

She nodded, though reluctantly, and made her way back toward the schoolhouse and the crowd assembled on the front steps, watching Gideon's humiliation play out. He summoned his best look of amusement, despite not being at all amused, and waved merrily to them. There would be fewer questions and fewer pitying looks if he hid the true extent of his frustration and disappointment.

He turned back to Miriam and willed himself to see this current predicament through to some kind of conclusion. He was tired. Tired of the unending line of problems he had to address. Tired of women deciding they'd rather not marry him. Tired of returning home to an empty house day after day.

"The hotel has vacant rooms," he told her. "You can stay there until the stage comes through on Tuesday."

She didn't look at him. "I was whisked here so quickly, my trunk and traveling bag were left behind."

Whisked here. Everyone *had* been extremely excited. That had made the prospect of marrying a woman he hadn't met a little less nerve-racking. The bureau had provided him with a lot of information about Miriam. He'd been absolutely convinced they could have been as happy together as any married couple could reasonably expect to be. Happier than his parents, at least, which had been all he'd ever truly hoped for.

"I will ask after your trunk," he said.

"That is the hotel, just there above the restaurant?" She pointed at the building sitting at the corner of the street.

"Yes."

She didn't wait for further discussion but moved swiftly up the road, nearly at a run. Yet another would-be bride had decided she didn't want him. Three in a row.

Gideon let out a frustrated breath. This was not how the day was supposed to have played out. This was not how his *life* was supposed to have played out.

Chapter 3

Gideon lay on his sofa, staring up at the ceiling and wondering what horrible childhood misdeed had earned him the wrath of every vengeful god in existence.

Harriet Fulton had been the first to reject him, laughing coldly when he had asked for permission to court her. Eleanor Bainbridge had taken the experience to new heights, accepting his offer of marriage after a four-month courtship, only to change her mind mere days before the wedding, leaving him to make what explanation he could to their friends and family.

There hadn't been enough jests in the world to laugh his way through *that* nightmare. He'd had to grit his teeth, seethe, sigh, hurt, and swear he'd never set himself up for that kind of pain again.

And now Miriam Bricks, who was supposed to have been a perfect fit based on a logical, unemotional evaluation of the situation, had waited until they were actually in the church, in front of everyone, in the middle of the ceremony, to jilt him.

This was definitely the work of a spiteful deity or two.

The front door, out of sight of the parlor, squeaked as it

opened. He had long ago decided not to oil the hinges, preferring a bit of warning before bleeding and broken patients stumbled inside. This newest arrival, however, sounded neither ill nor injured.

Gideon knew the rhythm of Cade's confident stride. Everyone in Savage Wells did.

"You ain't dead, are you?" Cade asked. "It was only a jilting from a mail-order bride. It wasn't as though you were desperately in love with her."

"This is not a broken heart, Cade. This is exhaustion." He laid his arm across his eyes. "I need a nurse, badly. And I want a wife, because your ugly mug is the only one I see with any regularity, and that is more than any man can be expected to endure."

"You ain't the only one suffering." Cade's booted footfalls took him to the nearby chair. "You're near about the only company I'll have until the end of next week. Hawk's got my Paisley knee-deep in some difficulty or another out toward Laramie. I swear that man's purposely giving her overly long assignments."

Gideon appreciated the distraction from his own problems. "Hawk is probably punishing you for not following Paisley's lead and becoming one of his deputy marshals."

Cade humphed. "Hawk can keep right on asking. Won't do him any good."

Gideon lowered his arm, looking over at his friend. "You're very cross whenever your wife's away."

Cade tossed his hat onto an end table. He gave Gideon a look of clear warning. "If I hear you've whispered a word of my grumblings to her, I'll skin you alive. Slowly."

"Women are a great deal of trouble, my friend."

"That they are," Cade said. "What do you mean to do now?"

Gideon took a long, deep breath. "I'll go down to the cellar and fetch a bottle of MacNamara whiskey and drown my sorrows."

"I ain't no dull-witted clod, Gid. You're too responsible a doctor to incapacitate yourself, knowing a patient might arrive needing your help."

"I'll tell them there's a nurse at the hotel. She can see to them." There was a fair bit of irony in that. "See how simple I've made my life by bringing her here? I can finally rest when I'm ill, travel to other towns without leaving this one helpless, maybe even sleep now and then. It all worked out so perfectly."

"I'm sensing a touch of sarcasm, there, Doc."

"I'm applying a rather thick layer, Sheriff." Gideon sighed. "The Western Women's Bureau looked for six months before finding a nurse willing to come to this backwater. I have my doubts they'll be able to find another."

"I'd wager it wasn't the town that the women were unsure of."

Meaning, of course, it was marrying him that had given any possible candidates pause. "Maybe the bureau could tell them they're welcome to come and leave me at the altar. That seems to appeal to large swaths of the female population."

"You know, Miss Bricks is here already, and you need help. Have you thought about offering her the job she thought she was coming here for?"

"Are you cracked?" Gideon sat up enough to look over at Cade. "I can hardly think of a more awkward situation."

"You lying here crying about how tired you are ain't exactly comfortable," Cade muttered.

"Truth be told, I can't afford to pay her." Gideon wasn't about to be sidetracked. "A wife would have benefited from the income of the practice *and* the comforts it provided here in our home. That's far different than finding the money for a regular salary."

He dropped onto his back again, eyes trained on the ceiling. "I'd have to pay her enough for room and board. She certainly couldn't live here—not after today's disaster."

"It was a daft idea to begin with." Years of soldiering and sheriffing had all but drained Cade's well of empathy. "No matter how many details the bureau sent you, you'd still have been marrying a stranger."

"But so would she. We'd both have come into this expecting the same thing. There would have been no emotional complications, no heavy history to overcome." He shook his head. "It should have worked perfectly."

"'Should have' don't matter, friend. All you have is 'did,' and what your plan *did* was fail."

Gideon rolled himself off the sofa. As cathartic as the admittedly dramatic posture had been, he really didn't have time for theatrics. In deference to his wedding day, the town had solemnly promised not to suffer any illnesses or injuries, but he wasn't foolish enough to actually expect any such reprieve. It hadn't been a great day for making vows, after all.

"I suppose I'd better prepare for the inevitable flood of patients." He loved his job, but he wasn't feeling particularly fond of it in that moment.

Cade raised a single golden eyebrow, eyeing Gideon with annoyance. "Even if all you can give Miss Bricks is enough for room and board, it might suffice for now. What other choices does she have?"

There was some logic to his argument. And who wouldn't want to spend every day with a woman who had taken one look at him and promptly run away?

It would likely be deeply unpleasant. But what was a little

discomfort if it helped the town? Truth be told, it would help half the territory. That was why he became a doctor: to help.

"Do you think she'd consider it?" he wondered out loud.

"Only one way to find out."

Think, Miriam. Think. She'd worked her way out of stickier situations than this; surely she could sort this one out as well.

She paced the floor of the hotel room she was temporarily calling home. There had to be another doctor looking for a nurse. One who lived somewhere remote and relatively far from civilization and who was desperate enough to accept her first three years of employment history without batting an eye at the two-year gap that followed it. One who cared only that she could suture a wound and find a heartbeat. It would also be helpful if that doctor didn't expect her to marry him.

She sat on the bed, exhausted and overwhelmed. Finding employment was crucial; she hadn't money enough for a full week's lodgings.

Women in her situation, but without her knowledge and education, had few choices, none of which were pleasant. They would either be forced to marry whomever would take them, or earn their keep in the only profession available to unprotected and unskilled women. Miriam could find respectable work. In theory, at least.

Maybe Dr. MacNamara knew someone else in need of an employee. But how did one go about starting such a conversation?

"I don't want to marry you, but would you please help me find a job?"

She let her shoulders droop. This mess was not at all her fault, yet she was paying for it. All she'd wanted was the tiniest taste of freedom.

"The barest bit of it," she whispered to the empty room. "No more bars on windows. No locked doors. No hallways echoing with sobs and screams." She took a shuddering breath. "I just want to live again."

A knock at her door stopped Miriam mid-thought. Who would possibly be looking in on her? She didn't know anyone in town. And she'd taken such pains to cover her tracks. Surely she couldn't have been found so quickly.

She tucked her sketchbook in a bureau drawer. It wasn't particularly well hidden, but it wouldn't be immediately found.

Heart pounding, she opened the door an inch, peeking through the small opening. Dr. MacNamara stood on the other side. His unexpected but well-timed arrival could either be a good sign or a terrible omen.

"Miss Bricks." He gave a tiny nod of acknowledgment. "May I speak with you for a moment?"

"I haven't changed my mind," she warned.

"I have given up on matrimony, I assure you." He sounded entirely sincere. "I wish only to talk with you for a minute or two."

Seeing as she needed to talk with him as well, letting him in was more than reasonable. Why, then, was she so nervous? She had certainly faced more daunting situations.

She opened the door the rest of the way and motioned him inside. Life had taught her not to be too trusting, so she left it ajar.

"This is going to be uncomfortable," he said, turning to face her. "I want to establish that from the beginning so we can proceed with the same expectations." He stood with his hands shoved into the pockets of his coat, his shoulders hunched. "I need a nurse. Badly. And even with everything that happened this afternoon, I am hoping to convince you to stay."

Stay? Work *here* as she'd originally planned? That couldn't possibly be what he was suggesting. It seemed best to make certain she fully understood what he was asking, especially in light of the enormity of their earlier miscommunication. "You promised this wasn't a marriage proposal."

He held his hands up in a show of innocence. "It's not. I am offering you a job."

It seemed far too good to be true, and far too many people had lied to her over the past years.

"I need help." He pushed out a breath. "The town is growing, and with it, the number of patients I tend to. They also come in from surrounding towns, and I often travel to see those living in the far corners of the territory. I am only one person, and I am quickly reaching the limit of what I can do. I was hoping for a wife, but I need a nurse more."

She was never this lucky. "You're offering me the job I came here for originally?"

"More or less. But I can't pay you well, only enough for room and board. And, in the interest of full disclosure, I should tell you that at least part of your salary will likely be paid in eggs and fruit preserves, since that is how my patients generally pay me."

Work for a man who'd fully intended to marry her sight unseen? There had to be an angle in this, something more he was aiming at. Else, why would he be willing to subject himself daily to the very discomfort they were both feeling?

"I would simply work as a nurse? That's it? Nothing else?"

"I assure you, that is all." He sounded just annoyed enough at the idea that she found herself believing him.

He was offering her a job, which she needed desperately. She could work for him, earn enough to see to her basic needs. She would be living a safe distance from Blackburn Asylum in a town few had ever heard of, let alone would think to search. Her stomach flipped a little. It was exactly what she needed, what she thought she'd come here for in the first place.

"I—I accept."

"Well, then. It is all settled." He didn't sound very enthusiastic. "I will see you at nine o'clock tomorrow morning."

She nodded. "Nine o'clock."

He moved his mouth, but didn't say anything more. His eyes darted around the room. His hands remained in his coat pockets.

After a moment, he nodded quickly and made his way from the room. The moment the door closed, she exhaled with both relief and anxious anticipation.

"This will work," she told herself.

She had to believe it. Without a safe haven, she was as good as dead.

Chapter 4

Miriam spent a half hour the next morning attempting to tame her tresses. She tried a bun, a knot, the front pulled back with the back left loose, all of it tied with a ribbon. In the end, only a tight braid would keep it in submission. Curly hair, she'd learned quite young, was not for the faint of heart.

It was not the best day to be fighting with her hair. Starting a new job was always nerve-racking. New people. New schedules. This time "We were almost accidentally married" and "I have reasons for being here that I am not being forthright about" contributed significantly to her discomfort.

She reached the front porch of Dr. MacNamara's house with only a minute to spare. His house was the largest she'd seen outside of New York. It stood three stories high, with a bay tower and a covered porch, the roof of which served as a balcony for the room above. Flowers grew along the short front walk. This was far more welcoming than the facade of Blackburn Asylum, which had resembled a prison on the outside. Inside, it had quite literally been one. No matter how awkward working with Dr.

MacNamara might prove, it could not possibly be worse than her two years at the asylum had been.

She tightly held her sketchbook, kept securely closed by a thin strap of leather. New beginnings were always unsettling. Heaven knew she'd had too many "new beginnings" to count. But what choice did she have?

She climbed the steps to the front porch and crossed to the door. Her courage didn't desert her. After a deep, reassuring breath, she knocked. The door opened.

"Right on time." The doctor even seemed happy to see her.

She stepped across the threshold, unsure what to expect. The interior was no less impressive than the outside. The banister and wood paneling could, perhaps, use a polish, but taken as a whole, the entryway was very fine. She hadn't expected anything like it in the wilds of the West.

"We'll be in here." Dr. MacNamara motioned her through a doorway to the left. "The parlor also acts as my medical office."

A sofa and two armchairs flanked the nearby fireplace. A desk and examination table sat at the far side of the room, where the windows formed the rounded bay tower. A tall, glass cupboard and shelves held vials and jars and tins of powders and ointments. She would wager that the drawers of the lowboy held bandaging and medical implements.

It was a nice arrangement, with plenty of space for both of the room's functions.

"There is a small room just past the staircase with a bed where patients can go for a little extra rest or recovery." Dr. MacNamara next pointed at the ceiling. "The two upper floors are all bed-chambers awaiting patients."

"You have room enough for an epidemic," she said.

He assumed a look of overdone pride. "That is the MacNamara

medical method: over-prepare for when things go incredibly wrong."

"'When,' not 'if'?" That seemed an important differentiation.

His mouth twisted in thought. "'When,'" he said after a minute. "I'm going to stick with 'when.'"

There was enough humor in his tone to tug a tiny, fleeting smile to the surface, despite her continued nervousness. He smiled as well. It was an unexpected moment of lightness between them. It helped.

He waved her over to the doctoring side of the parlor. "The vials and powders and such are all labeled. In the bottom drawers of the desk are the patient files. Anyone I've ever seen or treated has a file with everything anyone might need to know about their medical history."

He clearly kept meticulous records, and his workspace was tidy and organized. She would wager he was equally particular about medical matters. Dr. Blackburn had been the most fastidious doctor Miriam had ever known. The moment of connection she'd felt with Gideon disappeared. That he shared any characteristic with a man like Dr. Blackburn was reason for wariness.

"Over here is the washstand," he said, "the most important part of the room."

"The washstand is the most important?" She thought he was kidding, but a quick look at his expression told her otherwise.

"I would be ridiculed by most of my colleagues for my opinion on this, but I've extensively studied the writings of Semmelweis and Lister. They postulate a connection between the lack of cleanliness and a prevalence of disease and infection." He tapped the spine of a book in the bookcase behind his desk. "Semmelweis's proof isn't entirely conclusive, even combined with Lister's observations, but since the nearest hospital is days away, and I am the only help anyone in this area has, if there is any chance that washing my hands and instruments will help, I'll do it."

There was wisdom in that. "It couldn't do any harm, at least."

His sigh was one of relief. "I thought I'd have to spend the entire morning convincing you of that."

"To wash my hands?" How uncooperative did he think she was going to be?

"People aren't always receptive to new ideas," he said. "Or even 'different' ones."

"Believe me," she answered, "I know."

The front door squeaked, and footsteps approached. "Your patients walk in without warning?" She had never seen that before.

"One thing a small-town doctor gives up is any degree of privacy. Every moment of my day, and an exhausting number of my nights, belong to this town."

She couldn't tell if he happily made that sacrifice or if he was complaining. Dr. Blackburn at the asylum had never stopped complaining about his patients. Never.

Mrs. Wilhite stepped into the parlor. Miriam undertook a quick assessment. Though the woman didn't move agilely, she didn't seem to be truly struggling. Her coloring was pale, but not in a way that indicated illness. Miriam heard no labored breathing.

"Mrs. Wilhite." Dr. MacNamara greeted her. "What brings you around?"

"I have a tickle in my throat." Her voice didn't seem affected, though. And her eyes continually darted to Miriam, a look of shock and distrust on her face.

"You seemed well yesterday." Dr. MacNamara set to washing his hands straightaway. "When did your throat begin bothering you?"

"Last evening." Mrs. Wilhite's gaze settled on Miriam. "I didn't expect *you* to be here."

A dozen different responses sprang immediately to Miriam's mind. *After yesterday afternoon, neither did I.* Or *If not for Dr. MacNamara's odd matrimonial notions, there would be nothing unusual about my presence here.* Or perhaps an abject apology, though what she would be begging pardon for, she wasn't at all certain.

In the end, she only nodded.

Dr. MacNamara returned to his patient's side, motioning for her to sit on the examination table. Once she was situated, he began feeling her neck. "Does swallowing hurt? Or speaking?"

"Swallowing, a little."

He raised his examining lantern and checked her mouth. "Have you experienced any coughing? A blocked nose?"

She shook her head.

He set the back of his hand against her forehead. "You aren't feverish."

A lot could be learned about a doctor by watching him with his patients. Dr. MacNamara was forbearing, calm, and thorough.

"How have you been sleeping?" Dr. MacNamara asked Mrs. Wilhite.

"Not well. Even before the sore throat." She sighed deeply. "I don't know what is the matter with me. Perhaps I'm simply old."

That might very well have been the difficulty. But extreme exhaustion in a woman was sometimes interpreted by the medical community as a sign of madness. Did Dr. MacNamara share that view? She truly hoped he wasn't one to jump quickly to that conclusion.

He pulled up a stool and sat facing Mrs. Wilhite. "What enjoyable activities have you indulged in lately?"

"I have my ribbons."

He shook his head. "That is your livelihood. I am speaking more of a hobby."

Her brow furrowed. "I like tatting, though I haven't made lace in ages."

Dr. MacNamara nodded with approval. "I suggest you take it up again."

"How will that help my throat?"

Miriam wondered the same thing.

He gave Mrs. Wilhite a look of such compassion that it momentarily stole Miriam's breath. "I suspect you are feeling unwell because you are a little unhappy."

Without warning, Mrs. Wilhite began tearing up. Miriam was immediately on alert. Excessive melancholy was also a reason some women were deemed mad. She had seen far too many women locked away at Blackburn who should never have been there. She'd learned not to trust that any member of her sex was entirely safe from that fate.

"Mrs. Wilhite does not seem *overly* unhappy to me," Miriam interjected.

She immediately received looks of censure from them both. Apparently, she was meant to be a silent helper.

"Forgive me," she said, though she wasn't truly repentant. "I won't interrupt again, Dr. MacNamara."

"That would probably be best," he answered. "And I have asked you to call me Gideon."

"I will endeavor to do so from now on," she said.

His attention returned to his patient. "Take up your tatting again, see if it lifts your spirits, even a little. If by week's end you aren't feeling better or, heaven forbid, are feeling worse, please come back and see m—us."

Mrs. Wilhite's horrified gaze—it truly *was* horrified—flew to Miriam at once. "She will still be here?"

Gideon smiled, but the gesture was noticeably strained. "That is the plan. We are in need of a qualified nurse in this town."

"But she jilted you before all your friends and loved ones."

If Miriam wasn't already quite accustomed to hearing herself discussed as though she weren't present, she might have felt self-conscious. She'd grown up with the experience, however. Her mother and father had often discussed her at length, within her hearing. She'd learned to listen without comment.

"If it does not bother me, it need not bother the town," Gideon said.

"I know you too well to believe for a moment that this doesn't bother you a great deal." Mrs. Wilhite looked Miriam up and down, dignity rolling off the older woman in waves.

Gideon caught Miriam's gaze. "I did warn you this would be awkward."

"Yes, you did."

By the time noon rolled around, Gideon's use of "us" had proven itself to be terribly premature. Every person who came in the door treated Miriam as though she'd arrived in Savage Wells for the sole purpose of causing their beloved doctor misery. She seemed to have been deemed their mutual enemy, all because she hadn't agreed to marry a stranger on a few seconds' notice.

This was far more like her usual luck: quick judgment, followed by almost instant dismissal. Perhaps it was for the best, though. While she would have liked to have made friends in her new town, the degree to which Savage Wells invaded Dr. MacNamara's privacy did not bode well.

She had far too many secrets.

Chapter 5

Gideon started his morning the way he always did, medical emergencies permitting: with music. Mother had insisted that all of her children learn to play an instrument. Gideon's oldest brother, Ian, had chosen the violin. James, the middle son, had spent two years threatening to choose the bagpipes before finally settling on the clarinet. For reasons he still couldn't pinpoint, Gideon had always been drawn to the cello. And, despite Mother's insistence that men of refinement preferred classical pieces, he'd spent hours learning popular tunes. He could play both; he preferred the latter.

One thing Mother *had* been right about: music was soothing. He spent thirty minutes at it every morning. It calmed him and prepared him to face whatever chaos came his way. This morning, he'd been at it a full hour.

Miriam had said and done little the day before. She hadn't had much opportunity, really. He'd seen a number of patients, and every last one of them had made their dislike of her clear. There'd been something gratifying in being defended so vehemently, and, though it was petty, a part of him had enjoyed it as

29

well as felt a little vindicated that she'd been as humbled by their patients' disapproval of her as he had been by her very public rejection of him. But clarity and the loud voice of his conscience had come with the sunrise.

He was not a vengeful person; he didn't particularly want to become one. Hurting Miriam because she had, inadvertently, hurt him—his pride, at least—would do neither of them any good. From a professional standpoint, he needed to find a way to help the town accept her, or there'd be no point in her being there.

As he played through "My Old Kentucky Home," he thought his way through a few strategies. Throwing a "We Didn't Get Married" party would likely be overdoing things, as would requesting Mr. Endecott preach a sermon on loving thy neighbor even if that neighbor doesn't love thy bachelor doctor. Bribery also seemed likely to fail; he had little to bribe anyone with.

He needed an actual plan.

The town would never be comfortable with her until *he* was. Comfort required familiarity. If they had been married, as he'd originally planned, he would have immediately begun working to know her better. There was no reason he shouldn't move forward with that course of action, though on a less personal basis.

Making friends had always been a strength of his. Why not put that talent to use now when it mattered so much?

He would be friendly. He would ask about her family, her hometown, her education, her likes and dislikes, how likely she was to murder a jilted fiancé in a fit of rage. The crucial things.

That was his plan for the day. He only hoped it was a good one. He set his cello carefully back inside its case. There was no way of repairing the instrument so far from "civilization" if anything happened to it, so care was essential. Enough had gone wrong without adding that to his list.

The mantel clock in the parlor struck half past eight as he made his way down the stairs. He moved directly to the front door and pulled the "Please Knock Loudly" sign from the side window, replacing it with "Please Come Inside." He then turned the bolt, unlocking the door. His established hours didn't begin until nine o'clock, but the world of illness and injury was seldom predictable and almost never convenient.

A clanking from the kitchen pulled him that way rather than toward the parlor. The kitchen's exterior door led into the side yard, but it was locked at night. The only people in town with a key were Paisley, who was in Laramie at the moment, and Cade. And, he realized quite suddenly, Miriam. He'd given her a key the day before.

But why was she there thirty minutes early? And why was she in the kitchen?

She was standing at the stove when he stepped inside. She looked up. "I hope you're hungry."

She was cooking him breakfast?

"I am absolutely certain I didn't ask you to cook meals," he said.

"You didn't." Did she always speak so softly? She didn't seem bashful. She continued stirring whatever was in the pan. Eggs, if he didn't miss his mark. "I simply thought it would be helpful."

"What can I do?" he asked. "I am particularly good at making toast."

"The charred crumbs on your mouth yesterday indicated otherwise." The tiniest hint of amusement tugged at her lips. That was encouraging.

He took the bread knife out of its drawer and pulled the loaf of bread over to the cutting board.

"You are very talented," Miriam said.

"You haven't even seen me slice the bread yet."

"Not the cutting." She shook her head. "The cello."

He inwardly sighed. She had heard him play. Now even that part of his private life was to be invaded. It would have been if they had married, but this felt different. "I didn't realize I had an audience."

"I attended a great many symphonies growing up. I always enjoyed the sound of the cello."

She'd had a life of some privilege, then. He ought to have suspected as much, considering her education and her very proper manner of speaking. "Not many people here know that I play the cello. I would prefer to keep it that way."

"Why is that?"

Because it is too personal, the only thing that is entirely mine. Everything about him belonged to his neighbors and associates and even complete strangers throughout the territory. His wedding plans had been open to their scrutiny. His subsequent rejection would be discussed at length for weeks. Months. Probably even years. The town could claim his time, his efforts, his concern, his energy. But his music was his alone.

Miriam was not his wife; he wasn't about to confess all of this to her. "It is an uncommon instrument this far west. The townspeople might find it odd." That was a reason he could admit to. "It is like the wax seals my mother sent to me, or the bone china she sent, or the high-polished furniture I insisted she not send. All of it is out of place."

"And you, as a doctor, need your patients to feel that you belong here, so they'll trust you." She'd grasped that quickly.

"They took their time deciding to accept me when I first arrived," he said. "But they did, eventually."

She scooped scrambled eggs onto a platter. "Perhaps they will warm up to me in time, as well."

He hoped they would, but he could not be certain. Jests seemed more advisable in that moment than the blunt truth. "Provided you don't do something truly shocking, like play the cello in public."

She set the eggs on the table. "How does the town feel about someone who sketches?"

"Is that what your leather notebook is for?" He'd noticed it on the sideboard. She'd kept it with her the day before as well. It was the only thing she'd carried with her to the church the day of their aborted wedding.

She sat. "I like to draw. I do it often. But if the town will think it a peculiarity in me, I'll be circumspect."

He set a spoonful of eggs on her plate. "I don't know what their opinion is of drawing. I can't think of anyone in town with that interest."

"And what they might embrace in someone else, the town is likely to consider a failing in me." She smiled at him, but not with amusement. "They must like you a great deal to have decided to hate me so quickly and so entirely."

Oh, the guilt of that all-too-accurate observation. "You'll win them over. I'm certain of it."

"How?" She poked at her eggs with her fork, but showed no sign of intending to eat. "And I'm not being petulant. I will be of no help to you or this town if they think the worst of me."

He swallowed a bite of eggs. "I've been giving that some thought. Yesterday, you were a silent observer." He'd insisted on it, like a peevish toddler. "Beginning today, you will be a nurse, involved in treatments and discussions. They'll see that I want you to be part of this practice and that you're competent." He shot her a theatrically concerned look. "You are competent, aren't you?"

"It seems the Western Women's Bureau didn't provide you with quite enough information," she said lightly.

"Of the two of us," he said, "I don't think *I* am the one most likely to lodge that complaint."

She held back a smile, but her eyes lit with it. What a fascinating change in her. The moment of humor between them was promising. He'd far prefer to spend his days with someone he could laugh with now and then. Perhaps this wasn't going to be a complete disaster after all.

"I have a patient coming in today who broke his leg a while back," Gideon said. "As much as I'd like to believe he'll be cooperative, he has the unfortunate tendency to be a very wiggly, very wary six-year-old boy."

"Have you plaster bandaged it or taken the more traditional splint-and-bandage approach?" she asked.

It took a moment for the shock of her question to settle. Not many people within the medical community were familiar with plaster bandaging; it was a relatively new approach to broken limbs and one not seen much outside of battlefield medicine.

"Where did you learn about plaster bandaging?" he asked. "You can't be old enough to have been a nurse during the War between the States."

"I worked in a hospital where the doctors were eager to learn and to try to improve their methods." Her enthusiasm for that was tempered by wariness. "Which approach did you use on the boy's leg?"

"Splint and bandage," he answered.

She nodded in what looked like approval. "What would you like me to do?"

"I'll need your help if I'm to have any chance of getting a good look at the little terror's leg. He isn't a bad sort. He simply needs some reassurance and distraction. So, if you could prepare a song and dance, perhaps a dramatic recitation, that would be helpful."

"I don't sing." Her voice was calm as ever, but adamant.

"You're that terrible?" Somehow Gideon doubted it. "Or do you simply prefer not to?"

"My voice could likely be considered a weapon."

He'd finished his breakfast. "So if you are ever invited to sing a solo in a town musicale, I should—"

"Run, Doctor. Run for your very life."

This was his first real conversation with her and, he admitted, he was enjoying himself. She was sharp and witty. Her humor was subtle and well-hidden, but it was real just the same.

A few minutes after Gideon and Miriam had finished their breakfast and set up the parlor for the day's patients, Mrs. Fletcher, with little Rupert clutching her hand, arrived. The poor boy's large eyes shimmered with unshed tears. His last visit had been a painful one, despite Gideon's best efforts.

"Mrs. Fletcher, Rupert, this is Miriam Bricks. She is a nurse and has come to work here."

Rupert eyed Miriam with blatant curiosity. "I saw you at the schoolhouse when you were running away."

The faint pink on Miriam's cheeks turned to a deep, burning red, nearly matching her copper curls.

"Hush, Rupert," Mrs. Fletcher whispered.

Gideon jumped in before Miriam could be further embarrassed. "Mrs. Fletcher, if you would please help Rupert up onto the table." He turned to face his young patient. "And you, young man, give Nurse Bricks your best 'howdy' while I go wash my hands. She's here to help, and you would do well to make yourself her friend."

Rupert turned slowly once more toward Miriam. Gideon watched the exchange surreptitiously as he moved toward the washbasin. He was interested to see how she dealt with frightened children.

"Howdy." Rupert's greeting was very nearly a question.

"Howdy to you as well," she said.

Rupert pointed at his bandaged leg. "I broke my bones."

"Dr. MacNamara told me that."

Mrs. Fletcher lifted her young son onto the table, all the while keeping a decidedly suspicious eye on Miriam.

"Did you ever break your bones?" Rupert asked Miriam.

"I once dislocated my shoulder."

The boy's brow pulled low. "Is that like breaking it?"

Miriam moved to the examination table, her demeanor as calm as ever. It seemed like such a contradiction: a redhead with so little fire. "It is more a matter of the bones pulling too far apart."

Rupert's face twisted with disgust. "Did your arm fall off?"

"Not all the way, but it hung wobbly at my side as if it had come off inside but not outside."

Slowly, inch by inch, Rupert's expression transformed into interest, even excitement. "Did it blow around in the wind?"

Miriam shook her head. "The doctor who fixed it put my arm in a sling before the wind could do anything. I suppose it might have waved about otherwise."

Rupert made a sound of absolute awe.

Gideon breathed a sigh of relief. Miriam had expertly seized Rupert's attention. She would do fine in this job. He dried off his hands and turned to the examination table.

"Lay back, young man," he instructed.

"Did Nurse Bricks's bones come apart inside?" Rupert asked the moment his head hit the small pillow.

"Not completely." Gideon had seen enough dislocations to know exactly what would have happened. "They pull away from each other like the stretchy part of a slingshot."

"Do they pop back together like a slingshot?" Rupert asked earnestly.

"With a little help from a doctor," Miriam said.

Gideon carefully lifted Rupert's splinted leg from the table. Rupert's lip began to quiver. Mrs. Fletcher hurried closer, but Gideon waved her back. He met Miriam's eyes and gave a subtle nod, hoping she would know what he wanted her to do.

She set her hand on Rupert's. The boy wrapped his fingers around hers. Gideon slowly unwound the bandaging on Rupert's leg.

Rupert kept his eyes on Miriam. "Did blood come out when your bones pulled apart?" What a sordid bit of questioning, but so perfectly appropriate for a boy his age.

"Yes, but not because of the bones."

"Why, then?" Rupert's eyes were trained on her, fascinated.

Gideon quickly worked at the bandaging. The task was best done while the child was distracted.

"I hurt my shoulder in a fall. That fall also cut my head. The blood poured out everywhere from that wound. Down my face. All over my hair."

Mrs. Fletcher gasped quietly, pressing a hand to her heart. It was likely more graphic than she would have preferred, but Miriam had taken Rupert's measure straight off. The boy enjoyed hearing the ghastly details, provided they didn't apply to him personally.

"Were you scared?" His little voice broke. No doubt it was no longer only *her* injury he was thinking of.

Miriam kept her focus on him. "A little. Falling can be a frightening thing."

"I bet I wasn't as scared as you," Rupert said.

Gideon quickly covered a laugh with a cough, but didn't manage to smother his grin.

"You must be very courageous," Miriam said to Rupert, "because I was quite scared."

Rupert's brow drew in. "Well, I didn't have blood coming out of my face. Maybe that's why you were so scared."

"You may be right."

A bit of the bandaging stuck, and Gideon had to tug harder than before. Rupert's brow wrinkled with concern and what looked like a bit of pain. Perhaps the limb was still more tender than Gideon had expected.

Miriam squeezed Rupert's hand. "You are being very brave, young man. I fussed and fussed when the doctor put my bones back."

Rupert didn't answer. Very real worry clouded every inch of his face.

Gideon pulled back the last layer of bandaging. The smell was unmistakable: gangrene. What in heaven's name had happened?

Rupert held tight to Miriam's hand. "Are my bones pulled out?" he whispered anxiously.

"Nothing appears to be missing or dangling about," she said. "What is your expert opinion, Doctor?"

He wasn't about to tell the boy his leg was rotting. "At first glance, I would say Rupert was good about staying off his leg as he was told."

"I'm no blockhead," the boy insisted.

"I have a feeling, Rupert, you are smarter than all of us," Miriam said.

Rupert grinned up at her, hardly even noticing that Gideon was holding his leg, feeling the bones. The break appeared to have healed, which was reassuring. The gangrenous sore, though, was worrisome.

"How did you break your leg?" Miriam asked.

"I falled out of a tree," he answered. "I like to climb trees. I'm almost as good as Andrew."

Gideon leaned closer to Rupert's leg.

"Is there anything in particular that makes a tree good for climbing?" Miriam asked Rupert.

"Oh, sure."

Rupert launched into a very detailed account of climbing trees, pausing now and then with a wince when Gideon's prodding drew close to the sore. Miriam nodded at all the right moments in the boy's account, but much of her attention was on his leg.

"How long ago did the sheep's wool come out of the splinting?" Gideon asked Mrs. Fletcher in a low whisper.

"I don't remember exactly," she said with a shrug. "Everything else seemed to stay in place, so we didn't fret over it."

"I did tell you that it needed to be there, did I not?" He knew he had. He was certain of it. *This* was precisely the reason he'd been specific with his instructions.

"Is something wrong, Doctor?" Mrs. Fletcher's voice wavered. She wrung her hands, her mouth pulled in a tight line.

Something was most decidedly wrong. He needed to help Rupert, but Mrs. Fletcher wouldn't do well if she had to watch.

"I need you to go across the street and ask Mrs. Wilhite for a length of her puce ribbon."

Rupert was still rattling off information about trees. Miriam was likely the only one paying him any heed, and even she wasn't listening closely.

"I must insist, Mrs. Fletcher," Gideon added in a firm tone. "Give your boy a hug first, though. I think he'd appreciate it."

As Mrs. Fletcher stood by her son and whispered something to him, Miriam moved to stand by Gideon, a step removed from their small patient.

"I know that smell," she said.

He pushed out a tight breath. He'd assumed the hardest part of today's visit would have been keeping Rupert still. Things were far more complicated than that.

"The splinting rubbed against the side of his leg. Without the wool to act as buffer, it left a sore. That sore stayed warm and moist because of the wrapping, and was continually rubbed open by the splinting."

"How extensive is the rot?"

"It doesn't appear to be widespread, which is a relief."

"And the puce ribbon?"

"Anytime I send someone to Mrs. Wilhite asking for puce ribbon, she knows to keep him or her there until I send word." The system worked brilliantly. "In this case, a distraught mother who will likely fall to pieces when I start cleaning out the wound in her son's leg."

"A wise decision," she said. "How much tissue will you have to remove?"

"I won't know for certain until I begin cleaning." He took a deep, slow breath. He couldn't allow his worry to cloud his judgment. "Have you assisted in surgeries?"

"I have." Miriam looked back at the little boy. "You do intend to use ether, don't you? I have seen too many patients endure excruciating operations without any effort to relieve their suffering."

She'd worked for a doctor who made no efforts at pain relief during surgery? Gideon felt ill at the thought. "I will do everything possible to ensure his comfort."

She nodded with palpable relief. "I'd best wash up. I know that is a requirement of yours."

"Perhaps we'll get along better than everyone is predicting." The moment he said it, he realized how unintentionally accusatory it sounded. Her suddenly closed-off expression told him she had heard the complaint hidden in his words. "Miriam—"

"We should get to work." She turned back to Rupert, effectively ending Gideon's attempts to explain that he'd been attempting humor.

Mrs. Fletcher left as requested. Rupert's pale features indicated that he knew something was wrong. Gideon did his best to appear reassuring, while still working to get the information he needed.

"Has your leg been hurting up by your knee? Now, no fibs, young man."

"Uh-huh," Rupert admitted.

Gideon leaned his elbows on the examination table, his hands clasped. The posture put him more on level with his small patient, something he hoped would ease the boy's worries. "Why didn't you tell me or your ma or pa that it'd begun hurting?"

"I didn't want you moving my bones again." Tears started from his eyes.

"Listen, son." Gideon took hold of the boy's hands. "You and I are going to be acquainted for a lot of years. I need you to tell me if you're ever hurt, ill, curious about something, or afraid." He met and held Rupert's gaze. "I give you my word that I will never cause you pain if I can at all help it. My solemn vow, Rupert. Have I ever given you reason not to believe my solemn vow?"

Rupert gave it very real thought. "No, Doc."

"I know visiting with me isn't always a pleasant experience, but I don't want anything bad to happen to you. I can't help you if you don't come see me."

"I will."

"Even if you're scared?" Gideon pressed.

"Even if I'm scared."

"And if I'm not here, will you talk to Nurse Bricks?"

"I will."

Miriam returned to her stool, hands newly washed. "I am ready when you are, Dr. MacNamara."

"Make yourself comfortable, Rupert," Gideon said. "You are going to take a nap."

"I don't like naps," Rupert muttered.

"Well, I don't like toast, but I ate some this morning," Miriam said, "because the doctor said I should."

"I think Nurse Bricks is a troublemaker," Gideon said. "What do you think, Rupert?"

He smiled shyly. "I like her."

"And I like you, Rupert," Miriam said.

The boy's expression turned earnest. "Promise not to leave while I'm sleeping?" he pleaded with her.

"You are not the first person to ask me that, Rupert. And I will tell you this, I never left any of them. Not a single one."

Chapter 6

Miriam scrubbed at the examination table for all she was worth. Though she wasn't convinced that Gideon's strict adherence to the theoretical belief that cleaning hands and linens and surfaces to within an inch of their lives would truly prevent infection, if there was any truth to those theories, it was worth the effort. Still, her arms and back ached, and she wasn't at all sure she'd recover from the eye-wateringly strong odor of his chosen soap.

The morning had already gone better for her than the entire previous day had. Little Rupert had declared that he liked her. She had shown herself competent and capable. And Gideon was sticking to his intention to show the town that he trusted her and wished her to be there. She wasn't certain he actually felt that way, but he was doing a fine job of giving that impression.

The front door squeaked open. Gideon's practice was a busy one.

The steps that entered the parlor were soft, but not hesitant. Before Miriam could sneak even the briefest glimpse, the new arrival spoke, a woman, one whose voice she didn't recognize.

"You are Miriam Bricks?"

"I am." She looked up, and anything else she might have said died on her lips.

The new arrival, likely not much older than she was, wore a badge pinned to her flower-print dress and a gun slung low on her hips. Her gun belt boasted a seemingly endless supply of bullets.

"I had expected you to be Miriam *MacNamara* by the time I met you." She eyed Miriam with unmistakable disdain.

Her lack of a name change was a sore spot for the entire town. She had spent too many years being punished for things that weren't her fault, so it somehow seemed fitting that the pattern was going to continue.

"*I* hadn't expected my name to be anything other than what it is." Miriam spoke firmly. "But Gideon has hired me as a nurse, so what can I do for you? You don't appear ill or injured."

"Where is Gideon?" The question was so filled with distrust that Miriam wondered if this unnamed, fully-armed stranger suspected her of having done away with the good doctor.

"He is upstairs, with a patient."

The woman spun on her heel, then strode from the room, heading upstairs without so much as a "Goodbye" or a "Pleased to meet you." Miriam probably should have been offended, but found her reaction fell somewhere far nearer relief.

She returned to her scrubbing, but her eyes continually wandered to the bookshelf behind Gideon's desk and the many nearby filing drawers. An idea had begun to form in the back of her mind that she couldn't entirely shake. Gideon kept abreast of developments in medical science. Perhaps somewhere among his books and papers was a new, miraculous treatment for her particular condition. She had lived in fear of her own body for too long.

"If these episodes have no cause or physical explanation, then they must be the manifestation of an illness of the mind." Though the doctor who had made the diagnosis hadn't said anything she hadn't already read, his words had been chilling.

No amount of arguing that her mind functioned properly or that she felt perfectly sound had made the slightest difference. He hadn't listened, and Dr. Blackburn had wholeheartedly agreed. She had spent the next two years of her life as an inmate in Blackburn Asylum, fighting just to stay alive.

Plotting her escape had required the full two years and several failed attempts, the punishments for which had been excruciating. Even her current, brief moments of freedom came at the cost of near-constant fear. What if her condition were discovered? What if Dr. Blackburn found her?

And now she had to worry about Gideon. If he were to witness one of her "episodes," he would know the accepted diagnosis. Tension twisted inside her every time she allowed herself to even think about the precariousness of her situation. She'd spent so many years running, and she was exhausted.

Footsteps sounded on the stairs beyond the parlor, more than one set of them, in fact. Gideon was returning, either with Mrs. Fletcher or with the gun-toting, badge-wearing woman who'd gone upstairs looking for him. Either way, Miriam meant to present a professional demeanor.

She finished wiping off the table and set the last of her used rags in the basket. She returned the gloves she'd borrowed to protect her hands from the harsh soap to the spot where Gideon kept them. She gave her work apron a quick smoothing and tucked a flyaway strand of hair behind her ear as Gideon and his guest stepped inside the parlor.

His nose scrunched up. "Strong, isn't it?"

Miriam, seeing the question was directed at her, nodded.

"Rupert is resting," he said. "Mrs. Fletcher means to stay with him until he can return home. I'll move a cot in there for her before nightfall."

There was little else to do but nod again. The woman with the gun and badge stood nearby, watching Miriam too closely for comfort.

"Miriam, this is Deputy US Marshal Paisley O'Brien." Gideon glanced fondly at the lawwoman. "She's married to our good sheriff and counts herself as a particular friend of mine, though she's almost required to be. We are family, after all."

Family. Gideon was related to a deputy US marshal, who was married to the town's chief lawman. Two close associates with a great deal of power and influence. They had the authority to see to it she was returned to the nightmare she'd desperately fled. Which made keeping Gideon in the dark about her condition all the more important.

Gideon nudged Paisley with his elbow.

"Pleased to meet you, Miss Bricks." Paisley offered the greeting through tight lips. "Gideon says you are in need of a place to live, and we have empty rooms at our house."

It was likely supposed to have been a friendly offer, but Miriam was not so thickheaded as to believe it was anything remotely resembling one. Gideon had, no doubt, somehow forced the begrudging show of support.

"Thank you for your generosity." If Paisley could pretend it was a kindness, so could Miriam. "But I was hoping to find someone who takes in lodgers as a matter of course." And she would prefer one not so closely associated with the law.

"Mrs. Allen takes in roomers," Gideon said. "But she is full up."

That was unfortunate. "Then I will have to remain at the hotel, I suppose."

He stepped up beside her and lowered his voice. "I cannot pay you enough for you to live there long-term, especially since you have no means of cooking for yourself."

An idea emerged, fully formed and ready to pounce on. "What if I took my meals here? I cooked breakfast this morning and ate lunch here as well. Adding dinner wouldn't be so much to ask." The audacity of the suggestion hit her, and her heart dropped to her feet. Two days on the job, a job she desperately needed, and she was already suggesting she be permitted such a luxury. "Forgive me, that was presumptuous—"

Gideon cut off her apology with a wave of his hand. "No, it's a good idea. I don't know why I didn't think of it myself. My original arrangement would have had you taking all of your meals here. Why should that change simply because we're not married?"

Simply. Was there anything about this arrangement that was truly simple?

"You would still barely make enough to cover the cost of your room at the hotel," he warned.

"I understand." The purpose of this job had never been to grow wealthy. She was starting a new life and escaping her old one. Only those who had never known true oppression would value riches over freedom.

Gideon turned back to Paisley. "It appears your hospitality will not be necessary, after all."

She raised an ebony eyebrow. "I offered a room, not hospitality."

"Paisley," he scolded under his breath.

"I know I'm being unkind." Paisley directed the half-hearted admission to both of them. "But, at the moment, I am put out with *you*"—she pointed at Gideon—"I don't yet know what to think of *you*"—she indicated Miriam—"and I haven't seen my husband in weeks. So social niceties are not a priority."

Miriam far preferred Paisley's candor to the rest of the town's glares and often unspoken disapproval. "Although I know a great many people who would argue that social niceties ought never to be set aside, I, for one, find your directness refreshing."

Paisley's forehead lined with surprise and deep contemplation. "You must be from back East; you talk like Gid."

Too many secrets were tucked in the corners of her past for personal discussions to be truly comfortable, but this part she could admit to. "I'm from New York."

Paisley set her hands on her hips, though the posture was more curious than confrontational. "Are your family also whiskey barons who secretly run the country?"

Miriam's face turned cold. She addressed her next question to Gideon. "Your family are politicians?" People with influence were dangerous, she knew that all too well.

Gideon grinned. "You know, it's usually the 'whiskey' part that people find shocking."

She didn't care how they made their living, only what they were capable of accomplishing. "Paisley said they 'run the country.' She would know; you said you are family."

Gideon shook his head. "She is exaggerating."

"A *little*," Paisley said.

Gideon's shrug was more of a confirmation than a dismissal. *Goodness gracious.* His circle of acquaintances was broader and more influential than she could have imagined. She would have to be extremely careful.

"I see that having politicians on my family tree is a mark

against me in your book," Gideon said. "Perhaps if you told me about a skeleton in your closet, we could be even."

How had this discussion gone so wrong so quickly? He was teasing about her spilling a secret, but how long would it be before he asked in earnest? How long could she keep those skeletons hidden?

"I'll slip into the kitchen and see to dinner." It was not an elegant departure speech, but desperation had robbed her of any semblance of grace.

She snatched her sketchbook off the corner of Gideon's desk and escaped to the relative safety of the kitchen. She lowered herself into a chair at the table. Hers hadn't been the quiet, unobtrusive arrival she'd depended on. And this isolated backwater was, apparently, filled with people of widespread influence.

She set her sketchbook on the table, rubbing her hand over the top of it. *I need to stay calm. If I stay calm, no one will suspect anything.*

She untied the leather strap and opened the notebook, pulling her sketching pencil from its loop. Careful not to dislodge any of the loose papers, she flipped to the first blank page. She began with broad strokes, forming the barest outline of a face. Rounded cheeks. A tiny upturned nose. She bent over the paper, focusing all her effort on the eyes. Pleading, worried eyes.

"Promise not to leave me while I'm sleeping?" he'd begged.

How like the desperate plea she'd made two years earlier to a fellow nurse when Dr. Blackburn had come to claim her. "Please don't let them take me away." She'd been ignored and abandoned and resigned to the cruel fate that awaited her at the asylum.

"I'll look after you, Rupert," she whispered. "And everyone else here who will let me."

Chapter 7

"She's hiding something."

Gideon could have predicted that very declaration from Paisley. "Simply because she wasn't keen to discuss her personal life with a gun-toting stranger and a man she met only three days ago doesn't mean she's hiding something."

But Paisley shook her head firmly, eyeing Gideon thoughtfully. "I have spent the last six months traveling the length of this territory as a deputy marshal, and I have learned to tell when a person is being less than forthright."

"You made her nervous," he said. "I'm surprised you didn't keep a hand on your gun the whole time she was in here."

Paisley's gaze remained on the now-empty doorway. "She wasn't afraid; I noticed that straight off. Quiet; yes. A little overwhelmed, perhaps. But not truly frightened."

Gideon sensed there was a great deal of steel to Miriam Bricks. She would need it to survive the difficult life out West. He only hoped that life didn't harden her too much; he worried it had done exactly that to Paisley.

"I think you are being unnecessarily suspicious," he said.

"Cade didn't seem to think she was deceitful. He was the one who suggested I hire her even after she left me standing alone at the front of the church."

Paisley didn't seem impressed with that argument. "How much time did he actually spend with her?"

"Hardly any," Gideon admitted. "I still don't think he would agree with your suspicions."

"And I am certain he would."

Gideon caught a glimpse through the front windows of two men walking toward the house. "Shall we put that to a test? He and Hawk will be here in another moment."

"Cade is coming?" Paisley seldom looked as happy as she did at the promise of Cade's company.

Gideon stepped into the entryway and pulled the door open in time to see Cade and Hawk crossing the front porch. Even if he hadn't known them personally, he would have pegged them as lawmen from a mile away. They had the same swagger, the same posture of calculating confidence. They both wore their gun belts and ammunition as easily as they did their hats and boots. Their badges fit them as naturally as birthmarks.

"A fine evening to you both," he said. "To what, pray tell, do I owe the pleasure of your company, gentlemen?"

Hawk arched an eyebrow in dry disapproval. Cade ignored the remark. A show of impeccable manners never failed to irk the two of them. Heavens, but they were fun to goad.

"Mrs. Wilhite says you sent for puce ribbon." Cade held Gideon's gaze, waiting for an explanation.

"The Fletcher boy had a gangrenous sore on his leg," Gideon explained. "Mrs. Fletcher wouldn't have fared well watching me cut off bits of her son."

"Seems a lucky thing you had a nurse around," Cade said. "I'd wager that proved helpful."

"It did indeed." He waved them inside and toward the parlor, closing the front door behind them. "Though, at the moment, I'm a little overrun with 'helpful women,' so if you could take this one with you"—he motioned to Paisley—"I'd be forever indebted."

Cade headed directly to her. "You were gone entirely too long, love." His arms slid around her, pulling her flush with him, before he pressed a kiss to her lips.

Hawk caught Gideon's eye. "Do you ever wish the two of them remembered they have a place of their own to undertake this sort of business?"

"All the time, Marshal."

Cade pulled Paisley with him over to his usual spot by the window, keeping a lookout on the town. Savage Wells didn't appreciate enough how dedicated their sheriff was to his job.

Hawk dropped his black hat onto an end table and sat in a wingback chair. "I hear you're still a bachelor."

"I can't seem to find anyone who'll have me."

"You said the bureau told you she was a nurse at a hospital before coming here?" Hawk laced his fingers together and set his hands casually on his lap as he slouched lower in his chair. A person might be excused for thinking he was a layabout when he assumed that particular posture, but one look at his sharp, calculating eyes would convince that person otherwise.

"That is what they said, yes, but apparently they aren't the most reliable source of information."

"I mean to look into this agency you used," Hawk said. "Miss Bricks likely isn't the only woman they've misled."

"I telegrammed my brother about the bureau," Gideon

said. "As an attorney, he knows enough influential people in Washington to stir up a hornet's nest in St. Louis."

"But in the meantime, you have something of a mess on your hands," Cade added from his spot at the window.

Gideon shook his head. "Not really. I may not have a wife, but I do have a nurse, and that was at least half of what I was hoping for."

"If you ask me, her running out of that schoolhouse was a fine bit of luck for you, Gid," Cade said. "Marrying a stranger was a risk from the beginning. At least this way, if you find you can't bear her company, you can always fire her. It's a great deal harder to fire a wife."

Paisley tossed him a saucy look. "You've given this some thought, have you?"

Cade leaned against the window frame and crossed his booted feet at the ankles, folding his arms across his chest. "I might have."

She slid up closer to him. "And what are your thoughts on a wife firing her husband?"

His hand snaked around her waist. "Ain't gonna happen, love."

Gideon turned to Hawk. "Are they like this at the jailhouse as well?"

"Every single day." Hawk covered his mouth and pretended to vomit.

Gideon actually didn't mind; he suspected Hawk didn't either. Cade and Paisley had had a difficult courtship. That the ending had proven happy was a good thing, one worth celebrating.

Miriam stepped into the room. "Gideon, where is the—" Her words ended as her eyes settled on the gathering. "Forgive me. I didn't know you had company." She took a quick step back toward the door.

"A moment, please," he said. "You haven't officially met Cade O'Brien yet." He motioned toward the window. "Or John Hawking, US marshal." He tipped his head in Hawk's direction.

"Sakes alive, Doc," Hawk muttered, scrambling to his feet. "You didn't say she was a beauty."

"I've mostly been concentrating on her nursing skills," he answered dryly.

"For a doctor, you ain't too bright." Hawk sauntered to the doorway, where Miriam stood eyeing them all. "Good afternoon, Miss Bricks. I'm right pleased to meet you. I'm John Hawking, though most folks call me Hawk."

"I'm pleased to meet you as well." She was blushing deeply.

"Come rest your bones, miss," Hawk said. "I imagine Dr. MacNamara has worked you hard today."

"It has been an exhausting day," Miriam replied quietly.

"Cade, over there, may be the law in this town," Hawk said, "but I've a bit of say, myself. You come tell me if Doc gives you a lick of trouble."

She smiled warmly at Hawk. "I will bear that in mind."

"I hope you'll come by and say howdy regardless of what MacNamara, here, does," Hawk said. "I didn't get to meet you when you first arrived, an unfortunate circumstance I'd like to remedy."

Cade and Paisley eyed the two of them with much the same shocked interest Gideon felt. Hawk usually was so focused on his work that Gideon often wondered if the man noticed any woman who wasn't behind bars. But he was showing himself surprisingly suave.

Miriam clasped her hands in front of her, the blush spreading down her neck. Redheads never did seem to blush prettily, and yet, there was something inarguably endearing in the sight of it.

The door squeaked open.

"It seems we have a patient." He turned and faced the parlor door.

Andrew Gilbert, sporting his still-shiny deputy sheriff's badge, stepped inside. But had he come to see Cade, his boss—or Gideon, his doctor?

Andrew stayed back near the door. Though his mind had begun to recover from the impact of soldiering at far too young an age, he still preferred to keep his distance from most people. The way his brows pulled low and the tightness in his lips, however, told Gideon something new was weighing on him.

"Somethin' happen at the jail?" Cade asked.

"Paisley, your father . . . he's not acting right."

She was gone in a flash, Cade quick on her heels.

"Does he need a doctor?" Gideon asked Andrew, who still kept to the far end of the room.

"I don't think so." Andrew's worry hadn't eased.

Gideon crossed to the doorway, purposefully making the short trip slowly so Andrew had ample time to prepare himself for his approach.

"What happened with Mr. Bell?" Gideon kept his voice low.

"He couldn't remember the rules," Andrew said, shoving his hands in his jacket pocket.

He and Mr. Bell played checkers every day. They had formed an unexpected but mutually beneficial friendship. Andrew's mind had suffered in the war; Barney Bell's was succumbing to dementia. They understood each other in ways no one else did, or likely could.

Gideon stepped from the parlor into the entryway. Andrew followed, eyes downcast, his worried expression filled with a lingering loneliness.

"I had to tell him my name four times today," Andrew said. "He kept forgetting that he knew it."

Gideon motioned for Andrew to sit on the lower steps of the staircase, then sat next to him. "The last few times I've had him in for an examination, he hasn't remembered that we've met before. It will keep happening, I'm afraid."

Andrew picked at the threadbare knees of his trousers. "When I left, he was sitting on the cot in one of the cells, crying about how he couldn't find his dog. But he hasn't got one."

Gideon folded his hands in front of him, his elbows resting on his legs. "I think he did have a dog once, but he's forgotten that he doesn't any longer."

"Do you—Do you think it scares him when he can't remember things?"

Gideon gave it a moment's thought. "It might a little. In time, he won't realize he's forgetting, and that will take the fearful part away."

"When my mind starts hiccupping and I can't get it to stop, it frightens me." Andrew still hadn't looked up. That was his way when he spoke of these things. "It'd be a fine thing not to be afraid of my own head."

These were the moments when Gideon most wanted to put an arm around Andrew's shoulders, or give him a reassuring pat on the back. But Andrew didn't care to be touched. He didn't like people being near enough for contact.

"Though your brain has moments when it becomes confused about what it's meant to be doing, for the most part I'd say it gets along fine." Gideon filled the words with sincerity. Andrew was worried for Mr. Bell not only because the man was his friend but also because he saw so much of himself in his friend's struggles. "As Rupert Fletcher would say, you're no blockhead."

"Feels like it, though. I have a head that hardly does me any good."

Gideon thought for a moment. "Your pa has a knee that aches him from time to time, but would you say his entire leg is worthless?"

"No," Andrew answered.

"Having a bit of your brain that gives you trouble now and again doesn't make your entire head worthless, either." Gideon held his gaze. Andrew had made progress over the past months; Gideon wasn't about to let all of that go to waste because of self-doubt and worry. "Even Mr. Bell, whose mind grows more ill all the time, is not worthless because of it. He never will be. When he reaches the point that he doesn't remember any of us, or this town, or how to play checkers, he will still be important."

"I'll miss him, though," Andrew said quietly. "He is a good man. I like him."

"There are a great many people in this town who say the same about you, Andrew. That you are a good man, and that we like you."

His eyes filled with a painful combination of hope and doubt. "I have tried to be a good deputy. I don't want anyone thinking Cade's a fool for hiring me on."

"That decision was one of the best he's ever made. You've always been one to help people, you're good at your job, and everyone who knows you can't help but like you."

Andrew shrugged, a hint of a smile on his face. "You ain't half bad, yourself, Doc."

Gideon chuckled. "Off with you, Andrew, before I start puffing up with self-importance."

Andrew rose and slipped out the front door, no doubt headed back to the jailhouse, but Miriam remained by the parlor entrance, watching Gideon with an unreadable expression on her face.

Gideon stayed on his step. "What was it you needed to ask me when you first came into the parlor? You were looking for something, I think."

She didn't take up the topic. "Did you mean what you said to Andrew? About his brain having some parts that didn't work right, but that overall it was still valuable?"

Of all the things she might have asked, that was not one he would have guessed. "The brain is like most any other part of the body, really. It doesn't have to be perfect to be good."

If anything, her gaze grew more intense. "Then you don't intend to ply him with every cure or treatment you can imagine in an attempt to make his mind 'perfect'?"

"I know the limits of medical science, Miriam. Some things cannot be fixed." He rubbed at his face, suddenly quite tired. "I address what I can. Beyond that, I try to help people live happy lives."

"What about Mr. Bell?" She crossed to the stairs and leaned against the banister. "From what Andrew said, Mr. Bell's mind seems far more deteriorated and unfixable than does his."

Gideon opted for honesty. "His mind is utterly unfixable. As frustrating as that is, I have to be willing to acknowledge when there is nothing more I can do."

Her attention remained fixed on him. Something about this topic was particularly important to her. But what?

"And you don't mean to take more aggressive action?" she pressed. "Do something more drastic?"

His hackles rose. "Such as cutting into his brain? Digging around a bit?"

Miriam held her hands up in a show of innocence. "I didn't

ask in order to accuse you, but to further understand your character and your doctoring philosophy."

"And what have you learned of my character and philosophy?" He was a little nervous to hear her answer. It had been a long time since anyone with a medical background had evaluated him.

She leaned on the banister once more. Long tendrils of curly red hair hung over her shoulder, drawing his eye. He'd always had something of a weakness for red hair. Red hair and blue eyes, and Miriam had both.

"You care about your patients," she said, "and you see them as people rather than merely illnesses or injuries. That speaks well to your character."

She was impressed that he treated his patients like people? What kind of doctors had she worked for that something so basic surprised her? "Anything else?"

"You are fond of handwashing—alarmingly so." A small hint of humor touched her expression.

He wished her quiet humor would make an appearance more often. Perhaps in time she'd be comfortable enough for that.

Hawk stepped out of the parlor and into the entryway. "Miss Bricks?"

She turned toward him immediately.

"I need to head back to the jailhouse," Hawk said. "But I wanted to tell you again what a pleasure it was to meet you."

"And you." Her response sounded perfectly sincere.

Hawk held his hat in his hands. The usually bold US marshal looked almost uncharacteristically meek. "I'd be honored if you'd allow me to walk you home after you finish up for the evening."

"Home is actually the hotel." She sounded nearly ashamed of the fact, though she'd refused the offer to live in Cade and

Paisley's home. While Gideon didn't believe she was being deceptive like Paisley did, he found she *was* something of a mystery.

"I'd be honored to walk you there," Hawk repeated. "If you'll permit it, of course."

She gave a tiny, silent nod.

"Until this evening, then." Hawk dipped his head, then popped his wide-brimmed hat atop it.

Miriam's eyes met Gideon's, and immediate embarrassment touched every feature of her face. She slipped quickly away in the direction of the kitchen.

A mystery, indeed.

Chapter 8

Mrs. Endecott stepped inside the parlor a little ahead of suppertime the next evening. Gideon struggled to summon a smile for her. He liked the preacher's wife, but he'd passed a difficult twenty-four hours and was too exhausted to summon excitement at seeing another patient. Rupert's surgery had been a gruesome and delicate undertaking. The concentration it required had drained him. The inevitable bouts of self-doubt that had followed meant he hadn't slept well.

He wanted nothing more than to simply walk up to his bedchamber, drop on his bed, and sleep for days on end. But he was all this town had, and they needed him.

"Good evening," he said. "What can I do for you?"

"I've done something to my wrist," she said. "It's swollen and paining me."

Simple enough. "Come have a seat. I'll take a look at it."

She watched him with concern as they crossed the room. "I've heard that woman is here."

Gideon glanced around, half expecting to find a woman lurking in the corners.

"The one who refused to marry you," Mrs. Endecott whispered.

Ah. "She is working as a nurse." He patted the examination table. "We need a nurse in this town." How often had he told people that the past three days?

Mrs. Endecott used the step stool to climb up. "But how miserable for you to have to see her day after day."

He was, apparently, destined to be a martyr in the eyes of the town. How depressing. "She is proving herself to be a competent nurse," he said.

Mrs. Endecott nodded. "So, you are willing to endure it for our sakes?"

"Something like that."

With a sigh, she said, "You poor man."

"And your poor wrist." He could see it now, decidedly swollen and bruised. "What happened?"

"I am not entirely certain."

That seemed unlikely, considering how bad it looked. "Have you taken a spill lately or twisted your hand lifting something heavy?"

"Not that I can recall." Her expression turned contemplative. "Actually, I slipped on the stairs the other day, though I caught myself on the railing."

"With this hand?" Gideon motioned to the swollen one.

"I think so."

He nodded.

"Would you like me to write that down, Doctor?" Miriam's sudden question caught him entirely off-guard.

Mrs. Endecott even startled a little.

Miriam stood nearby, too close to not have overheard their conversation if she'd been standing there long enough.

"How long have you been in the room?" he asked.

Her eyes darted to Mrs. Endecott, and then dropped to her own hands, clasped in front of her. "A little while," she said quietly. "I heard someone come in and thought you might have a patient. I wished to be of help."

"Dr. MacNamara has been looking after us for years without your help," Mrs. Endecott said. Hers was not a criticism of Miriam so much as a defense of Gideon, though it amounted to the same thing.

"I haven't the least doubt in his abilities." Miriam looked to him. "Would you like me to make notes about this visit?"

He'd had her do precisely that with almost every patient who'd come by the past three days. One look at Mrs. Endecott's pursed brow told him that was likely not a good idea this time.

"I will make notes myself afterward," he said.

He was nearly certain he saw disappointment in her eyes, even a hint of hurt. But she tucked it away and simply nodded.

"I will see to supper, then." She turned and walked from the room. Ever in control. Ever calm. Who was she beneath that veneer?

"She assists with your patients *and* cooks for you?" Mrs. Endecott watched Miriam's exit with confusion. "If she is willing to do all of that, why would she dislike the idea of marrying you?"

"Perhaps because there is more to marriage than being a nurse and a cook." Gideon carefully took hold of her injured hand, checking for breaks.

She winced. "Regardless, she could not hope to do better. You are quite remarkable."

He offered her a smile. "I won't argue with you on that score."

"But then *you* certainly could do better—find someone who wants to marry you to begin with."

"That would be a refreshing change." He tied a knot in the corner of a triangle of cloth. "I want you to wrap your hand in a cool, wet cloth. The cold will help reduce the swelling. And while I don't want you to entirely stop using it, you should let your wrist rest for a week or so." He tied the two unknotted corners together, fashioning a sling, and slipped it over her head to hang around her neck. "Put your arm in so your hand is supported."

She did as instructed.

"If your wrist does not feel better in a week, come back and see me."

Mrs. Endecott briefly eyed the empty parlor door. Her voice lowered as she said, "I can come while she's cooking, then she needn't be involved."

This was not going well. Though he, himself, was still not entirely comfortable with Miriam, he needed the town to be welcoming and accepting.

"That won't be necessary," he said.

He walked Mrs. Endecott to the front door, waving to her as she left, then closed the door. He changed the sign from "Please Come Inside" to "Please Knock Loudly." It wouldn't stop patients from arriving, but it would allow him more time to smooth things over with Miriam. She was collected, yes, and hadn't seemed upset, but Mrs. Endecott was only the most recent in a long string of townspeople coming by and expressing their disapproval of her.

It wasn't Miriam's fault the bureau had lied to her. It wasn't her fault she'd disliked him so much on first sight that she'd run—literally—from the church. It wasn't her fault the town would probably never forgive her for it. None of that was *his* fault, either, but he was a doctor. When something was wrong, he fixed it.

He entered the kitchen, unsure what he meant to say but hoping the words would come. Miriam sat at the worktable, sketching in her notebook.

He recognized the face she had drawn. "That's Mrs. Wilhite."

She looked up at him briefly. "I can't get her smile right. It's both happy and sad, but I can't seem to portray that."

He hadn't noticed that before, but now that he thought on it, he knew Miriam was correct. "I wonder if she took my advice about the tatting."

"I hope so." Miriam continued drawing as she spoke. "I know my observation wasn't welcome that first day, but I meant what I said about her not being overly sad. I don't even think she is *mostly* sad."

"I agree." He sat beside her. "Unfortunately, the balance has tipped more toward sad of late. It breaks my heart to see it."

"You care about your patients." It was a statement, but with a touch of wonder.

"I'm a doctor."

"Not all doctors care," she said quietly.

First questions about his willingness to offer pain relief to patients in surgery, then questions about his philosophy on institutionalizing harmless people, now this observation. What kind of people had she worked for in the past that these were her feelings about doctors?

He set a hand on hers. "Do you want to talk about it? I'm a good listener."

"I'm a good listener too," she said. "But mostly because I'm a very poor . . . talker."

It was oddly comforting to hold her hand, this woman he hardly knew. "You don't seem inarticulate. Do you simply prefer not to talk?"

"I've generally found it best." That was an unexpected answer. She didn't offer any further insights.

"Have you drawn everyone in town?" he asked.

"I haven't met everyone."

She made no attempt to pull her hand from his. He was grateful for the connection. Despite people coming in and out of his house all day, he was lonely.

"I drew something you would appreciate," she said.

"Did you?" Perhaps she'd drawn a portrait of him. Did he too have a smile that was contradictory? Some kind of oddity in his expression?

She slipped her hand free and flipped back a few pages. He tried to hide his disappointment at losing that simple touch. A man didn't generally like looking pathetic.

Miriam found what she was looking for and held up the sketch for him to see.

He laughed out loud, and it felt wondrous. "You've drawn my washstand?"

His heart did a little flip at the hint of her smile he was afforded.

"You said it was the most important part of your practice. I thought that worth documenting."

"It is a very good thing, then, that I didn't say the outhouse was the most important part."

She smiled at him, fully and genuinely. Laughter sparkled in her eyes. Hawk had the right of it: Miriam was beautiful.

Beyond that, she worked hard. She showed their patients kindness, despite not being shown it in return. She was forgiving and optimistic. Her conversation was enjoyable and intelligent.

Somehow, he'd accidentally picked a wife, sight unseen, with whom he could honestly get along, and whose company he suspected he could thoroughly enjoy. Unfortunately, he'd also picked one who didn't actually want to marry him. Her rejection would likely sting less if he'd discovered they would have been ill-suited from the start.

"I'll make supper," he offered stiffly, stepping away while he collected himself. Had they actually married the day she'd arrived, feeling this tug toward her would be a welcome thing. But they hadn't, and he wasn't certain if forging a friendship would make things better or worse.

"I can draw you a picture of the outhouse, if you'd like," Miriam said. "You seem so disappointed."

Had he given that impression? He looked at her, ready to explain, but enough amusement remained in her eyes to tell him she was teasing him. How unexpected. Welcome, but unexpected.

"I will let you know if I ever desperately want a portrait of the privy."

"I am here to help."

That she managed lightness helped him to do so as well. "Why don't you help me with supper?"

She closed her notebook and tied it with the leather strap. She rose and crossed to the stove, but then she paused and looked at him.

"Thank you," she said.

"For what?"

Her fingers fussed and twisted around each other. She took a deep breath. "I know very little these past few days has gone the way you expected. I'm certain you've been frustrated. But you've also been kind and considerate. Thank you for that."

Her thanks came with a degree of surprise for his being a decent human being. An ache started in his chest. Though she hadn't said as much directly, such moments spoke of a painful and difficult past.

"You are welcome, Miriam."

She turned her attention to the meal preparation, again withdrawn and quiet. She was guarded, and it seemed for good reason. The town might not be warming to her quickly, and he still felt awkward around her, but he would make certain that, in this home, she was treated with kindness. And he would do what he could to make certain he showed her that not all doctors were the monsters she hinted at having known.

Chapter 9

Miriam's years in Blackburn Asylum had been filled with one misery after another. The patients wallowed in hopelessness, often left to suffer untreated by a doctor who saw them as less than human. A grueling amputation brought on by neglect. Burying so many poor souls who had wanted nothing more than basic compassion. She'd tried to help as many as she could, but her options had been horribly limited.

She could still see their faces, so many pale, gaunt faces. Eyes pleading with her. Expressions wrought with agony and fear. She had made every attempt to heal them and help them—even in the dark of night. Once Dr. Blackburn had declared that a patient had received his or her allotment of medical care for the day or week or month, Miriam had been forbidden to do anything more. "There must be order," the doctor had said. "There must be schedules and allotments." He had insisted on it.

She had nursed them anyway. In the end, it had done little good. They died, sometimes suddenly, sometimes fading by degrees, leaving behind nothing but Dr. Blackburn's records of their treatments and the portraits she'd drawn of them.

Gideon's words from a few days earlier remained with her: "I address what I can. Beyond that, I try to help people live happy lives."

Dr. Blackburn certainly hadn't lived by that philosophy. His patients' happiness had never meant anything to him. They were peasants for him to lord over. Their illnesses were opportunities for him to prove his worth and line his pockets.

Miriam had seen the asylum ledgers. Dr. Blackburn had received reimbursements for medications she knew he hadn't administered, funds for equipment he never purchased, and stipends for patients he no longer housed. He was growing wealthy while his patients were suffering. And dying.

He had considered those patients with persistent conditions as a personal challenge. He was unwilling to leave them alone to "live happy lives" if it meant admitting he couldn't cure them. Miriam had lived in fear that she would have one of her episodes in his presence and he would make curing her his next impossible task. The patients whose healing became a matter of pride to him never survived. Not ever.

So, as awkward as things were with Gideon and this town, she couldn't truly complain. She hadn't once felt herself to be in danger where Gideon was concerned. On the contrary, she'd come to truly enjoy his company. She'd even begun to trust him a little.

"Rupert is coming by today." Gideon always reviewed their expected and potential patients each morning in the parlor. "Paisley told me Hawk cut his arm deeply yesterday. He may come by and have it looked at. The Jepsons south of town had a mare foal last night. I'd like to go check on the new arrival this afternoon."

Nervousness seized her. "If someone comes by while you're gone, do you think they will even let me help them?"

He shrugged. "If they are desperate enough." There was a hint of laughter in his response that set her more at ease.

Mrs. Fletcher and Rupert stepped inside only a moment later. Miriam was happy to see the little boy. He'd been the first in this town to show her true acceptance.

"Hop up on the table, Rupert, and give Nurse Bricks a 'howdy,'" Gideon said.

He moved to the washbasin while Miriam helped Rupert climb onto the table. Even with the step stool, Rupert had some trouble. His leg wouldn't fully heal for some time yet.

"What mischief have you been undertaking, Rupert?" Miriam asked. "And don't tell me 'none.' I think I know you well enough now to be certain that can't be true."

Rupert's gap-toothed grin was all the answer she needed.

"Keep it up," she whispered, then joined Gideon at the washbasin. "He is walking a little better."

"He is." Gideon glanced at Rupert. "I only hope I found all of the rot. I'd hate for him to have to endure another surgery."

He was an odd sort of doctor. His patients' comfort always came before his own. Even his pride seemed less important than their convenience. Miriam admired it, even though she didn't know what to make of it.

"I am getting nothing but pensive looks from you today," he said quietly. "Has something upset you?"

She wasn't about to admit that she'd been pondering *him* to the point of distraction. "You don't actually think Rupert will require further surgery, do you?"

He shook his head. "He would be more miserable than he is if the gangrene were still there."

She finished washing her hands and returned to the examination table. "How are you feeling?" she asked Rupert. "Have you been keen to obey the doctor's instructions?"

Rupert puffed his chest out proudly. "I even told my pa I couldn't do my chores in the barn on account of Doc saying I wasn't to get my cut-up part all dirty."

Only with effort did Miriam keep a straight face. "A great sacrifice on your part." She lowered her voice. "Do you know what great sacrifice *I* made on your behalf?"

He shook his head, watching her eagerly.

Gideon must have recognized her efforts as the distraction she meant them to be, because he set quickly to work unwrapping the boy's leg.

"I have hidden away a cinnamon cookie where Dr. Mac-Namara will never find it," Miriam said. "All so I could give it to you today if you had been good and obeyed his instructions."

"Doc didn't find it?" Rupert's eyes widened hopefully.

"He did not."

Gideon peeled back the final layer of bandaging. Miriam watched his expression for signs of concern but saw none.

"You have been using the tincture I gave you?" he asked Mrs. Fletcher.

Her brow lowered, heavy with worry. "Exactly the way you said to. I've been very careful."

"I can see that," he assured her. He wetted a bit of cloth with the same mixture he'd sent home with Mrs. Fletcher nearly a week earlier.

"It smells bad," Rupert said.

"I hope you are referring to the tincture and not Nurse Bricks's cookies." Gideon dabbed the wet cloth along the stitched-up wound. Rupert winced, but didn't object. No doubt he was used to it after nearly a week of treatments.

"Nurse Bricks's cookies don't smell bad," Rupert said once Gideon was finished. "Hers are the best cookies ever."

"Other than your mother's," Gideon whispered. "Make sure you say that part."

"Other than my ma's cookies," Rupert said, though with some hesitancy.

"Well done, Doctor." Miriam thoroughly enjoyed his sense of humor.

Gideon stood up. "Now, Nurse Bricks, I believe this brave young man has earned himself a cinnamon cookie, though I object to you hiding them from me. I spent half the night looking for the last one."

"You have to get your bones broken," Rupert said. "Then you can have all the cookies you want."

"That's a pretty stiff price. I think maybe I ought to try talking sweet to the cook instead, and see if that works." He winked at Miriam.

Heat immediately stole over her. She wasn't one to blush easily, but, when she did, it was always at the worst possible moment. She wanted to keep a strictly professional tone between them. Friendliness was dangerous.

She looked away from him and spoke to Rupert. "Don't you fret; I won't give him your cookie." She took his wrist in one hand and the pocket watch Gideon had lent her in the other. "I will give you Rupert's numbers, Doctor, if you'd like me to."

They had this part down to a flawless routine. She had a knack for finding a pulse; she was even quicker at it than Gideon was. He jotted down Rupert's pulse when she told it to him. Miriam had the boy lie flat on the table and measured his length, calling that number out as well—Gideon only measured the height of children, wanting to make certain their growth was continuing at the correct rate.

Having finished her part, Miriam took Rupert to the kitchen for his cookie.

"Is Doc gonna have to cut off more bits of me?" he asked as he climbed onto a kitchen chair, despite his heavily bandaged leg. Little ones were remarkably resilient, adapting quickly to their limitations.

"It doesn't seem so." Miriam set his cookie on the table in front of him.

Rupert grinned. "I like Doc. He's nice."

"Yes. He does seem to be."

Rupert took a generous bite of his cookie, obviously content with his reward. "Maybe you should marry him like you were supposed to."

Somehow she managed not to choke on her next words. "It isn't that simple."

"Sure it is." Crumbs flew from his mouth as he spoke. "You like him, and you are already here."

What would Gideon say if he heard that argument? Considering he had intended to marry someone who *wasn't* guaranteed to like him and who *wasn't* already there, he would probably find Rupert's ill-conceived plan a fantastic one.

"You make good cookies." Rupert took another bite. "I bet Doc likes your cookies."

The mischievous little boy was playing matchmaker. She could find some amusement in his efforts. "Doc likes my drawings."

"You draw?"

She nodded. "It is one of my favorite things."

"Could you draw me?"

She already had, but that portrait captured a moment of worry. He wouldn't enjoy seeing that. "If you will sit here very still, I will draw you a quick picture."

He nodded enthusiastically. Miriam took her notebook from the shelf she'd begun keeping it on. She withdrew a page from it and took up her pencil. Rupert must have truly wanted the picture. He kept quite still; only his eyes moved, darting to her again and again.

She made a quick sketch, nothing elaborate. It captured him though. His broad smile. The mischief in his expression. She even included his half-eaten cookie.

She slid the paper to him. "What do you think?"

His face lit with excitement. "That's me!"

She laughed quietly. "Of course it is."

He climbed off the chair. "I'm going to show Ma!" He hobbled from the room, clutching the paper in his hand.

Miriam returned her pencil to its rightful place, then quickly checked to make certain nothing had fallen out of her notebook. Everything was as it should be.

She crossed paths with Mrs. Fletcher as she made her way back to the parlor. "Did Rupert show you his picture?"

The woman watched her a moment, brow drawn. Was she upset?

"Would you rather I hadn't drawn it?"

"It was very kind of you," Mrs. Fletcher said. "He was so pleased with it."

Yet, Mrs. Fletcher still looked dissatisfied. "Is something the matter?"

"You and Dr. MacNamara seem to get along well." That was a weighted observation if ever Miriam had heard one. "He's a good man, you know. Exactly the sort a woman would be fortunate to—"

"Ours is a strictly professional relationship. Neither of us wishes for anything more."

"He still needs a wife." That was, apparently, supposed to be a strong argument.

Miriam forced her voice a touch stronger. "But I don't need a husband."

"You are opposed to marriage?"

Gideon had told her on her first day of employment that the town afforded him precious little privacy. Even little Rupert had been marching down this particular road.

She swallowed a lump of apprehension. What if they started asking questions she would have to refuse to answer? She might do best to address the things she could in the hope that they would leave her be if she satisfied their curiosity.

"I have no objections to marriage," she said, "and none to Dr. MacNamara in particular. I don't know him well, and, I will add, he doesn't know me either. I can tell you with absolute certainty that the more he knows me, the more grateful he will be for his escape." She pressed her lips closed on the instant. She'd inadvertently admitted more than she'd intended to. She was not usually so careless. Letting things slip was a good way to land herself in trouble. A quick exit seemed best. "If you'll excuse me."

Only then did Miriam discover Gideon standing in the parlor doorway, watching her. He'd overheard the entire exchange, no doubt, from Mrs. Fletcher's attempts at playing *re*matchmaker to Miriam's unintentional admission that someone actually acquainted with her was far more likely to be opposed to a match than someone who knew nothing of her.

Humiliation hit her like a bucket of hot water. What

little pride she possessed pooled at her feet. Perhaps if she moved quickly, she could reach the small recovery room behind the stairs and close herself in there to wait out the burning blush spreading over her face.

"I should—look into—" She couldn't formulate any kind of excuse, so she simply walked around the staircase. She slipped into the dim interior of the room and dropped her heated face into her hands.

"Miriam?" Gideon spoke from the open doorway.

Was she not even allowed to be embarrassed in private? After two years of near-total isolation, Miriam had expected to welcome some company and interaction. That was not proving to be the case.

She moved her hands away from her face and turned away.

"I am sorry, Miriam."

"What are *you* sorry about? I am the one who was caught talking about you behind your back."

"I am sorry this town is being difficult." He stepped around to face her. "I didn't realize they'd upset you this much." He took her hands in his. "I wish I could promise that they will eventually stop harping on the topic of our aborted wedding, but I suspect they won't for a long while yet."

His touch was comforting, reassuring. She even managed to look him in the eye. "You did warn me this arrangement would be awkward."

"Do you really believe *I* would have the biggest objection to a marriage between us?" His tone was as kind and soft as his touch.

"I know that you would." Men didn't generally care to marry women whose minds were broken and whose bodies offered evidence of it at unpredictable intervals.

"I would remind you," he said, "I happily contracted an

arranged marriage. That is not the action of a man who demands perfection in a union."

"It isn't a matter of falling short of perfection." She stepped away, and he released her hands. "If you truly knew me, you'd be thanking the heavens for how this all played out."

His slow smile shone with amusement. "I doubt that, Miriam."

"You shouldn't." She stepped to the doorway. "You really shouldn't."

With that, she moved to the kitchen, despite not having anything to do in there. She needed space. She needed time. In only one week, Gideon had begun chipping away at the walls that kept her safe. She couldn't afford to truly trust him, but she feared she was beginning to do just that.

Chapter 10

Late that evening, after Miriam had returned to the hotel, Gideon placed a sign in the window indicating he was next door at the jailhouse, then dragged himself across the small side yard with the express purpose of eating a large slice of humble pie.

Paisley sat in the chair at the desk. Cade sat on a stool beside her with his legs up on the desktop, crossed at the ankles.

"What brings you 'round, Gid?" she asked.

"You were right."

"I'm glad to hear it," Paisley said. "What was I right about?"

He sat on the edge of the half-wall that divided the jail cells from the rest of the room. "She's hiding something."

Hawk stepped out of the back room at exactly that moment. "We're talking about Miriam?"

Gideon eyed Paisley. "You told him about your suspicions?"

She held up her hands. "I didn't say a word."

"She didn't have to," Cade jumped in. "We ain't blind."

Cade and Hawk exchanged a knowing and amused glance. Gideon waited. Those two never needed encouragement.

"Your new nurse watches everyone as if she expects them to pounce at any moment," Cade said.

"She's nervous. That would make anyone a little stiff," Gideon said.

"I know 'nervous' when I see it," Hawk said. "There's more to it than that."

"Should I lock up my good silver, then?" Gideon paced to the window. He knew Miriam was being less than forthright, but found himself angry at hearing the others say as much.

"I don't suspect her of anything nefarious," Paisley said.

"Neither do I," Hawk added.

Cade switched his crossed ankles. "But she is keeping secrets, that much is clear."

"Maybe I should warn her, then, not to grow overly friendly with the law around here," Gideon said.

Paisley grinned as she rose, crossing to the open door. "We are terribly good at ferreting out secrets."

Not all secrets. None of them knew about Gideon's aborted engagement, nor the weight he felt at having fallen short of his family's expectations, nor did they have any idea that he was still haunted by the four months he'd spent working at St. Elizabeth's, an asylum in Washington.

Hawk pulled his black hat off its hook by the door. "So, Doc. Are you gonna cut out my liver if I ask that nurse of yours to the town sociable?"

"You're going to ask her right this moment?" Gideon inexplicably disliked the idea.

"I was considerin' it."

Cade unfolded himself, standing with easy, fluid movements. "If the two of you mean to have a shoot-out in the street, would you wait until I've a chance to clear things out first?"

"No one's shooting anyone." Gideon shook his head. "Though I can't imagine why Hawk would ask someone he thinks is being deceptive to a social."

Hawk remained unconcerned. "We're all deceptive about something, Doc. I doubt her secret is something degenerate. And I imagine there's a lot more about her I'd enjoy learning."

This sounded like more than merely a desire to be fair. "You're actually courting her?"

"Why shouldn't I be? Rumor has it, she ain't married."

Gideon heard the teasing in Hawk's laughing tone, but he refused to be goaded. "I've heard that rumor myself."

"Then why does this have your trousers in a knot?" Hawk's jesting timbre was beginning to give way to frustration.

"I am merely looking out for her." Gideon had seen firsthand the pain and vulnerability in her eyes that afternoon. She was hiding something, yes, but she was also afraid.

"I don't know that it's your place to champion her," Hawk said. "She turned you down, after all."

Cade set a spindle-back chair a few feet from where they stood and sat in it, facing them. "Don't stop on my account," he said. "I only want a better view when fists start flyin'."

"Miriam's coming this way," Paisley said.

Miriam was coming? Had something happened? Gideon watched the door as she stepped inside. She seemed hale and hearty. He opened his mouth to offer a greeting, but her gaze settled immediately on Hawk.

A bashful smile touched her face. "I had hoped to find you here."

"Had you?" Hawk sauntered to where she stood, tossing Gideon a smug look as he passed. "What can I do for you, Miriam?"

Gideon sidled toward the desk. He didn't want to leave, but neither did he care to stand nearby while Hawk flirted with Miriam. Public displays of affection were always uncomfortable. And it was the discomfort he objected to, not the twinge of envy or the undeniable confusion. The discomfort.

"You didn't come by to walk me home today," Miriam said to Hawk.

That had, it seemed, become quite a ritual between the two of them. It was a ninety-second walk, for heaven's sake. It wasn't as though she had miles and miles to cover.

"My apologies for that," Hawk said. "I received a telegram from my counterpart in Nebraska and needed to send an answer."

She froze. "Nebraska?" The single word emerged broken and choked.

Every eye in the room was suddenly on her.

"Nebraska," Hawk repeated. "He had an update about a band of train robbers. Nothing of immediate consequence, but worth being aware of."

The news would have alarmed most people, but Miriam, however, showed relief. What dire thing had she been expecting Hawk to reveal that word of train robbers was a relief?

"I heard you cut your arm," she said. "You didn't come by to have it looked at."

"And you were hoping to get a peek?"

Miriam's eyes darted to Gideon. "Unless Dr. MacNamara already has, that is."

"Doc and I have discussed a few things since he wandered over," Hawk said, clearly enjoying himself, "but my arm wasn't one of them."

Gideon had seen enough. He paused at Miriam's side on his

way toward the door. "If you see any signs of infection or a need for suturing, bring him by the house."

"I will." She didn't have a soft smile for him like she'd given Hawk, nor a grin of amusement like she'd offered him now and then.

He did his best not to think about that as he made the short trek back home. They got along well enough, which was more than he would have expected the day she'd run out of the church. He could be happy about that. Probably.

"Hold a minute, Gid."

Cade. Exactly the person he didn't need. Gideon flung him a look of severely tried patience.

Cade wasn't cowed in the least. "I'm the closest thing to neutral you've got in all this, amigo. Best not turn on me."

"Neutral?" Gideon climbed the steps to his front porch. "You wanted a fight so badly, you pulled up a chair in order to watch it."

"Only trying to cut the tension a bit."

Gideon leaned against one of the porch posts. "Is that what you're doing now as well?"

Cade mirrored his stance. "What made you suspect Miss Bricks of hiding something? You didn't seem to think it before."

"It was nothing, really. She said something about how anyone who knew her well wouldn't ever want to marry her." The more he thought about it, the more ridiculous it was to suspect her of deceptiveness based on something so small. And, yet, there'd been such insistence in her words, something that went beyond mere humility.

"I'd wager Nebraska has something to do with her mystery," Cade tossed out.

"You noticed it, too." Gideon didn't think any of them had missed it.

Cade nodded slowly. "But what is in Nebraska that she's so worried we'll hear about?"

Gideon shrugged. "Nothing the Western Women's Bureau sent me about her mentioned Nebraska."

Cade adjusted his hat so it sat lower on his head. His gaze turned to the street. Gideon recognized his "thinking" pose, and knew it was best not to interrupt.

"What if something happened there that she didn't tell them about? Maybe she falsified things in order to get this job."

He'd worried about that possibility the moment he'd realized the Western Women's Bureau had misled one or the both of them. "Her knowledge and abilities are extensive enough that I'm certain she's had training. She couldn't be lying about that."

Cade's gaze returned to him. "But she is lyin' about something."

Tension twisted inside. All he'd wanted was some help and some company, and now he had a potential disaster on his hands. He was meant to go out of town the next week to make visits, but could he leave Savage Wells to Miriam's care not knowing what she was hiding?

Cade straightened. "I'll see if I can find out if she's a wanted criminal or something."

"Thanks," Gideon muttered as he stepped inside his house.

What a mess. He'd told himself after Eleanor had called off their wedding that he would be better off not growing overly attached to a woman again.

He'd made the decision to arrange for a wife, taking a risk and letting some of his guard down. He hadn't ruled out the possibility of love growing between them, but would have been happy with a marriage based on mutual respect and trust. For that reason, his growing suspicions bothered him. He'd wanted to trust her.

And he'd only been proven foolish again.

He paced the parlor. Paisley had said she didn't suspect Miriam of anything truly sinister. Hawk hadn't either. But that was before she'd paled at the very mention of Nebraska. What did his friends think now? What did *he* think?

"She is a good nurse." He'd seen the proof of it again and again. "She is particularly good with children. She is patient with this town that's so determined to dislike her." Though perhaps the town had the right of it.

Gideon made another circuit, his thoughts spinning right along with him. He would have to keep an eye on her. And, out of necessity, would have to cancel any out-of-town visits until he knew for certain if he could leave the town in her hands.

He made a mental note to send a telegram to Garretsville letting them know he would have to postpone his trip. He would have to go to Luthy, though. There was a patient there whom he couldn't delay seeing.

"And I need Miriam to go with me," he realized, his stomach dropping. He muttered a few colorful words.

The door squeaked open. The flood of patients never seemed to slow down. It was little wonder he was exhausted. And why he needed a nurse. A *reliable* nurse.

The newest arrival, however, *was* the nurse.

"Is Hawk going to live?" It was a more petulant comment than he'd intended to make.

She ignored it. "You seemed out of sorts when you left the jailhouse. I wanted to make certain you weren't upset with me."

He was put out with her, but that wasn't quite the same thing as upset. "My mind is a little heavy. I have a patient in Luthy I'm concerned about." He hoped she wouldn't realize this was a change of topic and not an answer to her inquiry.

"Where is Luthy?" she asked.

"A few hours' drive from here." He lowered himself into an armchair. If he stayed on his feet, he would keep pacing.

"If you need to check on your patient, I can keep an eye on Savage Wells." She seemed eager enough to take on the responsibility. But he couldn't hand it to her yet. Not until he knew the truth.

"I fear she has an abdominal tumor," he said. "I can't be completely sure without an examination, but her husband won't allow a man to touch his wife, even in the context of a medical evaluation."

Miriam sat on the sofa. "What do you mean to do?"

"I am relatively hopeful that her husband would allow *you* to do the examination."

"I don't know the first thing about tumors," she admitted. "I wouldn't have any idea what to look for."

"I don't mean to toss you in there alone and tell you to do your best," he said. "Before driving out there to see her, I would let you know exactly what you would be looking for, in excruciating detail if need be. And you can read up on the topic in my medical books between now and then. During the exam, I would be nearby, and you would be able to ask questions of me as well."

Her gaze drifted away from him. She clasped her hands on her lap, her fingers clutching each other. "What if I make a mistake? I couldn't bear it if I hurt someone."

Gideon moved to sit beside her on the sofa. "Nothing about this visit would be life-and-death, Miriam. The situation is not that desperate yet. I am in need of more information so I can tell her and her husband what they ought to do next."

"You truly think I can do this?"

"I haven't a doubt in the world." *Not about this, anyway.*

"I'll do my best." She punctuated her statement with a firm nod.

She was such an odd mixture of calm confidence and deep doubts. He would have ample time during their long journey to study that contradiction, though he was a little nervous about what he might discover. He hoped the answer was less dire than he feared. "I'd like to go day after tomorrow, if that will work for you."

"Let me check my social calendar." She paused for the briefest of moments. "You're in luck. I've no prior engagements."

"Perfect."

Despite everything, he was beginning to like Miriam. He didn't want to have to send her away.

Chapter 11

Mr. Driessen agreed to Miriam's examination of his wife, but only if Gideon remained in a different room. Miriam hadn't expected to undertake the task without him directly beside her. Thank heavens he'd let her study his medical books over the last two days. She at least had some idea what she was looking for.

"Do you think it's somethin' bad?" Mrs. Driessen asked as Miriam felt around the swelling.

"Dr. MacNamara is far more experienced in this area than I am, but I will gather all the information I can so he can determine the state of things."

Mrs. Driessen nodded, though her anxiety didn't lessen. "My Frank has been so terrible to him. He doesn't trust doctors—thinks they're all snake-oil salesmen."

Miriam concentrated as she pressed her fingers along the outermost edge of the tumor. She'd wager it measured nearly three inches end-to-end. Very little of the tumor pressed upward. Mrs. Driessen winced repeatedly during the examination.

"Does it hurt more when I press on it?" Miriam needed to be certain the information she gave Gideon was correct.

"It does," she said. "I know you're helpin' me, though, so I'm tryin' not to complain."

"I appreciate that, but I do need to know all I can. Dr. MacNamara can't help you if he doesn't know everything." Miriam began checking for signs of swelling around the tumor. "Is there anything else unusual you've noticed that he doesn't know about? No matter how unconnected it might seem to you, please tell me."

She spoke of a diminished appetite and of needing to run to the outhouse more frequently. Miriam listened even as she continued her examination. She could find no signs of further tumors, no swelling elsewhere.

"And—" Mrs. Driessen's face flushed on the instant.

Miriam recognized the embarrassment for what it was— something of a more personal nature. "Please, go on. It may be important."

"My monthlies've been odd. There's bleeding between them, and when they come, they come heavy."

If Miriam didn't miss her mark, that symptom was a significant one. She jotted down every bit of information she had gathered, afraid she would forget something crucial. Once she'd finished, she turned back to Mrs. Driessen, still lying on her bed, pale-faced. "Is there anything else you think I ought to share with the doctor?"

She shook her head. "Do you have to tell him about my monthlies?"

"I think I had better."

Mrs. Driessen's color faded further. "But men put so much store by that sort of thing. What'll he think of me?"

She squeezed Mrs. Driessen's hand. "I know without a doubt that some doctors would use that as an excuse to dismiss your suffering or justify mistreating you, but I don't for a moment believe Dr. MacNamara would do either." She was depending on it, in fact.

"He is very kind," Mrs. Driessen said. "He didn't give up on me, even after all the grief my Frank has given him."

"Precisely." Miriam stood, grabbing her paper and lead pencil from the bedside table. "I'll pass this information on to Dr. MacNamara and let him discuss with you and your husband what it means and what you ought to do. Take a moment to collect yourself or take a quick nap or whatever appeals most. Doctor's orders," she added with a smile.

Mrs. Driessen sighed. "A nap does sound heavenly. And the children are next door."

"Then I suggest you get to it right away."

What wouldn't Miriam give to return to a time when sleep was heavenly and not filled with nightmares of Blackburn Asylum?

Miriam closed the door softly, then made her way across the room. The small house had only one large room with a bedroom to one side and a loft. This was not a wealthy family by any means.

Gideon rose as Miriam approached, his expression focused and serious. She handed him the paper. His eyes scanned it without hesitation.

Mr. Driessen crossed toward the bedroom with loud, heavy steps.

"Your wife is resting," Miriam said. "A medical necessity." She spoke as firmly as she could manage.

Without even being prodded, Gideon spoke up. "It would be best if you let her sleep for however long she needs. An examination can be quite exhausting."

Though he didn't seem to understand the reason for the dictate, Mr. Driessen moved away from the bedroom door.

Gideon returned his attention to Miriam's notes. "The tumor is three inches across?"

"Perhaps a little smaller than that, but very close."

"Larger than I thought," he said, obviously to himself. His eyes continued to fly over the page. He must have been rereading; there was not that much written there. He dropped his voice to a low whisper. "Her monthly cycles have changed?" Gideon's posture spoke of tension. "This is not good, Miriam."

She slipped her hand around his arm and pulled him aside enough for their conversation to be more private. "I realize that disruptions in a woman's cycle are often seen as a symptom of madness." Several of the women at Blackburn had been sent there for precisely that reason. "Her body is ailing, but she seemed in complete possession of her faculties."

"There are few things that, in and of themselves, are a sign of madness," Gideon said. "Insanity is a rather drastic diagnosis to make based on one symptom alone." He folded the paper and slipped it into his vest pocket. "I must talk with Mr. Driessen. He and his wife have a few decisions to make."

He stepped away, quite as if he hadn't said something shocking. He didn't believe in making a diagnosis of madness based on a single physical symptom. The possibility was unprecedented. Her diagnosis had been based on just one thing—an unignorable, unexplainable, incurable, frightening one, yes, but only the one. Maybe he wouldn't have resigned her to the same fate others had. It was a theory she didn't dare test yet, but even the idea offered the first bits of hope she'd felt in years.

She looked over at Gideon as he spoke to Mr. Driessen. Something Gideon said left that mountain of a man visibly shaken. He lowered himself to a nearby chair, his color ashen. Their conversation continued in low tones, their words too quiet to be understood from a distance.

"I didn't realize she was so bad off," Mr. Driessen said. "Can't you do anything for her?"

"She needs a surgeon experienced in this particular difficulty," Gideon said. "She needed one weeks ago, but the nearest one I would trust with this is in St. Louis. You would do even better to take her to New York or Boston."

Mr. Driessen's shoulders hunched forward. "I haven't the money for a trip like that."

"You drive for the stage occasionally," Gideon said. "Perhaps you could take on a few extra driving jobs."

Mr. Driessen looked up, his eyes bleak. "What should I tell the surgeon is wrong with her?"

"When you're ready to make the trip, send word. I'll write up the information you'll need."

"Thank you, Doc." Mr. Driessen turned and looked at Miriam. "And thank you, Miss Bricks. If I can ever repay you . . ."

She waved that off. "I'm glad I could be of help."

Gideon turned to Mr. Driessen. "Let me know what you decide."

He received a silent acknowledgment in response.

They let themselves out.

They began their journey back to Savage Wells, and in no time at all, Luthy was but a dot on the horizon.

"Thank you for what you did today, Miriam." Gideon kept his eyes on the path and his hands on the reins as he spoke. "Mrs. Driessen has weighed on my mind for weeks."

"Is there anything that can be done for her?" She rubbed a hand against her temple.

"There is a surgeon in Cheyenne who could *try* to remove the growth. Surgeries are risky, however, especially this far West."

"And *not* having the operation? Is that a risk as well?" Miriam asked.

"A tremendous risk."

Poor woman. "Do you have any other texts I could read? I have a sinking feeling that, when you are away, people will come by with complaints I haven't the first idea how to address."

"Every book I own is at your disposal, and you may ask me any question you have," he said. "I don't claim to be the best teacher, but I will certainly try."

"You don't mind me thumbing through your papers and such?" Dr. Blackburn had expressly forbidden such a thing. The rule hadn't stopped her—access to his records had been her only hope of helping the others in the sanatorium—she'd simply had to do it in the dark of night, at great risk. Being caught meant . . .

She wrapped her arms around herself. Her hand rested on the lump of her sketchbook in her coat pocket. It was still there. Still safe.

Gideon guided the buggy off the road with no explanation.

"Another patient?" she asked, but she didn't see any signs of a home nearby.

"No. We're going to have supper while the weather is holding." He eyed the leaden sky. "The road is treacherous in the rain."

"I would rather not be driven off a precipice, if you don't mind." She wasn't usually one for jests, though that had begun to change since she'd come to Savage Wells.

"What a pity it would be to keep to the road when precipices are so much more adventurous."

All of the other doctors she'd known had been ceaselessly serious, to the point that they often added to the burden of worry their patients carried. Gideon was so wonderfully different from the rest. His humor lightened her burdens.

He stopped in the shade of a small group of trees and wrapped the reins around a low branch. He stepped around the buggy and handed her down. Then, with a quickness that spoke of practice, he spread a wool blanket on the ground and set down a basket of food.

"This is the point where I usually go for a walk around the pond," he said, motioning to a small body of water not far distant. "It helps me clear my mind. Please don't think you have to wait for me. I'm certain you're hungry."

Her stomach was rather desperate for attention. Her nerves had dampened her appetite at breakfast, and she'd worked through lunch. "Enjoy your walk. I will try to leave some food for you."

His smile was distant. Clearly his mind was heavier than he was letting on. "The mercantile in Luthy always sends me home with more food than I can possibly eat. Have as much as you'd like."

"Thank you. I will."

He tucked his hands in his coat pocket and walked away. Stretching his legs brought him calm and relief. Sketching brought her that same peace.

She sat on the blanket, her back against an obliging tree. With her feet flat against the blanket, she propped her notebook against her bent knees. She'd often sat that way on the floor of her room at the asylum, her legs acting as a desk. The position felt almost whimsical in the fresh air of the meadow.

There had been a moment with Mrs. Driessen when the woman's expression had lightened, when the worry that had filled her seemed to ease. That was the look Miriam wanted to capture: hope.

She worked at the sketch as the minutes stretched on. There never was time to clean up the drawings and make them anything but rough pencil strokes. Still, she was happy with them. Drawing had seen her through some very difficult times.

When Gideon returned, he said, "You didn't eat."

"I was distracted."

He sat beside her, which she hadn't expected. She liked it, though. His company was comforting and enjoyable. She wasn't afraid of him the way she was of nearly every doctor she'd ever known.

"You are very talented," he said, looking at her sketch. "I can't say I've ever seen that expression on Mrs. Driessen's face. She only ever looks tired and defeated."

Miriam filled out the hair in her drawing. "She looked this way for only a moment, when she was telling me that she was grateful you didn't give up on her."

"Giving up is not in my nature," he said. "That frustrated my mother to no end."

"We have that in common, it seems. I frustrated my parents to the point that leaving home was my only option."

He watched her with drawn brows. "They tossed you out?"

"I left." Heavens, how was he managing to get her to talk about this? She closed her sketchpad. "Shall we eat?"

He didn't accept the change of subject. "If you were to draw your parents in your book, what expression would they be wearing?"

"Disappointment." She spoke without even thinking.

He took her hand, as he had once before at his kitchen table. It was a kind and gentle gesture. She'd needed kindness these past years.

She let her gaze take in the small meadow, a line of trees

meandering along its edge, and the pond in the distance. The stiff breeze drowned out any noise the water might have made.

"This is a lovely spot," she said.

"It is." He leaned against the other side of the same tree she was using, still holding her hand. "If I didn't need to be easily found by townsfolk at all hours of the day and night, I would build myself a house right here."

She turned her face toward the wind, closing her eyes. Too many long days spent shut up indoors at the asylum had granted her a deep appreciation for the invigoration of fresh air. She had often stood at the windows of Blackburn, desperately watching the horizon, wanting to leave, even if only for a moment.

"We should probably eat." His breath tickled her ear.

Far from flinching at the nearness, as she would have with anyone else, she leaned toward him, resting her head against him. His arm slipped behind her, settling around her waist. She pulled her sketchbook to her heart, her hands crossed over it, and tucked herself into his unexpected embrace.

"Thank you for your help today, Miriam. I couldn't have done a thing for Mrs. Driessen without you."

"It was nice to be permitted to help."

"Did you work for a doctor who didn't allow you to do your job?"

She adjusted her position, growing more comfortable nestled beside him. "I worked for a doctor who didn't allow me to be a human being."

There was a pause. A long moment. "Was this doctor in Nebraska?"

She stiffened. Her heart pounded in her neck. She sat up straight, and eyed him. "Why would you ask that?"

"Something about Nebraska rattles you. I've been at a loss to discover what."

He was too sharp for her peace of mind.

She scooted away, every nerve on edge. She kept a tight hold on her sketchbook.

He watched her closely. "I've told you before I'm a good listener. And I'm trustworthy. If something is weighing on you—"

"There's not." The falsehood sat uneasy on her lips. If anyone who knew her history realized where she was, her entire world would come crashing painfully and dangerously down around her.

Gideon looked away. "I guess it's a good thing we didn't get married after all. I don't think I could have been happy with someone who can lie to me so casually."

"That is your assessment of me?" It shouldn't have bothered her, but it did.

"I know you're not telling me the truth." He stood and took a step away. "It is difficult to trust you with my patients' lives when you won't trust me with any of the details of yours."

He had no idea what he was asking of her. "I am entitled to my secrets, Gideon."

He sighed. "If you ever decide to sketch a picture of me, you can draw me disappointed, as well."

A sharp turn in the wind chilled her, even as his words seared through her. She had let his gentleness lull her into feeling safe. Had life not shown her often enough that she was never safe?

Miriam stood, a white-knuckled grip on her sketchbook. "It is a little cold. I think I will wait in the buggy."

"You haven't eaten." His tone had softened, but it did little to ease her anguish.

"I'm more tired than hungry." She moved swiftly toward the buggy. "I'll just close my eyes and see if I can't fall asleep."

He watched her, brow pulled. After a moment, he nodded and hunched down by the picnic basket.

"I'm sorry I'm a disappointment." Her voice broke on the words. "It's another of my talents."

She climbed into the buggy and set herself on her side of the bench. She tucked her sketchpad into her pocket, then buttoned her coat against the biting wind. Gideon sat beside the picnic basket, eating his supper alone. She'd lied about more than Nebraska; she was actually very hungry. But she didn't like to cry in front of people, especially people who could hurt her as quickly and deeply as he had.

Her first tear fell in the very moment rain began tapping against the roof of the buggy. She turned so she faced away from the spot where Gideon would, thanks to the rain, be sitting in a moment's time, and feigned sleep.

He climbed inside in the next instant. He didn't say anything, though he must have known she was awake. In silence, he set the horse in motion and pointed them toward home. *His* home. She didn't truly have one. Perhaps someone like her was never meant to.

Chapter 12

Gideon kept the horse to a reasonable pace: slow in deference to the mud, but quick in light of the dangers of getting stuck overnight in such weather. He'd never had much of a temper, yet he was struggling to hold back his frustration. If he couldn't trust Miriam to give him an honest answer, even if that answer was "I'd rather not say," how could he entrust her with the well-being of hundreds of people?

The rain came down in sheets too strong and too constant for even the roof of the buggy to keep them entirely dry. What he wouldn't give for some isinglass curtains for his buggy.

Miriam sat with a blanket wrapped around herself. She'd not said a word since they'd resumed their journey. For the first thirty minutes, she'd sat facing away from him. Then she'd moved closer to him, though likely because the weather had turned so miserably cold. He didn't for a moment believe things were patched up between them. And he couldn't for the life of him explain why he wished they were.

When she'd sat in his arms under that tree, content and comfortable, he'd had the most unexpected sense of serenity. The isolation he so often felt had disappeared, not merely because someone was beside him, but because *she* was.

Then he'd reached out to her with tenderness and sincerity, and she'd responded with a lie. An unhesitating, determined lie. He had, it seemed, only been fooling himself. Again.

The mud was growing thicker, but they weren't too far from home. He could work out his tension with an hour or two on his cello.

He felt her brush against his shoulder. He looked over just as her head bobbed against him.

"Sorry," she slurred as her head bobbed again. Twice more the exact scenario played out.

"Lean your head against me," he said. "We still have a few miles to go."

"Sorry." But she let her head settle on his shoulder. As they continued down the wet road, she silently grew heavier against him.

This was what he'd hoped for when he'd sent for a wife. Someone to sit beside him, to talk with, to chase away his loneliness. Someone to argue with hadn't been on his list. He'd seen enough tension between his parents to know he didn't want to live that way.

The vast nothingness spread out on either side as the rain continued and the day grew dimmer until, at last, they reached the outskirts of Savage Wells. Gideon guided the buggy down the main street, pulling to a stop in front of the livery stable.

"Miriam." He gently nudged her.

Her eyelids fluttered a few times before opening.

"I have to stable the horse and buggy. We'll have to run back to my house in the rain."

She nodded, though he couldn't guarantee she fully understood.

He hopped down. "Be right back." He ran inside, braving the downpour. It took but a moment to let Jeb know he was back. The man was a wonder with horses and equipage; he'd have the wet, soggy mess sorted out in no time.

Gideon returned to the buggy. He reached up for Miriam. She allowed him to lift her to the ground. He moved the blanket from around her shoulders so it covered her head, then he grabbed the picnic basket.

"Run like your life depends on it."

They ran across the narrow gap behind the buildings on Main Street. Mud splattered everywhere, squishing into his boots and piling heavy on his trouser cuffs. Neither of them slowed until they came around the side of his house and onto the front porch.

He pulled his house key from his pocket. As he began sliding it into the lock, the door inched open. Why wasn't it locked?

"Someone is in my house," he said under his breath, peeking around the doorframe. "Wait here."

"And freeze to death? Not a chance."

He stepped inside, Miriam right on his heels, eyeing the entryway for signs of an intruder. Heavy footsteps approached from the parlor. Gideon reached behind himself, taking hold of Miriam's hand, reassuring himself she was there and safe. A broad-shouldered figure stepped out.

Cade. What was he doing there?

"You ought to know you can't leave town without some kind of disaster happening while you're away," Cade said.

"What disaster?" He didn't release Miriam's hand, though he no longer suspected any danger. He was, it seemed, a glutton for punishment, allowing himself to imagine the comfort he felt in that simple touch wasn't going to hurt him in the end.

"Barney wandered off," Cade said. "He's been found; he's not in danger. But he took a thorough soaking, and Paisley's worrying herself into a whirlwind, afraid he'll develop an inflammation of the lungs like he did the last time he was drenched to the core."

"I'll have a look at him." He turned to Miriam, pulling his hand from hers and holding the basket out to her. "Change and warm up, then have a bite to eat."

"But there's a patient," she said.

"I don't need your help with this."

Color splotched her cheeks, just as it had in the meadow when he'd admitted to his disappointment. She lowered her eyes. "I understand."

She turned and stepped into the small room beneath the stairs and closed the door. A chasm was growing between them, and he didn't know whether to try to bridge it or simply accept that this was what happened anytime he let himself grow fond of a woman.

Chapter 13

Gideon rubbed his face, trying to shake off the bone-deep exhaustion he felt. Barney hadn't grown ill, though he'd remained in one of the upstairs rooms overnight, mostly to calm Paisley's worries. Her father had coughed a little during the night, which had pulled Gideon from his own bed to check on him. He was painfully deprived of sleep, with no end in sight.

The front door opened. Gideon didn't look up immediately. Someone needed a doctor, and he wasn't sure he had it in him to be one just then. Except he didn't have a choice. *This* was what he'd come to Savage Wells to do. It was what he'd devoted his life to, and exhaustion couldn't be permitted to get in the way of his work.

"Oh, Gideon, you look so tired," Mrs. Wilhite's voice greeted him.

He looked up. She seemed quite hale for a woman in her seventies, who had been complaining of a sore throat only two weeks earlier. That was a relief.

She held up the basket she carried in her hands. "I've brought breakfast, and I will not leave until you and Barney Bell have eaten your fill. I promise there is enough for everyone."

Except she hadn't listed *everyone*. "What about Miriam? She is here, as she is every day."

The town still hadn't forgiven her for something which had, in all honesty, not been her fault. And they didn't seem willing to acknowledge how much she had done for them in the two weeks since her arrival.

"There is enough for her as well."

Miriam ought not to have been an afterthought. But he was too weary to argue. "Miriam is in the kitchen with Mr. Bell. I can't say how she did it, but there was none of his usual fear with her."

Gideon didn't mean to look that particular gift horse in the mouth, but he wished he knew how she'd managed it. Easing Mr. Bell's worries grew trickier as his mind further deteriorated. Miriam's approach might work with Andrew. Perhaps when he was less exhausted, he could sort that out.

And then maybe he could get to the bottom of Miriam's connection to Nebraska, then he could understand her propensity to lie to him, then decide when and if to make his journeys around the territory, and a hundred other things that weighed on him day in and day out. He hadn't had a chance to play his cello in days. If ever he'd needed a minute or two with his music, it was now.

"Come into the dining room, Gideon." Mrs. Wilhite offered the invitation with a mixture of firmness and empathy. "You can sit and eat and not think about anything else for a few minutes."

"That would be heavenly."

He stood and allowed himself to be led to the dining room. Mrs. Wilhite served him a generous helping of sausage, boiled eggs, and corn bread drizzled with honey. He breathed in the mouthwatering aroma. Bless Mrs. Wilhite.

She took up the basket once more. "I'll take this to the kitchen for Miss Bricks and Barney."

"Thank you."

She slipped out. He dove into his meal, devouring it in moments. His stomach no longer empty, sleep deprivation quickly caught up with him.

He pushed his plate to the side and laid his head on the table. The position was anything but comfortable, but at least it required no effort. He closed his eyes and took a deep breath, letting the tension slip from his shoulders. The house stood, for once, still and quiet. Blissfully, blessedly quiet.

You have a patient, he reminded himself. For a long moment, his body refused to bow to the dictates of his mind. He sat there, head on the table, unable to move. When he felt himself beginning to drift off, he sat up and shook himself awake.

He took his empty plate and used utensils with him to the kitchen. Mrs. Wilhite was gone, but Miriam and Mr. Bell were at the worktable, sitting on opposite sides. She'd known enough, then, to give him some space.

"Of course you don't have to eat all of it," she said to Mr. Bell. "If you aren't hungry anymore, you can be done."

Mr. Bell nodded vaguely. "I think I'm not hungry. Maybe. I might be, but probably not."

Gideon's gaze fell on Miriam. How would she respond to his indecision? Too many people reacted with annoyance or frustration.

Miriam didn't look the least bit bothered. "Is there anything else you think you might be?"

"Tired." He answered quickly, decisively.

"Perhaps you'd like to lie down for a while," Miriam suggested.

His mouth turned down. He looked around the kitchen, searching for something. "I don't sleep here."

"Your bed is upstairs." Miriam stood, smiling at Mr. Bell. "You can sleep up there."

His shoulders relaxed on the instant. "A good idea, Lizzie. Upstairs."

Lizzie? That was a name Gideon hadn't heard Mr. Bell use before. Who did he think Miriam was? A sister, perhaps? A childhood friend? It was impossible to know where in his lifetime Mr. Bell's mind was from one moment to the next.

Miriam and Mr. Bell walked toward the door, and she paused by Gideon's side. "I'll see that Mr. Bell finds his bed, then I'll return and clean up."

"I can clean up," he insisted. "You look every bit as tired as I feel."

"We'll work together," she suggested. "Then we can both get a moment's rest that much sooner."

"I accept."

Then he was alone in the kitchen, left with little to interrupt the silence beyond the lingering guilt of seeing Miriam still withdrawn and guarded. Until yesterday, she'd smiled at him now and then, jested a little. She'd been lighter and happier, and so had he. All that was gone now.

He pulled another slice of corn bread from the basket. He wasn't particularly hungry, but Mrs. Wilhite's corn bread was impossible to pass up. One bite at a time, he made his way through the bit of heaven. He refused to let his mind think about anything other than each morsel of food and the promise of his bed. He wasn't delusional enough to think the effort would continue to work. Worries inevitably worked their way through the cracks in his defenses.

"Mr. Bell was confused, but I convinced him the room was, indeed, his," Miriam said as she stepped into the kitchen.

"Thank you for being patient with him. Not everyone is."

She carried the plates from the sink to the table. "There was a man, a patient I worked with, named George, who spent day after day, hour after hour, asking for an apple. Only ever an apple." She scraped the leftover bits of food into the scrap bucket. "He was never violent or angry. He always seemed sad. His family grew weary of hearing about apples and, in their impatience, turned him over to a doctor whose solution was to ply poor George with one concoction after another."

Gideon knew all too well the inhumanity too many doctors showed to those whose minds were struggling. "Did George stop asking for an apple?"

Miriam pulled her sketchbook from the shelf where she'd begun keeping it. She flipped through until she reached a particular page. She turned it around so he could see the drawing. A man, slumped in a chair, mouth hanging open, eyes utterly empty.

"This is George, as he is now—or when I last I saw him, at least. This is him every hour of every day." She pulled the sketchpad back and gazed at it, her expression one of sadness. "He no longer asks for apples. He no longer speaks. Or interacts. He sits day after day, staring at walls. He was rendered a shell of a person—in deference to his family's preference and to the delight of his doctor, he is a *silent* shell."

Miriam's story didn't surprise Gideon, but it still wasn't easy to hear. Doctors had the potential to do so much good in the world. Why did some choose to inflict pain instead?

"The sight of him so empty still haunts me," Miriam said.

"Then why did you draw him like that?"

Her eyes snapped back to him. "So I won't forget." She closed her book. "So I won't forget that people like George and Andrew and Barney Bell and so many others who are at the mercy of their struggling minds don't deserve the misery too many people heap upon them. So I never forget that they are worth fighting for."

Her impassioned declaration chipped away at the lingering frustration he felt over the secrets she was keeping from him. She was a good person in addition to being a good nurse. But he wasn't certain how they would build true trust between them.

"When I ducked over to the hotel earlier to fetch my shawl, I noticed Andrew was sitting in a tree," Miriam said. "I offered a hello, but he didn't respond. He didn't even seem to hear me, though he must have."

Gideon's heart dropped. Andrew hadn't retreated to the trees in weeks. "He spent most of the war up in trees, acting as lookout. He returns there when he is overwhelmed or afraid."

Heartache entered her deep blue eyes. "He hides there from the broken bits of his mind."

That was it exactly. "He used to spend every waking hour in the trees, but he'd been doing better these past months."

"He will come down when he's ready," she said. "Let us hope it is sooner rather than later."

He pulled the broom from the corner and began sweeping. "I worked in a sanatorium for six months," he said. "The hardest six months I've spent as a doctor."

"I was at one for two years," she said.

He didn't like talking about his experience, but if he opened up to her, she might do the same.

"I worked at St. Elizabeth's in Washington."

She wiped down the tabletop with a rag, not looking at him. "I was never there."

"Where was the asylum you worked at?"

Still bent over the table, she whispered, "Nebraska."

Nebraska. This was her secret, then. He seldom discussed what he'd seen and experienced at St. Elizabeth's. She likely felt the same.

He returned the broom to the corner and moved to the table. He reached forward and took her hand. "I'm sorry I've pushed you about this. I have a few memories of my own that I can't bear to relive. It was wrong of me to try to force you to do so."

"You have no idea," she whispered.

He gently turned her enough to face him. He needed her to see that he was sincere. "If you ever want to talk, know that I will listen. But I won't broach the subject again unless you wish to. And I will do my best to give you the benefit of the doubt when other subjects arise that you aren't comfortable discussing."

"Won't that 'disappoint' you?" Though she clearly tried to make the remark sound offhanded, the pain beneath it was all too obvious.

"I have spent most of my adult life being lied to by women, which is something I don't think I've ever confessed to anyone before. Feeling misled is a particular sensitivity of mine."

Her gaze turned concerned. "I ought to have at least told you that Nebraska was where I worked as a nurse and a place I don't have fond memories of. I should have said that, rather than pretend there was nothing significant about it. I am sorry for that."

"We are getting quite good at apologizing." He let himself smile a little. "Perhaps we should make a habit of it."

"Or *not* make a habit of doing the things we have to apologize for in the first place."

He smiled more fully. "I like your idea better."

"Who are these other women who have been lying to you?"

Though he'd guarded his history since coming to Savage Wells, he found himself unexpectedly willing to speak of it. At least a bit. "Let us just say that you are not the first woman I intended to marry who, in the end, decided against it. Although you are the first one I never directly made the offer to."

"We can reasonably blame this on the Western Women's Bureau." A hint of mischief touched her expression. "They should apologize to us."

"Another excellent idea."

She set her other hand around his, clasping his between both of hers. "I'm sorry those women deceived you, Gideon. And I'm sorry you are disappointed in me."

"I shouldn't have said that. Certainly not the way I did." He'd regretted it ever since. "My parents and I don't get along for exactly the same reason."

Her gaze dropped to their hands. "Likely not *exactly* the same."

He brushed the thumb of his free hand along her jaw. She raised her eyes to him. "Will you give me a chance to prove to you I'm not a terrible person?"

"I've watched you with your patients. I know you're not a terrible person."

He touched a stray curl hanging loose from her braid. His heart pounded so hard she must have heard it. He tried to take a breath, but his lungs fought him.

"Miriam, I—"

She stepped back. His hand dropped away.

"I should finish my cleaning," she said.

With a little distance between them, his heart calmed, but

only a bit. "And I should update my patient files from our visits yesterday."

She nodded and turned away, grabbing the broom he'd left in the corner. He slipped from the kitchen. One step into the hallway, though, and he stopped.

What in the world had just happened?

Chapter 14

Miriam's first trip to the mercantile began on a cold footing. Mr. and Mrs. Holmes, who ran the shop, hadn't yet forgiven her despite some of the townsfolk having warmed to her. The Fletchers said hello when she passed, the preacher and his wife had smiled at her after services on Sunday, and Paisley and Cade tipped their hats and asked after her health when they crossed paths. The rest of Savage Wells was making the transition from adversary to ally much more slowly.

Having received her first pay, Miriam reconciled her bill with the hotel, and then set money aside for next month's bill. She had a small amount left and meant to treat herself. For two years, she'd dreamed of a colorful ribbon for her hair or an anise candy. On her truly desperate days, she'd even let herself imagine having a dress that wasn't gray, the only color Blackburn's inmates were permitted to wear. She'd escaped with only two of the drab, shapeless dresses—the dresses she was still wearing. She wore them every day, but secretly dreamed of something colorful and beautiful.

A pink dress, edged in lace, hung in the window of the

mercantile. Her hair was too red for wearing pink, yet it was tempting.

Mrs. Holmes passed by. She had done so several times since Miriam had arrived at the mercantile but had noticeably ignored her.

"Pardon me," Miriam said.

Mrs. Holmes paused, but with the posture of one fully intending to move along quickly.

"How much for the dress in the window?" she asked.

"Two dollars and seventy-five cents."

She couldn't justify such an expense. Perhaps eventually. Mrs. Holmes moved on, helping another customer, and Miriam wandered toward the table of notions. She couldn't afford a dress, but a ribbon for her hair might be within her reach. The table held no ribbons. She didn't see any nearby.

No ribbons, then.

A rainbow of candies filled the row of lidded jars on the countertop. She stepped up to the jars. The black candies looked like anise. Her mouth instantly began watering. She'd craved the candies, favorites of hers since childhood, for two years. Two years.

Mr. Holmes was behind the counter but didn't acknowledge her.

"How much are the anise candies?" she asked.

"Two for a penny."

She didn't bother to hold back her delight. "Four, please."

Mr. Holmes yanked off a small square of paper, then pulled out four pieces of anise candy. With brusque, annoyed movements, he folded the paper around the candies. Miriam's eyes fell on a small spool of fine ivory thread, just the right thickness for tatting.

"What is the cost of this thread?"

"Two bits." Her questions clearly irritated him.

Twenty-five cents. That wasn't too expensive. "I'll take the thread as well, please. And do you have lead pencils?"

"A penny a piece."

"Two, please."

Mr. Holmes set the tatting thread on the counter with a thud, then fetched the pencils.

She counted out twenty-nine cents. Having spent a few weeks working for Gideon, and seeing how and what he was paid by the people who came to see him and those he traveled to treat, she knew with certainty he would never grow wealthy; he would likely never be anything other than comfortable. In light of that, her meager salary felt quite generous.

She thanked Mr. Holmes and slipped the candy and pencils into her coat pocket, but she kept the tatting thread in her hand. She'd told Gideon she would only be gone for a quarter hour. Though she felt certain he wouldn't begrudge her a few extra minutes, she didn't care to be late.

Fortunately, Mrs. Wilhite did not reside far from Gideon's house—almost directly across the street. Miriam made her way there quickly. The front of the house was a millinery shop, though she hadn't been inside yet.

On the front step, she hesitated. Mrs. Wilhite had been cordial during her brief visit to Gideon's house a few days earlier, but the woman was by no means warmly welcoming. Yet, Miriam could not forget the memory of her sad, careworn eyes the day she'd come complaining of a sore throat.

Miriam had had no apple for George. She'd not been able to determine what Mr. Bell was craving during his brief stay at Gideon's home. But she could give something to Mrs. Wilhite, something to lift her spirits.

She pushed open the door. The shop was utterly chaotic. Bonnets hung from hooks and nails and sat on tabletops, surrounded by a mishmash of silk flowers, feathers, and the largest assortment of ribbons Miriam had ever seen. She had frequented the millinery shops of New York in the years before her parents stopped allowing her in public. Not one of them had carried so much ribbon.

Mountains of ribbon, and she hadn't a single penny to spare. She ought to have passed up the candy or perhaps purchased only one pencil. Then she might have had, at last, a ribbon for her hair.

An older woman, sitting near the far wall, looked up at Miriam. Her smile faded quickly. Most of the town went through that transformation when they saw her. Disapproval. Disappointment. Miriam hid the pain of their rejection behind a mask of serenity.

"Is Mrs. Wilhite here?" she asked the woman.

"She's lying down."

In the middle of the day? "Is she unwell?"

"Wilma's been tired lately is all."

Being tired had been one of Mrs. Wilhite's complaints when she'd come to see Gideon. Miriam would have to mention this to him.

The shop door opened. Hawk stepped inside. He slipped his wide-brimmed hat from his head, nodding to them both. "Howdy, Mrs. Carol. Miss Bricks."

Mrs. Carol. Miriam committed that to memory.

"Wonderful to see you again," Mrs. Carol said. "Did you need something?"

"Only a moment of Miss Bricks's time. Once she's completed her business, of course."

Miriam hadn't intended to undertake this with an audience.

She set the spool of thread on the table where Mrs. Carol sat. "For Mrs. Wilhite," she explained. "She said she liked tatting. My mother does as well, and this is precisely like the thread she most prefers."

Mrs. Carol was clearly surprised by the offering. "For Wilma?"

Miriam nodded. "You needn't tell her it's from me."

Mrs. Carol didn't say a word, didn't look away. Nothing about her pinched expression spoke of approval. It seemed Miriam had overstepped herself.

She took a step backward. "I will leave you to the rest of your day."

She turned and faced Hawk. "What was it you needed me to do?"

He eyed her with blatant curiosity. "Do you always assume people seek you out because they want you to do something for them?"

"Being useful is not a bad thing." Indeed, it was the only thing that convinced people to keep her around.

"Well, Miss Bricks, I've not come with a task for you." He motioned her toward the door. "We can talk while we walk back to Doc's house."

She nodded and fell into step alongside him.

"The town's hosting a social day after next," he said. "I'd be honored if you'd considered going with me."

She stopped a single pace from the door. He couldn't have shocked her more if he'd asked her to join the marshals. "You want me to go with you to a social? Are you certain?"

He smiled at her. This was a man who likely broke a few hearts while enforcing the law. "I'm not one to issue idle invitations."

They stepped out of the millinery. "Why would you want to go with me? You hardly know me."

"That's the point of socializing, ain't it?" Hawk said. "Getting to know the other person."

He offered her his arm as they crossed the wide street toward Gideon's house. Hawk did that sometimes when walking her to the hotel at the end of the day. She appreciated the considerate gesture.

But, though she only vaguely admitted as much to herself, his was not the company she most longed for. He was kind and thoughtful, but he didn't warm her through or bring her a sense of peace and comfort. Her thoughts didn't spin when she was with him. Her heart didn't pound.

"Now, if you're of a mind to accept my invitation," Hawk said as they reached Gideon's front porch, "I'll make a few things clear up-front. Single women are few and far between in Wyoming. You'll have plenty of offers to dance, and I'll not begrudge you any of them. If there are any offers you'd rather not accept, why, you merely toss me a look, and I'll clear out the pests. Secondly, there is always a chance that, owing to my work, I might be called away without warning. I have a good group of deputies who take care of most everything, but there are no guarantees."

Miriam reached out and opened the door. "So, you are inviting me to a social where you're not going to dance with me— assuming you even show up?"

Hawk's usually stern mouth twisted in a grin as he followed her into the parlor. "That ain't at all what I said. And now I've half a mind to ask someone else."

"Is that so? Because I had heard rumors that single women are few and far between in these parts." She did appreciate that Hawk kept their conversations light.

Hawk looked over at Gideon. "Are you hearing this, Doc?"

"Sounds to me as though you're being turned down." Gideon's eyes remained on the book he was reading. "You could always arrest her, I suppose, but you won't haul her out without a fight."

Hawk chuckled and turned back to her. "You'd fight me, would you, Miriam?"

"I didn't mean *she* would fight you," Gideon muttered.

Heaven help her, her heart fluttered. "You wouldn't let him drag me to jail?"

He closed his book, but didn't rise from the chair by the fireplace. "The only thing rarer around here than single women is competent nurses. More to the point, if you're a jailbird, I'll have to go back to burnt toast for every meal." He gave her a look of absolute horror.

Her smile came easily after that. She liked when he teased her. There'd been so little of that in her life that she sometimes wondered if she even remembered how to laugh. But she liked even more when he held her hand, when he brushed his fingers along her cheek, when his smile turned soft and gentle.

"What do you say, Miriam?" Hawk asked. "Will you go to the social with me?"

She appreciated his offer; she truly did. And he would be an enjoyable companion. Why, then, did she feel dissatisfied at the invitation? Perhaps she was simply nervous.

"I haven't anything nice to wear. I don't even have a ribbon for my hair. I'll look as drab as a hatchling."

Hawk held his hat to his heart. "Miss Miriam Bricks, you couldn't look drab no matter what you wore, nor how ribbon-less your hair was. I've never thought otherwise, and I'd wager there's no one in all this world who has."

It was one of the kindest things anyone had said to her. How was it this town could be so cold and so welcoming at the same time? "I would very much enjoy going to the social with you," she said.

"I'm looking forward to it." Hawk plopped his wide-brimmed hat on his head. "Doc, if you have a moment later on, would you step over to my office? I've a bit of information for you."

Gideon frowned in confusion. "May I ask what about?"

Hawk's eyes darted to Miriam. "A clue in a mystery," was all he said.

A clue in a mystery. Instinct told her Hawk's clue had something to do with *her*.

"I have a minute now," Gideon said.

Hawk nodded. "Walk with me over to the jailhouse."

A moment later, they were gone. She stood in the middle of the parlor. Hawk had uncovered something. About her. Depending on what it was, she might lose her job. Worse by far, she might lose her freedom.

Chapter 15

"It seems a great deal of sour grapes to me." Gideon had listened to Hawk relay the information he'd received from the Western Women's Bureau. He didn't like what he'd heard. "They've been caught being deceitful and are trying to lay the blame at someone else's feet." Namely, Miriam's.

Hawk was unmoved by the argument. "They're likely panicked. A certain Mr. Ian MacNamara, lawyer and up-and-coming star in Washington's political circles, has been making his own inquiries."

Gideon's brother had gladly agreed to investigate the agency, but Ian had never been one to do things quietly. He'd likely made quite a ruckus in St. Louis.

"Knowing the bureau was possibly covering their tracks, I did a little more digging," Hawk said.

Gideon stepped over to the windows of the marshal's office and looked out over the town. The window, directly above the jail, provided a view of one end of the L-shaped Main Street. The wall to the right had a window that did the same for the other leg of Main. It was little wonder Hawk had claimed it for the marshals. He could monitor all of Savage Wells from this one room. And, judging by the amount of information he'd gathered, half the country.

Gideon wasn't certain he was ready to hear what else Hawk had uncovered; what he'd heard so far was discouraging. The bureau insisted that Miriam had been let go from five of her last six positions for being unfit to perform her duties as a nurse, something she'd kept from them, and that only an investigation on their part had revealed it. She'd known of the marriage arrangement, the bureau added, and that with her history no doctor would hire her so marrying one was her only option.

He wanted to believe that the bureau was being untruthful. He needed to believe it. Miriam had admitted she'd been less than forthright about Nebraska. She'd even apologized, expressing regret. He'd thought that had cleared up the lies between them. But what if she was hiding so much more?

Hawk remained at his desk. "If you'd rather I not tell you the rest, I'll understand. Sometimes a drop or two of ignorance is better than a full measure of truth."

It was tempting, more so than Gideon would have guessed only a few short weeks earlier. But his doctor's conscience would not allow him to leave potentially crucial information unrevealed. "What else did you discover?"

"That she was, indeed, dismissed from five of her last six positions, though only the doctor she worked for five years ago expounded upon the reasons for her dismissal."

The confirmation didn't sit well at all. He needed to know, though.

Rupert Fletcher walked by on the street below, a limp to his gait. *I'll have to look into that; he shouldn't still be limping.*

Weariness settled heavily on him. "What did this doctor give as his reason for letting Miriam go?"

"He said she was ill in a way that interfered with her work."

Gideon paced away. An illness could be dismissed as a *temporary* impediment, not one that would last for years. Five of her last six positions ending in dismissal was a pattern he could not, as a doctor responsible for the well-being of half a territory, overlook.

"The doctor in New York, the one from five years ago, said he'd rather not give details of her illness," Hawk said. "He and his wife had grown fond of her. They don't want to impose on her privacy."

That brought Gideon up short. "The doctor believes this illness is still afflicting her after nearly half a decade?"

Hawk leaned back in his chair. The man never seemed ruffled by anything. "Seems that way."

Few things were that long-term without being obvious, especially to someone with medical training. But he hadn't seen anything that would make him suspect even a minor illness, let alone something catastrophic.

"I'd wager at least some of the other doctors would be willing to answer our questions." Hawk's steely gaze stopped Gideon's pacing. "It's possible you'll learn things you'd rather you didn't know."

Miriam did good, competent work. She cared for their patients. He was growing fond of her. What if he discovered she was hiding something truly devastating, that she'd been lying about something more than her past employment, perhaps had even deceived him about her ignorance of the arranged marriage? Could he ever trust her after that? What choice would he have but to fire her as the others had done?

"Something of a dilemma, ain't it?" Hawk at least sounded empathetic. "Tell me how you want to move forward. I can either leave things as they are, or I can contact more of her former employers."

Gideon resumed his pacing. "As a doctor, I need to know what this illness is, and as her employer, I need to know the reasons she has been fired so often, but I can't help thinking that opening this particular Pandora's box might be a grave mistake."

She'd claimed a piece of his heart. Seeing her walk inside his home on Hawk's arm discussing their intention to go to the social together had brought to light just how real his affection was for her. He'd been rendered instantly jealous, frustrated, dejected. He'd fallen the first, tiniest bit in love with her. But he'd been horribly wrong on matters of the heart before, and the degree of deception Hawk was hinting at would shatter him. He knew it would. But, as painful as it would potentially be, the truth was crucial.

"You need to make more inquiries."

Hawk raised an eyebrow. "You're prepared to be the sixth doctor to dismiss her if what you learn necessitates it?"

"I won't put the well-being of my patients at risk."

"What about *her* well-being?" Hawk asked.

"I know you're not indifferent to her," Gideon said. "I'm— I'm not entirely, either. But I have to know for certain that this town is safe in her hands."

Hawk stood. "I'll send some telegrams today. We should know more soon enough."

Gideon left with that dire pronouncement echoing in his mind. Paisley was in the jailhouse, sitting at the sheriff's desk, when he passed by a side window at the bottom of the outer staircase. Andrew sat across from Barney at their usual spot near the cells, a checkerboard between them.

Barney would need a great deal of care soon enough. Gideon had been impressed with how Miriam had interacted with him. She was not only kind and patient, but she also understood the best way to help him.

There was the rub. She was, in so many ways, exactly what this town needed—what *he* needed—and he'd just asked Hawk to open a proverbial can of worms.

Chapter 16

Wearing blue was the nearest thing to heaven Miriam could imagine after two years of gray.

"Thank you, Paisley." She carefully smoothed the bodice of the dress she was borrowing for the night. "Wearing gray to a town social would likely have offended someone. Everything I do seems to be taken as an affront."

"If anyone gives you a lick of trouble, you need only tell me. I'll set 'em straight." Paisley sat in the only chair in the room. She wore a finer dress than she usually did, though she still wore her deputy marshal badge. The contradiction in her appearance was echoed in her personality. Paisley was both tender and tough, kind and dangerous.

She was also becoming something of a friend. It had begun with a heartfelt expression of gratitude for Miriam's attention to Paisley's father, and had continued with quick and friendly conversations in the days since. Miriam was grateful for a friend, but she was also terribly unsure how to proceed. Friendships eased some of her loneliness, but they were also a risk.

The sound of scraping table legs and voices calling out

instructions floated up from the restaurant below, where preparations for the social were well underway.

"I think Gideon is upset with me," Miriam said.

"Why do you say that?"

"A few different reasons." She did her best not to fret, but she was worried. "He hasn't teased or jested much these past couple of days. His patience with me has grown thin. Just this morning, I couldn't recall the name of a tincture and, rather than simply remind me, he leapt into an endless stream of questions, quizzing me about things that he must surely know that I know. It was almost as if he expected to find out that I've only been pretending to be a nurse."

Paisley tapped her fingers on the arm of her chair. "I can't imagine he doubts your training entirely. Perhaps he's only worried that it isn't as extensive as he'd hoped. He *is* planning to leave you here to treat his patients in his absence."

While the argument made sense, it felt incomplete. "He's curt with me at other times, as well. We used to share stories and interact more lightheartedly during meals or between patients." He used to hold her hand, speak tenderly. For one brief moment in his kitchen a week or so ago, she'd even thought he might kiss her. "I know his terseness isn't a matter of him not feeling social. He is talkative with his patients. He and Mrs. Wilhite spent a full hour last evening laughing about something."

"It does seem like this is something about you."

Miriam rubbed at her mouth. She was certain it had everything to do with whatever Hawk had pulled him aside to tell him the day he'd asked her to this social.

"I fear he is going to fire me, and I haven't the slightest idea why." At least all of the other doctors who'd dismissed her had had good reason. Gideon didn't even know of her condition.

"The last few weeks haven't gone the way he expected," Paisley said. "I suspect he's trying to sort out where to go from here. Having so much on his mind, and most of it involving you, may be wearing on him."

Miriam leaned against the wall. How many years had she spent putting down roots only to have them pulled up again? The experience was growing soul-dampening. And dangerous. There weren't many tiny, tucked-away towns like this one where she could find work. Staying hidden was her only chance of staying alive.

"I'll keep an eye on our good doctor and see what I can discover," Paisley said. "In the meantime, we have a couple of handsome men waiting for us downstairs. We owe it to ourselves to go enjoy their company."

Miriam wasn't about to argue with that. Hawk was kind to her, and she appreciated that. Far too few people in her life had been. And he had invited her to accompany him to a social event. She hadn't attended any kind of leisure function since she was sixteen years old. She fully meant to enjoy the all-too-rare treat.

"Everyone is shocked that Hawk is coming with you," Paisley said.

"I know the town doesn't have a high opinion of me."

Paisley waved that off. "No, they're surprised that he is being social at all."

"Speaking of which," Miriam said, "I cannot believe you convinced Cade to come tonight." She had heard him grumbling about the social at Gideon's house that morning.

Paisley's expression turned mischievous. "I told him I don't kiss men who refuse to take me to socials. He agreed very quickly after that."

"Brilliantly devious," Miriam acknowledged.

"I know."

The more Miriam knew Paisley, the more she liked her. Did Paisley feel the same way? Did Miriam even want her to? The past years had taught Miriam to question everything: her worth, her judgment, her hopes and dreams.

They reached the hotel lobby, which also served as the entrance to the restaurant. Even through the milling crowd, the men they were looking for were easy to spot.

Miriam could scarcely imagine a more intimidating sight. Both Cade and Hawk exuded authority, with eyes that didn't miss a detail, and stances that spoke of cool confidence. They wore gun belts at the ready, and bright silver badges declaring they were the law. Wouldn't she look odd, surrounded by three such intimidating people?

"How was your day, Miriam?" Hawk asked. "I hope Doc didn't work you so hard that you haven't the energy for dancing."

"I haven't danced in a very long time," she warned him. "Lack of energy might not be the biggest concern this evening."

"I have a little bauble for you—a tradition in Savage Wells." He held out to her a fancy bow made of yellow ribbon. "Mrs. Wilhite assured me it is a good color for your gray dress." He seemed to suddenly realize she wasn't wearing her usual attire; it was rather uncomfortable that he'd not even noticed until then. "That is not gray."

She gave him a reassuring smile. "Yellow and blue are generally considered a good combination."

"Well, then." He set the bow in her hand. "We'll take that as a good sign."

Hawk did not seem to be one who would ever truly lose his heart to a woman. He was too casual in his regard, too disengaged from his own social endeavors. If not for Cade's unabashed devotion to Paisley and hers to him, Miriam would have wondered if all lawmen were that way.

Hawk motioned to Paisley and Cade. "They're a bit too affectionate for comfort sometimes, aren't they?"

"I don't mind," she said. "Happy endings are too few to not be celebrated. Perhaps you'll have your own one day."

"Don't hold your breath, Miriam." The man was built as solid as a steam locomotive, and Miriam was certain he was every bit as unlovable when he needed to be. But the upturn of his lips and the sparkle it brought to his dark eyes softened him enough to render him entirely unthreatening in that moment.

"Are you that set against falling in love?"

"I was told by a saloon owner in Cheyenne that I have a heart of stone," he said. "Seems to me someone with a stone heart would be incapable of love."

The restaurant had been cleared of its tables and chairs and decorated with seemingly endless streams of ribbons. A good number of people greeted Hawk, many more offered a "Good evening" to Cade and Paisley. Miriam, herself, even received a few nods of acknowledgment. Either the townsfolk were warming to her, or they had been told to be nice.

Miriam eyed Hawk suspiciously. "You didn't threaten them, did you?"

His gaze traveled over the crowd. "Didn't have to. They're all afraid of me."

He was perfectly serious and, if she didn't miss her mark, not terribly happy about the situation.

"You don't want them to fear you?"

"'Want' has nothing to do with it. I *need* them to. A marshal has obligations, not friends."

Gideon stood across the room, dressed to stunning perfection, his lean form accentuated by his well-tailored coat. He was flanked by people with whom he smiled and laughed.

"They all love him, don't they?"

Hawk didn't need to ask or answer. "How's everything between you and Doc? There's been a bit of tension the last few times I've been by."

She sipped a glass of punch while formulating an answer. She'd spilled some of her worries in Paisley's ear, but she couldn't bring herself to confess to Hawk. "There is always a transition when learning to work with someone new. We'll sort it out in the end."

Hawk rocked back onto the heels of his boots. "If you don't want to discuss it, you need only say so. There's no need piecing together excuses."

"I was that obvious?"

"I've made my living and risked my life on the strength of my intuition. I've learned to trust it." His gaze was understanding and not accusatory. "I know life here has been a bit topsy-turvy for you. I hope it settles down, and that you mean to stay for a while. There are a great many people in this town who need you."

"Just not Gideon." As near as she could tell, he hadn't even noticed she'd arrived.

"You think Doc doesn't need you?" Hawk actually laughed. "I've lived in Savage Wells a few months now, and these past weeks are the first time I've seen him not look ready to drop from exhaustion."

She wanted to believe that. "Then why did he say just this morning that I make him tired?"

Hawk grabbed a cup of punch for himself. "Believe me, sweetheart, Doc wasn't lodging a complaint."

"That's all he ever does anymore, it seems."

Hawk hooked his arm through hers. "What do you say we not talk about Gideon MacNamara for a while, and enjoy the social instead?"

Her mind could use the respite, almost as much as her heart. "I would like that very much."

Chapter 17

Blue, Gideon decided, was definitely Miriam's color. Her eyes turned azure under its influence and her hair a captivatingly deeper shade of red. He'd watched her from across the room ever since she'd entered on Hawk's arm. Hawk said something to her. She smiled up at him. Cozy, weren't they?

He slipped his hand into the pocket of his formal jacket and wrapped his fingers around the length of ribbon there. Miriam had specifically bemoaned not having a ribbon for her hair. Something in the admission, coupled with her concern over her dress, had felt more significant than an offhand observation. Like a fool, he had rallied Paisley to the cause, hoping she had something Miriam could borrow, despite their difference in height and build. Somehow, she'd found something nearly perfect. And he had, quite by accident, picked a ribbon that almost perfectly matched the dress she was wearing.

There'd been no opportunity to give it to her before the social, when she might have had time to put it in her hair. He couldn't give it to her now. She'd accepted Hawk's far finer offering with such a look of pleasure. His wad of ribbon would be pathetic by comparison.

"Dr. MacNamara," Miss Dunkle, the schoolteacher, pulled his attention back to his own conversation. "I believe this is the dance you promised me."

He offered a small dip of his head. "So it is."

He slipped his hand free of the ribbon and attempted to clear his head of Miriam. He'd been trying to do that for days. Hawk's initial discoveries had planted seeds of doubt, and Gideon couldn't entirely ignore the evidence that kept sprouting up. She was uncomfortable about more than just Nebraska. Questions about her family were quickly brushed aside. Inquiries into her previous employers were only vaguely answered.

He danced with Miss Dunkle, then the Franklins' oldest daughter, then Mrs. Wilhite, then Mrs. Carol. Despite himself, his attention never strayed far from Miriam.

She danced with Hawk, and then sat out one set, speaking with Cade. Her only other partner was young Rupert Fletcher. For a town so lacking in young, unmarried women and so over-run with young, and not-so-young, unmarried men, it was hard not to notice that she spent so many tunes without a partner. Yet, she received welcomes from a few: the Fletchers, Andrew, who stayed only a moment, the Endecotts, even Mrs. Wilhite. She wasn't being entirely shunned, but she was decidedly being left out.

Gideon inched around the room, hoping to catch her before the next song began. There was nothing objectionable about him dancing with her. She had come with someone else, true, but that was perfectly acceptable in Savage Wells.

"Miriam."

She startled at his abrupt arrival. "Gideon." At least she didn't look unhappy to see him. "I'd wondered if you would ever come and 'give me your best howdy' as you're always telling Rupert to do."

"Yes, well, Rupert has offered you a howdy *and* danced with you." Gideon threw caution to the wind. "I'm hoping to be granted that same privilege."

"You want to dance with me?"

He couldn't decide if she sounded more surprised or horrified. "Why wouldn't I?"

"You've hardly spoken to me these past few days." She brushed her fingers over the ribbon she had pinned to her dress, the one Hawk had given her. The ribbon he had for her sat in a sad lump in his pocket. "Dancing with me would probably be even more unappealing than having a conversation."

He *had* been avoiding talking with her. None of the doctors he had inquired of had responded yet. He was relieved and guilt-ridden and worried and . . . frustrated. He just wanted to know what she was hiding and who she really was.

And he really, truly, wanted to dance with her.

The fiddles and flute struck up a waltz. He held a hand out to her. "Will you dance with me, Miriam?"

"I haven't waltzed in years." She spoke as if warning him, even as she set her hand in his.

"That is the wonderful thing about the waltz." He pulled her toward the dance floor. "You need only hold on tight and let me worry about the rest."

He expected her to laugh, perhaps even roll her eyes. Instead, she blushed and dropped her gaze from his. Now that was a decidedly interesting reaction. The last time she'd colored up so quickly, they'd been in his kitchen, her hand in his, his fingers brushing her cheek, his mind forbidding him to give in to the temptation to kiss her.

The other dancers had already begun their twirling trip around the room. Gideon slipped an arm around Miriam's waist and swung them out among the others. He knew some women insisted they lacked grace on the dance floor only to reveal their true skill, but Miriam had not been making light of her ability.

She clearly did not remember the steps or the rhythm of the waltz and struggled to keep up. How was it that her bumbling attempt only endeared her to him further? Perhaps because it fit her so well—she tried so hard, so earnestly, even when she was overwhelmed and unsure of herself.

She apologized each time she took a wrong step and either bumped into him or stepped on his toes. After a half-dozen mis-steps, Gideon decided it was time to take matters into his own hands and pulled her more firmly into his arms.

He drew her close and leaned near enough to whisper in her ear. "Don't fight the music, Miriam. Let it become part of you."

"I don't have your musicality, Gideon."

"You don't need to be a musician," he said. "Close your eyes and *feel* the music."

It said something of her trust in him that she closed her eyes immediately. His faith in her had been shaken of late, and for what? The fact that she hadn't eagerly admitted to being fired several times? He'd seen that she was a good nurse. That ought to have secured her a degree of his confidence. Instead, he'd con-demned her before having all the answers he sought.

He spoke low and quiet as they danced. "I am sorry, Miriam. I've been insufferable." The brush of his cheek against her temple sent unexpected shivers of awareness through him. "I just want to know you better, but sometimes that feels impossible."

He couldn't remember the last time his heart had raced so swiftly. She was leaning into him. She fit so naturally in his arms.

"I don't feel well. I—" She took a tight, worried breath. Her brow pulled as she swallowed, then winced at whatever she tasted. "I need to stop. I need—" She pulled away, and he released her immediately. "I'm not well."

One look at her told him she was not making an empty excuse. She was pale and swayed on her feet.

"Mir—"

"Pardon me." She made a headlong dash for the door.

If she was ill, he wanted to know. He wanted to help. He caught Hawk's eye as he hurried along Miriam's path.

"What happened?" Hawk asked, joining his quick exit.

"She said she isn't feeling well. I'll check on her, make certain."

Hawk allowed Gideon to continue his pursuit alone. He caught sight of Miriam's blue dress as she disappeared through the back door of the hotel lobby. Why wasn't she going up to her room if she was unwell?

He stepped outside as well. The dimness kept her hidden. "Miriam?"

She couldn't have gone far. He'd left close on her heels.

"Miriam?"

He stepped out further. Movement to the left caught his eye.

Miriam was on the ground. Every muscle in her body jerked and pulled, ripples of convulsions punishing her over and over. He stood paralyzed by shock for only a moment before jumping into action. He pulled off his jacket, folding it down to a pillow-sized mound of fabric, then, carefully turning her onto her side even as her convulsions continued, slipped the jacket under her head. He scanned the immediate area, making certain no rocks were near enough for her to strike an arm or leg or, heaven forbid, her head against.

He sat by her as the seizure ran its course. There was little else he could do. He had treated a few individuals with epilepsy and some of the other conditions that could cause seizures. Miriam might awaken having chewed her tongue to bleeding shreds or be bruised from her fall. Sometimes a seizure impacted the internal organs in potentially embarrassing ways. She would awaken disoriented and confused and, more likely than not, very much afraid.

The jerking in her limbs began to subside. He waited, watching. Once the tremors had stopped entirely, he could truly breathe again. Seeing a body turn on itself that way would strike fear into even the most stalwart of hearts.

He carefully brushed back the strands of copper hair that had fallen over her face, then removed the bits of dust and grass that stuck to it.

"Open your eyes, Miriam," he said quietly. "Let me know you're coming back to me."

She didn't immediately comply; he hadn't expected her to. These things took time. He made a quick examination of the back of her head. She didn't appear to have hit it against anything. A weight lifted from his chest. Gideon ran his hand up and down her arms but felt no breaks, saw no blood that would indicate she'd cut herself in her fall.

The danger past, his worry now turned to her comfort and recovery. She'd sweated during the episode, and the night air was chilly. He slipped his arms beneath her back and knees and pulled her close to him, hoping to stave off the inevitable shivering.

He rocked her back and forth, trying to comfort her and

settle his own thoughts. Thank heavens she was whole, and the episode had passed relatively quickly.

She'd chosen a spot away from easy view, and she'd known not to try climbing the stairs, which meant this had happened before. Further, he felt certain she had recognized some kind of warning of an approaching seizure. Not every condition afforded a warning. Even those that did, didn't always do so consistently.

She slumped against him, exhausted. He held her more tightly.

"Oh, Miriam. Why didn't you tell me?"

But he knew the answer. A nurse prone to seizures would likely be declared unreliable or a danger to patients. She believed if he knew, then she would be fired, a fear fueled, no doubt, by experience.

This was the mystery he'd been chasing. *This* was the secret she was hiding.

She grew a little less limp, a little less heavy in his embrace. Awareness was returning by degrees.

He wrapped his arms more firmly around her. "Rest a moment," he gently instructed.

His thoughts wouldn't focus. His mind was filled with the horror of seeing her convulsing, utterly unaware of her surroundings, and the helplessness he felt.

This was not a condition he knew how to treat. What had been tried? Had anything resulted in improvement? He had so many questions and not a single answer. How much more overwhelming must this be for her?

"Gideon?" Though her whisper was barely audible, he could hear the worry in her voice.

"Do not overtax yourself."

She made no attempt to sit up or escape his embrace. "What happened?"

He suspected she already knew the answer. "As it turned out, you were not merely overwhelmed by my breathtaking talent for waltzing. You really were unwell."

She took a shaky breath. "How long were you out here?"

"Long enough." He offered her a sad smile, not knowing the right words to say.

She looked up into his face. Her chin began to quiver. A hint of tears filled her eyes. "Did anyone else . . . ?"

"No."

She closed her eyes; a tear trickled down her cheek. Another followed close behind.

He brushed the moisture away. "You appear to have passed the worst of it."

"I—" Her voice shook. "I sometimes have more than one in close succession. There might be another."

"Let's get you home."

She sat up a bit. "The key to my room is in the cubby at the hotel desk."

He supported her as they both stood. "I was not clear enough, dear. I meant *my* home. If there is even a chance of another of these occurring soon, I want to be near enough to help." He fetched his jacket from the ground and set it about her shoulders. "We'll slip around back so you needn't speak with anyone."

She nodded silently.

"Can you walk?"

Another nod.

He set his arm across her back, supporting her as they walked. She stiffened at the contact. Was it embarrassment? Worry? Was

139

she in pain? She wasn't steady enough on her feet for him to leave her to manage on her own.

"Will you be able to rest?" he asked. "Or should I prepare a tisane?"

"So long as I don't have another . . . of these, I'll be able to sleep." She spoke low, almost mumbling. She leaned on him but kept herself as upright as one could with buckling knees and wobbly legs.

"Is there someone I can send to your room to fetch your nightdress or hairbrush or whatever you might need?"

She stopped short and looked up at him, at last. "I don't want anyone to know about this. Please. I would rather—" Her breaths were coming shorter and shallower. "Please, don't tell anyone."

"I wouldn't say anything other than you aren't feeling well."

She shook her head before he'd even finished. "What if I'm 'ill' while whoever you sent is nearby? Then everyone would know."

"What if I sent Paisley?"

"She's the law."

That was an odd objection. Still, he could respect her wishes. Heavens, she looked tired. Defeated. "Someone who isn't connected with the law, who isn't a gossip, and who could be trusted to keep a secret?"

"I doubt there is such a person."

"Doc?" Hawk's voice was unmistakable, as was Miriam's immediate, total panic.

"Please don't tell him." Her fingers dug into his arm. "Please."

"What did I do to convince you that I could not be trusted?"

"Doctors can't be trusted," she whispered.

Hawk reached them; there would be no avoiding his questions. "Miriam truly has taken ill," Gideon said.

To his credit, Hawk looked immediately concerned. "Can I do anything?"

"Would you locate Tansy for me and send her over to my house in a quarter hour?" Gideon asked.

"I will." Hawk's gaze returned to Miriam. "Nothing serious, I hope."

Gideon assumed his most reassuring tone. "She has taken a little ill, but she'll be feeling better soon."

Hawk eyed them both as if he didn't entirely believe Gideon's words. That was the risk one took when telling half-truths to any of the three officers of the law who called Savage Wells home. They saw through ruses the way ordinary people saw through glass.

As Gideon guided Miriam around the corner of the building, Miriam looked up at him. "Thank you . . . for being kind."

"It would seem I am not the villain you think I am, doctor or not."

Chapter 18

Doctors can't be trusted. She was ill, and he was a doctor, something that ought to have made him an ally, and yet it seemed to have made him her enemy. He likely had all of her previous dismissals to thank for that.

He knew he ought to be pulling out all of his medical texts and reading everything he could find on seizures, but his thoughts were spinning too rapidly for concentration. Though he'd witnessed seizures before, the experience never stopped being jarring, more especially when the one suffering through it was someone he cared about. The fear he'd felt in that moment still hadn't subsided.

Thank heavens for Tansy. When he'd told her Miriam was ill and preferred the details of her illness not be public knowledge, Tansy had merely shrugged and told him she wasn't a gossip. He'd expected precisely that response, but he'd been caught by surprise at the tender attentiveness she'd shown Miriam. There was a warmheartedness to Tansy that she kept well hidden.

He leaned back in his chair. His eyes, gritty with exhaustion, slid shut. He needed an escape. His weary body and mind easily conjured the remembered weight of his cello leaning against his chest and legs. Of their own volition, the fingers of his left hand pressed imaginary strings, while his right hand imitated in small movements the motions of bowing. He could hear the music in his mind, soothing and centering him. He couldn't play with Tansy in the house. His music was too personal to share with anyone else. Miriam only knew about it by accident.

A crash above Gideon's head pulled him back to the moment.

"Doc!" Tansy's shout carried down to him. "You'd best get up here."

He jumped up and ran. Even knowing what he was likely to find upon entering Miriam's room, he still stopped short at the sight of her on the floor in the same state as before.

Tansy knelt near Miriam's convulsing body. "She was fixin' to climb into bed when this came on. Knocked herself hard into the bedside table on her way down."

He would need to check for injuries again once the seizure stopped. He joined Tansy, watching and waiting.

"When you said she had a condition she didn't want anyone knowing about, I assumed you meant she was expecting a baby. Not being married, she would want that kept to herself." Tansy folded her arms across her chest.

That assumption hadn't even occurred to him. "Thank you for your help," he said, "and your discretion. Not everyone would be so understanding." Indeed, Tansy didn't seem distraught at the unnerving scene playing out before her. She kept as close an eye on Miriam as Gideon did.

"My brother had shakes like this every day. People said things about him—that he had a devil, that he'd been sneakin' the moonshine, that he was mad." Tansy shook her head. "But he was a good boy. He was ill, that was all."

"I didn't know about your brother." Perhaps her family knew of some kind of treatment or home remedy.

"He died when he was still young. Hit his head during one of these." She motioned to Miriam's quickly subsiding seizure. "He never woke up from that one."

"I am sorry to hear that."

"He was my best friend," Tansy said, "and the only one in my family who thought I was worth a hill of beans. Maybe because they were ashamed of the both of us, so we understood each other."

Gideon knew only snippets of Tansy's past, but what he did know tugged at him. It was little wonder she was, for the most part, hard and distant. People had been hurting her for too long. He firmly suspected the same could be said of Miriam. The treatment Tansy's brother had endured was not unique. Unexplained illnesses, especially those that manifested themselves in unnerving ways, frightened people. It wasn't fair, and it wasn't right. But it was far too often true.

The seizure ended faster than the previous one. Miriam lay there, still, pale, entirely unaware of her surroundings.

He leaned closer, eyeing her left shoulder. "I think she may have dislocated her collarbone."

Tansy nodded. "She knocked into that table hard, poor thing."

Miriam had told Rupert that she'd once dislocated her shoulder in a fall. It likely had been a seizure. How long had she been enduring these?

"I can fetch her another nightgown if she needs one," Tansy said.

"You really do have experience with this."

"Told you I did."

Gideon slid along the floor right up to Miriam's side. A quick examination confirmed his suspicions about her shoulder. He quickly assessed her head as well, then felt along her arms, then her legs.

"She has separated her shoulder," he said, "but her other bones seem whole." He looked across at Tansy. "I will need some help realigning her shoulder."

Tansy nodded firmly and confidently. "Tell me what to do."

"Hold her down."

Miriam turned her head in his direction. Though her eyes weren't fully open, there was inarguable pleading in them.

He set his hands gently on either side of her face. "This is going to hurt like the dickens, my dear, but I suspect it does already."

"Help me," she mouthed silently.

He pressed a kiss to her forehead. "I'll be quick," he promised her.

Gideon took hold of her left hand and set his foot in her armpit. He looked over at Tansy. Her grip tightened.

"Here we go." He pulled Miriam's arm quick and sharp. She cried out in pain. Gideon felt and saw the collarbone pop into place. She sucked in a sharp breath, the sound of her suffering suddenly silenced.

"Breathe," he instructed, but she either didn't hear or was unable to comply. "Breathe," he repeated, more sternly.

She obeyed, the air rattling as she inhaled. Her next breaths were shallow and quick.

"Where do you keep your bandages, Doc?" Tansy was on her feet, ready to fetch the needed supplies.

"Bottom drawer of the armoire. You have experience resetting shoulders as well?"

She crossed the room. "I've lived a full life."

Apparently. "Where were you six months ago when I began looking for a nurse?"

"Making moonshine. Where else would I have been?"

Gideon turned back to Miriam. He cupped her face, hoping the touch reassured her, comforted her. "Immobilizing the arm will help tremendously."

"Is it broken?" she asked.

"No."

"Did Tansy see?"

Tansy returned with a length of bandaging. "I saw, but I'm no gossip. Besides, it ain't nothing I haven't seen before."

Miriam closed her eyes tightly. Her breaths continued to shake, likely from a combination of exhaustion, frustration, and pain.

Gideon made short work of securing Miriam's arm to her side to keep the shoulder from separating again. He helped her to her feet and eased her to the side of the bed, assisting her as she sat.

"Are you hungry? Thirsty?" Tansy asked.

"I am a little thirsty."

Tansy snatched the empty water pitcher from its stand and headed out of the room.

Alone with Miriam at last, Gideon asked the question that had been weighing on his mind. "Why didn't you tell me?"

Her gaze remained firmly on her lap. "You would not have allowed me to stay if I'd told you. You would not have even allowed me to come."

He sat on the bed beside her, tired to his core. "I likely would not have offered you this position if I'd known. There are too many possible complications."

"What do you mean to do now that you know?" Emotion cracked through the words.

He hadn't allowed himself to think that far yet. "That is a question best left unanswered at the moment. You need to rest and recover, and I need to consult my books."

"I would rather you not study up," she said. "Just let it be."

He shook his head. "I can't help you if I don't learn all I can."

"I don't want you to help me." Beneath the firmness of her tone was a layer of fear.

He had to find a way to reassure her. "As a doctor, I—"

"Don't be a doctor. Just be Gideon."

"But 'Gideon' is a doctor. It's who I am."

She turned the tiniest bit away from him. He hadn't thought she could look even more exhausted, but, somehow, she did.

"Lie down," he insisted. "I'll pull the curtains so the sun won't wake you in the morning, and I'll fetch you an extra blanket."

The words had only just left his mouth, and she was already lying down, the quilt pulled up over her, her eyes closed.

He wasn't an expert on this condition by any means. He wasn't even certain of the exact diagnosis. It was likely epilepsy, but the seizures could be caused by something else entirely. What if he wasn't doing something he should have been? What if she needed medicine he didn't have?

"I worry about you, Miriam Bricks," he admitted quietly.

"I wish you wouldn't."

He shook his head at the illogical nature of her request. It was far too late for him to simply not worry about her, to not care.

Leaving her there was harder than he expected it to be, but he had questions that needed answers. If only he knew where to find them.

Chapter 19

Miriam made the agonizing trek downstairs the next afternoon, having slept far later than she'd expected. Her shoulder hurt, and she ached, but it was not her physical condition which slowed her steps. She knew what came next, and she dreaded it.

Every time a new doctor learned of her condition, one of two things happened. Either he sympathized with her plight but regretfully informed her that he was letting her go, or he informed her in crisp tones that he knew the mental ramifications of her ailment and, as such, would insist she be placed in an asylum for her own good and that of the people around her.

Her days in town were numbered. She would either leave in defeat or be forced once again to run for freedom.

She listened for voices, not wishing to intrude if Gideon had a patient, but the parlor was silent.

Her attempt to appear confident when she stepped into the room was no doubt undermined by the fact that she was still wearing her nightgown. The bandages holding her tender shoulder in place prevented her from lifting her arm enough to change

148

her clothing. The question of her future was too pressing, however, to wait for more dignified attire.

Gideon was at his desk, as she'd assumed he would be. And, as she had guessed, several books sat open for his perusal.

"Good afternoon." Her voice shook. That couldn't be helped.

He looked up, and his eyes widened. "Miriam? What are you doing out of bed?" He hopped to his feet. "You are supposed to be resting."

"I've slept away half of the day. I do not need more rest."

He reached her side, his concern not ebbing in the slightest. "At least sit down."

She opted not to argue; she had bigger issues to address. He led her to the couch and sat beside her.

"How are you feeling?" The way his gaze quickly scanned her face, her shoulder, and her overall demeanor, she guessed he didn't actually need an answer to that question. He was a doctor, first and foremost. That was the problem.

"I am a little tired and a little sore," she said. "But, other than my as-yet-unhealed shoulder, I am doing quite well." She chose to jump straight to the heart of the matter. "Now that you are aware of my condition, what do you mean to do?"

"I don't rightly know," he said. "I've been studying for hours, but I haven't come across anything helpful. So much about your ailment differs from case to case. I don't know enough about your history with these episodes, how long you've had them, how often, or what has been tried with or without success." He shook his head, his shoulders rising and falling. "I want to help, but I don't know how yet."

"I didn't mean as my *doctor*. What do you mean to do as my *employer*?"

He leaned against the sofa back. "This is why you've been let go from so many jobs."

He knew about that? Of course he did. That explained why he'd begun questioning her so intensely the past few days.

"It didn't matter how capable I had shown myself, how competent, how hardworking. Once *this* was known, none of that mattered." The experience had repeated itself so often that recalling those firings left her more tired than angry. "Is this to be next on my list of lost positions?"

He leaned his elbows on his knees, interlocking his fingers in front him. "I have been focusing on you as a patient, I hadn't thought of—" His eyes seemed unfocused. "Do you always have warning beforehand? Last night you seemed to know—"

"Not always. I feel a bit strange, and sometimes I get an odd taste in my mouth. But not always."

Her answer only clouded his expression further. "Then this could happen again at any moment, without warning."

"Yes." Experience kept her calm, despite the weight pressing on her heart. "Did you come across anything promising in your reading?"

He shook his head. "As much as I hate even saying it, this seems like an untreatable condition."

"Believe me, I know," she muttered.

He rubbed the back of his neck. "Even if we had nothing more than a way to predict when this was going to happen. You could take the remainder of that day off and rest or . . ." He threw his hands upward in a show of frustration.

The nervousness she'd felt since leaving her bed that morning gave way to a familiar resignation. Though she'd known this was the inevitable outcome, a part of her had held out hope. "At least I know you will fall under the first category."

He looked back at her, brows drawn and mouth turned down.

"Every doctor I have ever worked for has eventually discovered this about me," she explained. "And they all reacted in one of two ways. They either dismissed me with kindness or with cruelty."

"You're a good nurse," Gideon said, "but—"

"Please." She held up her good hand. "I know how that sentence ends, and I would rather not hear it again."

"Right now, you are resting and recovering. Nothing needs to be decided immediately."

That was a new response. "You aren't firing me?"

"I would prefer not to," he said. "There is a lot I haven't read yet. Until I learn everything I can, I don't intend to make a final decision."

Obviously, he hadn't yet discovered the link between seizures and insanity, otherwise a "final decision" would have already been made. While she didn't think he would send her to a mental hospital, she felt certain his open-mindedness would waver in the face of that condemning information.

The front door squeaked open. A forced smile appeared on Gideon's face. Miriam attempted to follow suit.

Paisley stepped in. Her eyes settled on Miriam. "How are you feeling?"

How much did she know? Surely Tansy and Gideon wouldn't have told all they knew.

In the next moment, Tansy stormed into the parlor. "I said I'd fix a meal for you and Miss Bricks, but I ain't feeding a queen."

"A queen?" Gideon sounded as confused as Miriam felt.

"Came right in the kitchen, making demands and assessing the place like she meant to take over. I'm not a servant; I won't be pushed around."

Who in the world is in the kitchen? Miriam had never known any of the townspeople to come in through that door instead of the front.

The swish of silk layers and the click of heels on the wooden floor pulled Miriam's thoughts back to New York City and the fine and fancy ladies Mother had socialized with. It was an odd sound to hear so far West.

A woman who would not have seemed the least bit out of place amongst the finest of East Coast society stepped inside the parlor. She held herself proudly, appraising everything with a critical eye. She didn't seem to miss a thing, little or great. Her piercing gaze settled on Gideon, who had frozen, mouth slightly agape, eyes wide and staring.

"There you are, Gideon," the woman said in a cultured but chastising tone.

His mouth moved wordlessly for a moment. Then, with a shake of his head and a quick clearing of his throat, he said only two words: "Hello, Mother."

Chapter 20

Mother. In Savage Wells. Nothing could have prepared Gideon for that. Nothing.

Her gaze settled on Miriam. "Why is this woman wearing her nightdress in your parlor?"

"She was injured last evening after growing ill." That was both true and the safest response he could think of. "I am a doctor, you'll remember. Treating the ill and injured is what I do."

"But she is wearing her nightclothes in a public room. I cannot—" Mother's eyes pulled wide as she caught sight of Paisley. "Merciful heavens. You're wearing a gun."

"And a badge," Paisley said. "And on less formal occasions, I've been known to sport a man's hat."

Mother pressed a hand to her heart, her mouth dropping open.

"You ain't back East any longer, dearie," Tansy said.

Mother leaned closer to Gideon and whispered, "That woman was speaking of moonshine only a moment ago."

Moonshine and guns and nightclothes were not remotely

the most pressing issue at the moment. "Why are you—? When did—?" He had too many questions to know where to begin.

Mother, however, did not wait. "Which of these women is the wife you purchased through the telegraph?"

Gideon choked. Paisley laughed out loud.

Miriam, to his astonishment, was the one who seized control of the situation. "I would like to go upstairs to rest," she said. "Would someone assist me?"

Gideon, grateful for the reprieve, crossed to the sofa.

Miriam shook her head. "You need to stay here and talk to your mother." She looked over at Paisley. "Would you?"

"Gladly." Paisley slipped between him and Miriam. She glanced at Mother, then met his gaze and whispered sarcastically, "Your mother's a gem."

"I know," he whispered back.

"I am reassured to realize she married into the family," Paisley said. "With Gid being my cousin, that makes she and I only vaguely related."

"Not a reassurance I can offer myself, Pais."

Paisley helped Miriam to her feet. Miriam was still unsteady. He would need to find a way to convince her to stay in bed, but her stubbornness would likely make that difficult.

Tansy stepped toward the kitchen. "I'll go finish lunch—*by myself.* I'm needing some quiet."

He nodded, and she escaped without hesitation.

As Paisley and Miriam reached the doorway of the parlor, Gideon said, "I'll check on your shoulder later, Miriam."

She gave him a look of severely tried patience. "I am a nurse, Doctor. I took a look at it myself, and it is precisely where it ought to be." Then she slipped out, Paisley assisting her.

"She is a nurse?" Mother repeated. "Then she is the woman you sent for? The one you married without the slightest—"

"We aren't married," Gideon told her.

Rather than relieve her anxiety, those three words only shocked her further. "Not married? Yet she's"—she lowered her voice to a whisper—"living here? Traipsing about in her nightclothes?"

The discussion only grew more awkward. "She does not live here. As I said, she was ill last night and injured herself in a fall. As a doctor, it is my duty to care for those in need. And, before you decry the scandalous nature of an unmarried woman and an unmarried man under the same roof—no matter that one of them was deliriously ill for long stretches of time—Tansy was here all night."

"The moonshine woman?" That did not meet with her approval. Little ever did.

"She is a fine person."

Mother lowered herself into the wingback chair and pressed her fingers to her forehead. "This town is even more backward than I had anticipated."

"Why *did* you come to this 'backward town'? And on your own, no less?" It was foolish in the extreme, and that was not like Mother.

"I'm not alone. Your father and the driver are making arrangements with the stable."

"Father is here?" Worry seized him. Something truly terrible must have occurred to bring both of his parents all the way to Wyoming. Had someone in the family taken ill? Or worse? "What has happened?"

She eyed him as though he were being ridiculous. "I had an informative discussion with Ian."

"And he told you to come to Wyoming?" That was unlikely.

"He told us that you had recently paid a company to send you a wife, and we could not imagine this approach would work any better than your last attempt to marry."

Gideon groaned. "Ian wasn't supposed to say anything."

"You are fortunate that he did," Mother said. "You are making a mess of your life, son. Your father and I mean to stay until you have yourself sorted once more."

A great many responses came to mind, none of which were appropriate to say in front of his mother.

The front door hinges squeaked.

"Mother, if that is one of my patients, I would ask that you—"

His father's voice cut off his words. "The sign in the window said to walk in. I've never heard of such a thing. Ah, here you are, Isabelle. I see you've run him to ground."

"Enough with the pleasantries," Mother said. "I have discovered that our son is not married."

Father's eyes darted between them a few times. "We are happy about this." He looked at his wife and tried a different answer. "We are *un*happy. We are neutral. Utterly and extremely neutral." He never expressed an opinion on any matter unless it met with Mother's approval first.

"None of your sass, William. You will only encourage him to indulge in his usual ridiculousness, and then we will never have a serious word from him on this important topic."

"Yes, dear." Father turned to Gideon, his grin making a sudden appearance. "I met a US marshal. Right out on the street."

"There is a deputy marshal upstairs," Gideon told him.

"She is a deputy marshal?" Far from impressed, Mother sounded appalled.

"*She?*" Father's gaze darted to the ceiling. "That's unexpected."

"This is Wyoming," Gideon said. "It is always best to expect the unexpected."

"The deputy—is she the one you meant to marry but didn't?"

"The deputy is your cousin Mary Catherine's daughter, Paisley," he said. "She's family, so, no, she was never someone I intended to marry."

"Ah." Father nodded. "It's a shame they never came to Washington for a visit. If she is at all like her mother, she is already a favorite."

"Paisley is a great gun," Gideon said.

"And, being a marshal, I imagine she *carries* a great gun."

Mother sighed. "Do sit down, William, and let us sort this out like civilized people."

"Yes, dear." He sat near Gideon, his gaze taking in the entire room. But, unlike Mother, he seemed almost excited at what he saw. "Is this where you do your doctoring?"

Gideon nodded. "All of my equipment is on that side of the room. I see my patients there."

"Our son is a doctor, Isabelle." Father had never vocally disapproved of Gideon's profession the way the rest of the family had, but this was the first time he'd sounded truly proud. "He takes care of an entire town."

"I actually take care of half of the Wyoming Territory. Twelve different towns and a vast area of ranches and farms. Thousands of square miles."

Father whistled appreciatively, his attention fully on Gideon. "How do you manage that?"

"I travel a lot. Sometimes my patients travel here."

"And you remember all of them?" Father leaned back against the sofa. "I don't know that I could keep all of that information in my head at once. I have to write everything down at the bank."

"A medical practice isn't entirely unlike a bank, really. Instead of depositors, I have patients. Instead of guarding their money, I guard their health. I, too, take a great many notes and write everything down." He hadn't ever shared the details of his work with his family members. He was enjoying the experience. "You occasionally visit other branches of the bank you work for. Traveling to other towns is much the same for me."

"We can discuss the particulars of Gideon's profession later," Mother said. "At the moment, we have his disastrous personal life to sort out."

Quick as that, Gideon's enjoyment vanished. "Mother, if I am capable of running a complicated and successful medical practice, surely I can be trusted to sort out other areas of my life as well."

Her posture grew stiffer, her glare more scolding. "You, son, have been twice engaged and are yet unwed."

Twice engaged. Thank the heavens he hadn't told his mother about Harriet Fulton's rejection.

"One of those failed fiancées," Mother continued, "is the belle of Washington society. The other, apparently, traipses about your parlor in her nightdress."

"She was not 'traipsing.'"

"Is she another deputy?" Father asked eagerly.

"No," Gideon answered. "She is a nurse."

"Your nurse works in her nightdress?" He sounded both shocked and intrigued.

"She was not working."

Mother harrumphed. "Makes rather free with your home, then, doesn't she?"

"I told you, she is ill."

Mother lifted her chin a notch. "She seemed perfectly healthy to me."

"I will take your diagnosis into consideration," Gideon answered dryly.

"Do not grow impudent with me. I am in an ill humor."

That was not the least surprising. "Where do the two of you mean to stay while you are in town?"

"Here, of course." Mother hadn't, it seemed, been entertaining the slightest doubt as to her welcome. "And, it is a good thing, since you are in need of a respectable chaperone."

"I am a grown man. I do not need a chaperone."

"What you need is a good shaking." Mother rose from her chair. "Come, William. Let us settle in. Straightening this young man out will likely take longer than we expected."

Gideon and his father both stood and assumed nearly identical weary postures. To say Mother was, at times, a bit overbearing was like saying the ocean was, at times, a bit wet. And Gideon could feel himself drowning.

Chapter 21

Miriam returned to her room at the hotel for the second night of her convalescence. She arrived at Gideon's house at half past eight the next morning to begin her nursing duties. Gideon had not officially fired her, and she meant to prove herself worthy of being kept on. She had no delusions of her plan succeeding in the long term, but she didn't know what else to do.

Stepping into Gideon's parlor to the sound of his mother asking why he'd chosen a cherry end table when his desk was mahogany told her as nothing else could that *she* was unlikely to be the first concern on Gideon's mind. That was reassuring, at least.

Gideon stood like a man at a mark, not responding to his mother's detailed suggestions for improving the look of his home. Gideon, a respected doctor who never seemed out of his depth, listened helplessly.

Had he not yet learned how to survive the attentions of such a mother? Fortunately for him, Miriam was an expert.

As soon as Mrs. MacNamara stopped for a breath, Miriam jumped in. "Good morning, Dr. MacNamara. What is on our schedule for today?"

His attention was immediately on her. "Miriam. Are you—?"

"Ready to review the day? I certainly am." She gave his mother a sweet smile. "You will excuse us, I hope. Organization is key to a well-run day."

Mrs. MacNamara sputtered a moment before settling into silence.

Gideon shot Miriam a grateful look, then moved to his desk and pulled out a sheet of paper. "Rupert was limping at the social, so I've asked his mother to bring him back by."

"His leg should be healed by now."

"I believe it is," Gideon said. "Both the break and the wound from the operation. Yet, he is still limping."

It was odd. "Six-year-old boys don't limp for no reason."

"My thoughts exactly." His gaze dropped to the paper again. "The Clarks' mare is likely to foal today—"

"Gideon," Mrs. MacNamara spoke over him. "I believe I have not yet been introduced to your nurse."

"You met her yesterday afternoon." Gideon really didn't seem to know how to best interact with his mother.

"But that was not a *proper* introduction," Miriam said. She faced Mrs. MacNamara, whose taffeta gown could not have been more out of place in such a small, no-account town. "A pleasure to meet you, Mrs. MacNamara. I am Miriam Bricks."

"Bricks? I know a few with that surname."

Her own mother was forever ranking families. This was no different. "I would be surprised if you were familiar with my father's family. He is British."

"I didn't know that," Gideon said.

"You never asked."

"And from where does your mother hail?" It seemed Mrs.

MacNamara was determined to assume control of the conversation.

Miriam knew better than to fight it. "My mother is from New York City. That is where I grew up, in fact."

That seemed to impress Mrs. MacNamara. "What does your mother's family do?"

"My grandfather is in shipping, as are several of his sons, though one is a banker."

Mrs. MacNamara nodded her approval.

"I didn't know that either." Gideon set down his paper. "What else haven't you told me about your family?"

Mrs. MacNamara didn't allow his question to be answered before asking one of her own. "What is your father's line of business?"

"He is an importer. He ships goods from England."

"Is that so?" Quick as that, Mrs. MacNamara was no longer dripping with disapproval as she had been the afternoon before.

Miriam had experienced such shallowness before; the same focus on the outward had thoroughly condemned her for having a condition "no one cared to witness." She disliked it, but she understood it.

"Who else are we expecting today?" She returned her attention to Gideon and the business at hand.

"No one, which is actually a good thing." Gideon folded his hands in front of him. "I need to decide what to do about my trip to Quarterville."

This was news. "When are you going to Quarterville?"

"I had originally planned to leave in three days." He leaned his elbows on the desk and steepled his fingers. "I was leaving the town in your care, but now, with you feeling unwell . . ."

"I am much better today, other than my shoulder."

"Miriam."

She held firm. This was her chance to prove herself. If she could convince him to keep her on, even temporarily . . .

"Paisley could stay here at the house," Miriam said. "She has assisted you before. Or Tansy. We both know she knows more about treating injuries and illness than anyone had guessed."

"It is not your competency that concerns me," he said. "I would be gone for nearly a week, and we don't yet know how fully recovered you are."

Mrs. MacNamara cleared her throat. Gideon stopped on a tight sigh.

"You are leaving?" Mrs. MacNamara clearly disapproved. "But your father and I have only just arrived. You cannot go running about the country when you have guests."

The usually jovial Gideon was anything but when talking with his mother. "This is my job. It's what I do, and traveling is part of it."

"But your father and I—"

"I didn't know you were coming, and I cannot stop doing my job in order to entertain you."

"We—"

"Mrs. MacNamara, have you had the chance yet to visit the millinery across the street? Mrs. Wilhite and Mrs. Carol, I am certain, would welcome your expertise on the latest Eastern fashions. And beyond that, they are lovely women. I believe you would enjoy spending time with them."

She didn't answer immediately. Miriam suspected Mrs. MacNamara was unaccustomed to not being in charge of every exchange.

After a moment, Mrs. MacNamara regained her composure.

"I *should* go visit. Knowing the people who are looking out for Gideon will help us accomplish our goal for this journey."

"Wasn't tyrannizing me the goal for this journey?" Gideon muttered.

Miriam shot him a warning look.

"I will go look in on the millinery," Mrs. MacNamara said.

"And will you ask Mrs. Wilhite if she will find me a length of puce ribbon?" Miriam added.

Gideon turned quickly away, biting his lips against an obvious smile.

"Puce?" Mrs. MacNamara repeated. "That is an odd color to request."

"Yes, but I need you to ask for that color quite particularly."

"Very well." Mrs. MacNamara looked to her son one more time. "We will discuss this trip of yours when your father returns from wherever he's gone off to. Likely the jailhouse." She shook her head in exasperation. "I do not understand his fascination with such morbid things. He is a respected banker in Washington and quite influential in political circles. A single day in this town has turned him into a little boy playing with toys. I do not understand it at all."

A moment later, only Miriam and Gideon remained in the parlor.

"I am sorry about that," Gideon said. "My mother has particular ideas about . . . everything."

"So does mine. I, however, am far more interested in discussing your cancelled plans."

He came around his desk and sat on the corner of it, facing her. "It is only the two of us now. Tell me honestly—how are you feeling?"

"I was honest. Other than my shoulder, I feel fine. And it may be months or years before I have another episode."

"Or it could be today," he pointed out.

"I have never had more than two in a row. Mine are more infrequent than many other people experience."

He rubbed his forehead. "I don't know that I can take that risk."

"If I find myself feeling unwell, I will retire for the day. I promise."

"There would be no one here to help you if you were injured again."

She was ready for that objection. "There is Tansy. She has experience with this. Better still, she is not bothered by it."

He shook his head. "I cannot ask her to spend even more time away from her home."

"But you *can* ask the people of Quarterville to go even longer without a doctor's care?" She held his gaze firmly. "At the worst, Gideon, you would be leaving Savage Wells temporarily without medical care, which is something you have been doing regularly for three years. You needn't pay me while you're gone if I don't see any patients."

He slipped his fingers around her good hand. "I am not concerned about the money, Miriam. I think you know that."

"Your concern arises from the belief that this condition makes me unworthy of the title of nurse." She'd been told that before, but never while the doctor saying it was holding her hand.

"No, Miriam." His other hand cupped her face, his touch so gentle, so tender. "I worry about the town, I always do. But *this* worry is for you. I don't know how to help. I don't know if I even can. And the thought of leaving you to face another seizure, alone, weighs on my mind. And my heart," he added quietly.

Hope bubbled, but reality stood ready to burst it. "Knowing what you know of me now, you can't possibly . . ." She couldn't force out the words.

His expression softened even more. "Is this what you meant all those times you said I couldn't possibly care for you and would be grateful to have escaped our arranged marriage 'if I knew you better'?"

A chill trickled through her, painful and dispiriting. "People have abandoned me over this, Gideon. People who claimed to care for me."

He raised her good hand to his lips and pressed a lingering kiss there. "I'm still here."

The front door opened. Gideon released her hand. Miriam stepped away, grateful for the chance to sort out her thoughts, but acutely missing his reassuring touch.

"If that is my mother, I will jump out the window," Gideon warned under his breath.

"She knows how to wind you tightly. My mother was the same way."

"How did you endure yours?" he asked with an exhausted sigh.

"I ran away from home."

He laughed, but when she didn't, his amusement faded quickly. "You truly ran away from home?"

"We really don't talk much, do we?" She began setting out his instruments for the day. "On my nineteenth birthday, I boarded a train that took me to a small women's college of nursing, and I never returned. Furthermore, I don't think my parents wanted me to."

"How could they not? They were your family."

She knew he would understand their objections if he gave it

much thought. "Let me put it this way: I was the cherry end table amongst the mahogany furniture of their lives."

Mrs. Fletcher and Rupert, still limping, stepped into the parlor, ending any further conversation.

"We've come as you requested," Mrs. Fletcher told Gideon.

Miriam pushed aside her personal uncertainty and focused on their young patient. No matter that her nursing skills had often been called into question, she knew how to care for patients, she knew how to love the people she was supposed to help. And she meant to do precisely that.

Chapter 22

Rupert was a mystery. Despite thoroughly examining his leg, Gideon could find no reason for the boy's limp. Miriam had taken Rupert onto the porch to watch the stage come in.

"I don't know what to tell you, Mrs. Fletcher," Gideon admitted. "His leg has healed, and, watching him walk, he seems to be limping with both legs. I can't account for it."

She wrung her hands. "Neither can I."

Gideon scanned the paper containing Rupert's medical history. "He seems in perfect health. He's energetic and growing as he should."

Mrs. Fletcher looked as bewildered as he felt. "He's had such a difficult few months. My heart aches seeing him still hurting."

"Has he complained that he's in pain?" The boy hadn't seemed overly uncomfortable.

"He seldom complains about anything."

Gideon hated not being able to help. First Miriam and now Rupert. What good was he if his list of suffering patients only grew?

"That deputy, Andrew, is some kind of checkers genius."

Father entered the parlor with no more introduction than that. "Hasn't lost a game all morning."

"He's also an excellent tree climber," Gideon said. "You should challenge him to that."

Father laughed. "I've not climbed a tree in years. I ought to give it a go while your mother isn't around to grow faint at the sight."

"Father, this is Mrs. Fletcher. Her boy, Rupert, came in for an exam today."

Father greeted her, a farmer's wife in drab clothing, with the same bow he would have given a fine lady. "Your boy is the one on the porch, I'd guess. He and the nurse seem to be good friends."

"Yes, Miss Bricks is wonderful with him." Something of Mrs. Fletcher's tension dissipated. "Between her and Dr. MacNamara, this town is well cared for."

"*Dr.* MacNamara." Father spoke as though he was feeling out the words, getting the taste of them. "Your grandfather would have thought that a fine thing. A doctor in the family."

If only Father had come to visit on his own. Mother was a harder medicine to swallow.

Miriam stepped inside. "I believe I can begin demanding a higher wage." Her gaze settled on Father and lingered a moment before jumping to Gideon, then back again a few times. "Good heavens, the two of you look alike."

Father pretended to pluck a bit of lint from his cuff. "Gideon always was a fine-looking lad."

Miriam's mouth shot upward on the instant. "You must be his father."

"I must be." Father gave her his usual deep-waisted bow. "And you are Nurse Bricks, I understand."

"At the moment, I am a solver of mysteries." She turned to Gideon. "I have discovered the reason for young Rupert's limp."

"How did you manage that?"

"I asked him." She cocked her head to the side in an overdone show of pride. "I told him he walked as though his feet hurt, and he said that they do, but only when he wears his shoes."

"Oh, what a fool I am." Gideon slapped his hand against his thigh as the entire picture became clear. "He has grown quite a lot since spring. It's right there in his history. Of course his shoes are pinching."

Miriam nodded. "Meaning, there's nothing truly the matter with him."

"I am so relieved." Mrs. Fletcher embraced Miriam, though she was careful not to disturb her arm hanging in its sling. "We'll not have the money for new shoes for some time, but before winter, certainly."

"He can go barefoot until then," Miriam reassured her. "Most children prefer that anyway."

"I'm so glad this was something simple." Mrs. Fletcher gave Miriam one more hug, then gave Gideon one as well. "I won't impose any longer."

"You are never an imposition," Gideon said. "And please don't ever hesitate to come see us if you are ever concerned about anything."

"Come see us." I hope I can keep saying that.

He saw Mrs. Fletcher out. When he returned to the parlor, Father was seated beside Miriam on the sofa, already deep in conversation.

"And they all love Gideon that way?" Father asked.

He ought to have slipped back out, but he wanted to hear Miriam's answer.

"Everyone loves your son. I don't think they can help themselves." Miriam seemed at ease in Father's company. It was a MacNamara talent, one Gideon had hoped would serve him well in gaining the confidence of his new nurse. "And, in turn, Gideon cares for and worries about them. He loses sleep and works all hours of the day and night. He travels for days at a time to reach towns even more remote than this one because he knows if he doesn't, there won't be anyone to help them."

She made him sound like a saint.

"Gideon was always like that," Father said. "He never was content to sit idly by. He always had to be doing something. He was exhausting."

"He still is," Miriam said.

That pulled a laugh from his father.

"He never stops moving," Miriam said. "He doesn't sit down for more than a moment, not even for the length of a meal. Always moving or talking or thinking. Even watching him think is tiring."

Father patted Miriam's hand. "I am happy he has you, Miss Bricks. Too many of the women in his life haven't understood him."

"Please, call me Miriam. And don't give me too much credit. I am convinced your son is not understandable."

It was time for Gideon to join the discussion. "That is a fine thing to say about a man you've asked to increase your wages."

Miriam turned wide eyes to Father. He gave Gideon a warning look. "Miriam, here, is my newest friend. You be nice to her, son. I hold the ear of the leaders of this nation, you realize."

"Not from this far away, you don't." Gideon sat on a nearby ottoman. He would rather have sat by Miriam. Truth be told, he would rather be holding her hand and caressing her face again.

He didn't know where the impulse had come from, but the feeling had been too strong to ignore.

"Has he played his cello for you?" Father asked Miriam. "He is very talented."

"He played 'Gentle Annie' the other day. I think it was the loveliest version of that tune I've ever heard."

He hadn't realized she was familiar enough with Stephen Foster's work to have recognized the melody. Something about her unabashed praise was a little embarrassing.

"Mother always felt I should have concentrated on more refined music," Gideon said. "She was probably right."

"Nonsense," Father said. "You learned to play both styles of music, so you should be permitted to choose what you keep playing."

"I'll go make us some lunch." Miriam rose from the sofa. "Don't get your hopes up, Mr. MacNamara. There is a reason I am a nurse and not a cook."

Once Miriam had left the room, Father said, "I like her."

"Miriam is wonderful," Gideon acknowledged.

"Is that why you wanted to marry her?"

"I had been looking for a woman who would be comfortable living in the middle of nowhere as well as who could be a helpmeet with my patients. Everything I had learned of Miriam told me she fit that mold perfectly. It was to have been a mutually beneficial arrangement."

"Marriage isn't supposed to be mutually beneficial—" Father held up a finger. "That came out wrong. Do not tell your mother I said that."

Oh, how he'd missed talking with his father. "It'll be our secret."

"What I was trying to say is that you don't pick a wife because she's the most convenient option. You choose a woman who lights you up every time you see her, who makes your heart lodge itself in uncomfortable places."

"Such a woman is not as easy to find as you seem to think."

"How difficult is it to walk into your own kitchen, Gideon?"

"My kitchen?" There was only one woman in his kitchen at the moment. "You mean Miriam?"

"I didn't mean the stove, lad."

Gideon sighed. "Ian, apparently, left out the part of the story where Miriam refused to marry me."

"Why did she refuse?" Father's calm question didn't set Gideon's back up the way Mother's demands for information always did.

"Because she didn't know. The agency that arranged the match told her she was coming here for a job."

"Oh, dear." Father shook his head. "Is that why you contacted Ian? To determine what legal recourse you had?"

Gideon shrugged. "I suppose. Mostly I was embarrassed, I think. And I would like the money back that I paid to the bureau." He winced at how mercenary that sounded.

"If you ask me, Miriam was wiser about this than you were. A marriage based on anything other than mutual affection and respect will never truly be convenient." Sadness touched his words, something Gideon seldom remembered hearing or seeing from his father. He was ceaselessly cheerful, sometimes to the point of seeming foolish. "But in the few moments I saw you together, I saw both respect and affection." Father stood. "Don't discard that."

He left on that declaration. Gideon remained behind, dumbstruck. He had never, in all his life, heard his father speak that way.

Chapter 23

"Thank you for your help with dinner tonight, Paisley." Miriam stirred a simmering pot of carrots on the stove. "Lunch was a disaster."

Miriam hadn't planned on her humble meal being served in the formal dining room on Gideon's best dishes, but Mrs. MacNamara had insisted.

"I cook a big meal like this here once a month." Paisley mashed a bowl of potatoes as they talked.

"Once a month?"

"Gideon does a lot for my father. Making dinner so he can invite people over is my way of repaying him in a small way." Paisley added some salt to the potatoes. "I know how to make only the one meal, and it's nothing gourmet, but he seems to appreciate it."

"At the risk of sounding awful, meeting his mother makes me wonder how he became such a—" How could she put her thoughts into words? "How it is that he doesn't—"

"—put on airs?" Paisley stirred a lump of butter into the

potatoes. "Miraculously, he's the best of men—except for my father and Cade, of course."

The guests were all gathered when Paisley and Miriam entered with the last of the food and took their seats. Every place at the table was occupied; Mrs. MacNamara had issued several invitations.

Discomfort settled over Miriam as she eyed the gathering. Her mother had forbidden her to dine with company after the seizures had begun. She hadn't sat down to a finely set table with dinner guests in years. Before coming to Savage Wells, she'd eaten alone in her room at the asylum.

Gideon tapped the side of his goblet with his fork as he stood at the head of the table. Heavens, this was bringing back memories. Father had always begun their dinner parties that way. Mother had been so particular about gatherings and etiquette and appearance.

"Thank you all for coming this evening," Gideon said. "And thank you to Miriam and Paisley for providing the meal."

Now and then, she saw glimpses of the society gentleman he must have been back East hidden beneath the rougher influence of the West. She couldn't say if she liked one better than the other. Indeed, it was the mixture she found most intriguing.

"I don't intend to make a big speech," Gideon said. "Enjoy your meal and each other's company."

Conversation was general and friendly as the meal got underway. Mr. Endecott spoke at length with his wife regarding his upcoming sermon. Miss Dunkle devoured every word Mrs. MacNamara spoke as though she, and not the preacher, was speaking of eternal truths. As near as Miriam could tell, their conversation centered around the latest Eastern fashions.

"I don't like these," Mr. Bell muttered, holding up a spoonful of mashed potatoes.

Miriam sat near him. "Would you prefer carrots?"

Mr. Bell's brow furrowed. "I don't know if I like those either."

"Do you want to try some?"

He pushed his plate a bit away. "I don't know."

Oh, how he reminded her of George. So earnest. So lost.

"If anything strikes your fancy, tell me. I'll find it if I can."

He neither agreed nor argued, but sat staring at his plate, his food nearly untouched.

"Maybe offer him a bit of my moonshine." Tansy sat on Miriam's other side. "Brought some with me, but Doc told me to keep it outside on account of his mother not understanding our ways yet."

Miriam liked that she seemed to be included in "our." She met Mr. Bell's gaze. "Do you like sweet tea?" That was the actual content of Tansy's "moonshine."

Mr. Bell shook his head.

"Sorry, Tansy. That doesn't seem to be what he's looking for, either."

Tansy took it in stride. "He'll hit upon it soon enough. He always does." After a bite, she said, "How's your arm? That was a nasty fall."

"It is improving by bits."

Tansy raised an eyebrow. "So, why is Doc still worried? I been sitting here wondering why he watches you so closely."

"He watches me?" She hoped no one else could overhear their quiet conversation. "Like he is trying to decide the fastest way to get rid of me?"

"More like every time he looks up he's afraid you won't be

there and is relieved that you are." Tansy waved in Cade's direction. "Hand over the potatoes, will you?"

He wants me here. She'd sensed that. She'd felt nearly certain those were his sentiments. But Dr. Blackburn's words, spoken so many times over the past two years, continually undermined her faith in herself. "Your mind is broken. It always will be. Broken minds cannot be trusted." She'd tried not to believe him, but his insistence made her question so many things.

Tansy saw something in Gideon that seemed to confirm, on some level, what Miriam thought she saw and felt. It afforded her a rare bit of optimism.

After supper had ended and the guests were beginning to dissipate, Gideon pulled her aside. "Can we talk for a moment?"

Did that portend good or ill?

"Don't look so terrified," he said with a laugh. "This isn't bad news."

"I'm accustomed to bad news. It is my first assumption."

"It doesn't need to be this time." He eyed his pocket watch. "May I walk you home so we can talk on the way to the hotel?"

"I would appreciate that."

He led her to the empty entryway. "But let's hurry. If my mother sees me, she'll want to talk, and I would really rather not."

They slipped out unseen. They were only a single step off the porch when Gideon launched into his topic.

"I have been pondering my trip to Quarterville and your insistence that you're well enough to see to things here while I'm gone."

She held her breath. Was he going to give her a chance?

"I think I have hit upon a solution."

"I'm listening." Quite closely, in fact.

"You suggested Tansy, but I didn't want to pull her away from home after she'd spent two days here helping. But, what if you stayed with her while I was away? I realize that means leaving the privacy of your room at the hotel to be a guest in someone's house for a week, but I would worry less knowing there was someone nearby who was aware of the possibility that you might need assistance and who would know what to do if you did."

He really was concerned about her. *Her.* Not his practice or his pride, but *her.*

"We could put a sign in the window at my home," he continued, "instructing anyone with medical needs to see you at Tansy's." They'd reached the hotel and stood outside the front doors. "What do you think? I believe it could work."

The tears started without warning. She looked away, hoping he wouldn't see.

"Miriam?"

"I'm sorry. I'm not upset; I promise I'm not. I'm surprised. I'm shocked and confused and—" She was rambling, but the right words refused to come.

He set his arms around her. Miriam held to him with her uninjured arm, leaning her head against his chest.

"Every other doctor has thrown me away, like I was worthless."

"I told Andrew that Mr. Bell's failing mind doesn't make him worthless. Andrew's struggles don't make him worthless," he whispered. "You will never be worthless either."

"You may be the only one who believes that."

"Including you?" he pressed.

Putting into words her deepest uncertainty was too vulnerable, too painful. She'd told herself throughout her two years at Blackburn that she hadn't belonged there, that it was a mistake. But the longer she'd been there, the less certain she'd felt.

"I am broken," she said. "I always will be."

"All of us are broken in some way, Miriam. How we respond to our troubles, the strength we show in our trials, is far more telling than any imperfection."

She took a shaky breath. "Will you help me believe that?"

"You have my word."

Chapter 24

"You know, Father, you *can* go back to bed." Gideon didn't usually have an audience when preparing to leave town. "The sun won't be up for another hour."

"I've enjoyed watching you work these past days. I want to see this part of it too." He sat at the desk while Gideon checked his set of traveling medical instruments. "Your mother is upstairs gathering all the stockings she can find."

"Why is she—?" But he answered his own question. "So I won't be cold. Mother needs to start trusting that I can take care of myself."

"She does, son. She simply worries."

Gideon took one more look through his travel-sized bottles of medicines. "She disapproves."

"Does her approval matter so much to you?"

Gideon buckled his case closed. "She is my mother. I want her to like me." He winced. "I sound like I am five years old."

"No. You sound like me," Father replied. "I have spent a great deal of my adult life trying to make certain that she likes me."

"Father—" Gideon began, but was cut off before he could say anything further.

"Now, about Miriam." Father leaned back casually, folding his hands in his lap. "I like her."

Gideon accepted the change of topic. "You also liked Eleanor Bainbridge, and that didn't work out so well for me."

Father didn't seem to be listening. "Miriam's tender and sweet, but she can be fierce when she needs to be. A man needs a woman who brings a bit of fight."

"Life has taught her to be a fighter." And to doubt her own worth. He wouldn't have guessed that about her when they'd first met. She'd shown some trepidation when asked to examine Mrs. Driessen, but outside of that, she had fiercely defended her knowledge and skills. He'd not realized that she had been working to convince herself as well as him.

"Do you know how your grandparents met?" Father's question came seemingly out of the blue, though Gideon's distraction may have been partly to blame.

"I don't think I ever heard the story." He set his bags by the parlor door.

Father motioned him toward the matching armchairs by the empty fireplace. Gideon joined him there.

"My father had opened his first shop selling MacNamara Whiskey and hired a local Irishwoman to clean it each evening. He lost his heart to her quickly, but she was having none of it. She'd come to America alone, with no one to look out for her, and she was wary. So, your grandfather didn't let on that she took his very heart with her when she left each day, leaving him silently wishing she would stay."

Gideon shook his head. "Even *if* that story is true—and you are far too much like Grandfather MacNamara for me to entirely believe you—my situation is different."

"Only because your grandfather, may he rest in peace, was a bigger idiot than you are, so he had a better excuse." Father didn't even finish the sentence before grinning.

Gideon had deeply missed conversations with his father. The man was one of the most successful bankers in Washington, with a keen mind and sharp eye for strategy. He was also one of the funniest and most charming people Gideon knew.

"Have you thought about courting her?" Father asked. "Tell me you've at least thought about it."

He certainly had thought about it. He'd even found himself "accidentally" attempting it, holding her hand without thinking, holding her in his arms when she needed comfort, only to realize how desperately he, as Father would say, needed her comfort as well.

"She turned me down," Gideon reminded him. "At the altar, I might add. And she hasn't seemed to regret that in the weeks since."

Father rolled his eyes, something he'd started doing when Gideon was little because it made him and his brothers laugh. "You, son, are far too much like your grandfather. Except, in the end, he chose the right woman. Took him five years, the great lummox. Mother never let him live that down."

Gideon stood. "I must be on my way. Take care while I'm gone."

"I like Miriam. And I think you like her too."

He tossed his hands up, turning back to face his father. "Of course I like Miriam. How could I not? She's caring and intelligent and funny and brave. And, since you seem intent on pressing salt into this particular wound, I'll tell you that I have been courting her. Rather, I have been trying. Every time I feel like I'm making progress, like maybe I am finally on track to claim some happiness in my life and, I hope, in hers, it falls apart. Every time." The admission stung, but it needed to be said. Father would only keep harping on the topic if Gideon didn't put an end to it.

"It is a good thing you have a lot of time to spend on your own," Father said. "You've some strategizing to do, and I'd suggest you formulate a plan before you get back."

Gideon stopped in the doorway and set his hands, fingers interwoven, atop his head as he released the tension from his lungs. In a quiet, resigned voice, he repeated the words he'd not enjoyed saying the first time. "I've had my suit rejected before, and I've had my heart broken. I can't endure that again." He hadn't admitted that before, not even to himself.

"You've the blood of warriors in your veins, lad." When Father started calling on his nonexistent Scottish accent, Gideon knew things were serious. "If you love her, you have to try. No matter the risk."

Gideon took up his medical bags. "Will you and Mother still be here when I get back?"

Father rose at last. "We will. James is taking care of everything at the bank, and he does a fine job of it. Ian is seeing to my duties with the party and attending various political functions in my stead." He walked with Gideon into the entryway. "I rather like this little town of yours. It's quiet. Washington is never quiet."

"You could retire out here, you know. Spend all day playing checkers."

Father slapped him on the back. "It's tempting. But your mother would never be happy so far from Washington society."

Gideon pulled on his outer coat. "Do her needs always trump yours?"

"Needs are a difficult thing to juggle, son." Father grabbed the doorknob.

Gideon took a single step out when Mother's voice stopped him short.

"Oh, Gideon. I was hoping you hadn't left yet." Mother descended the staircase, managing to look regal in her dressing gown and nightcap. "I found you some woolen socks."

He accepted them, but with an inward roll of his eyes. "I've made this trip many times before. You needn't worry over me."

"I'm a mother, Gideon," she said. "Worrying is part of my job. Be safe, son."

"I will." He shook his father's hand. "If anyone comes by with medical problems and doesn't or can't read the sign, send them to Tansy's. That is where Miriam is staying."

"I will."

"Thank you." He buttoned his coat and stepped out onto the porch. "I'll see you both in about a week."

"Think on what I said," Father added quietly. "Some things—some *people*—are worth fighting for."

There was a tremendous amount of truth in that.

Mother looked at the both of them. "Let him be on his way, William. He has a long journey today."

That journey took him down the road past Tansy's house. He hoped Miriam was sleeping well despite being in an unfamiliar place and faced with the prospect of caring for an entire town on her own for the first time.

He could only just make out the front door, but could swear it moved. He slowed the horse and took a better look. The door was, indeed, open. Someone stepped outside. And that same someone waved an arm a little frantically.

Gideon pulled the buggy to a stop. It was Miriam. Had something happened? She wasn't one for irrational panic.

He hopped down, then wrapped the horse's rein around a fence post. "What's wrong?"

She shook her head. "I knew you would assume there was a crisis."

"When a woman wrapped in a quilt comes running out of a house before sunrise and waves me down, I do tend to think something out of the ordinary is at play." He didn't see any signs of trauma or illness.

She kept the quilt firmly around herself and leaned against the fence. "Andrew was here last night, and he mentioned that two of the Clark children have fevers and sore throats, as does Georgette Abbott."

Gideon hadn't heard that.

"I've not seen any Ayer's Cherry Pectoral amongst your medicines," she said. "Do you prefer to treat children's sore throats with something else?"

He shook his head. "I don't use it often, so it is kept in the apothecary cabinet in my bedroom. If there's something you can't find, look for it there."

He reached across the fence and adjusted the quilt where it had slipped off her splinted shoulder. "Did you really wait up to see me go past?"

"Not for terribly long. I didn't think you would leave before there was at least a little light." She tipped her head to the side. "I thought about sleeping in the middle of the road and hoping you saw me before you ran me over, but this seemed like the safer approach."

"Much safer, yes."

Her hair hung down in long, intertwined curls. Mesmerizing. He brushed his fingers over a copper strand. "I didn't realize how curly your hair is."

"Excessively curly," she said. "It is the bane of my existence at times."

"I like it."

Her eyes were dark in the dim light of earliest morning. Her hair hung in riotous waves all around her face. It was the sort of goodbye a man could grow accustomed to. The sort of goodbye he'd thought his arrangements with the Western Women's Bureau would have provided. Although, who was to say any real warmth would have grown between them if they'd begun their acquaintance on that footing? He had a chance to court her, to truly win her affection. He simply needed to sort out how.

"Take care of yourself while I'm away," he said.

"I will, and I'll pray for an uneventful seven days. For both of us." She stepped back from the fence. "I'm going back inside. It is a little chilly."

"Good idea."

She nodded and took another step away. "I'll see you in a few days."

A moment later, she had slipped inside Tansy's house, and he was alone. He shook off his lingering thoughts of her eyes, the color in her cheeks. He needed to make good time to Quarterville so he wouldn't be caught in the dark. He also needed some time alone to sort out just what he meant to do with his life.

Chapter 25

"Miss Bricks?" Andrew stood a pace away from the clothes-line where Miriam was attempting to hang laundry one-handed. Tansy would likely have helped, but she had slipped out to the shed where she made her "moonshine."

"Good morning, Andrew." Miriam didn't step forward, giving Andrew the space he needed to feel comfortable.

"You said to tell you if the Clarks' little ones and Georgette Abbott were still ailing today. Clarks live a stone's throw from here, so I dropped in to check. Their girls looked miserable, all flushed from fever and such. I told Mrs. Clark she oughtta bring 'em to see you." His brow pulled low. "I hope that was the right thing to do."

Miriam summoned her most encouraging tone. "That was absolutely the right thing. In fact, if you would let Tansy know where I've gone, I'll drop in on the Clarks myself and save them the trouble."

Andrew's eyes darted toward the shed. "Tansy's a friend." The declaration was clearly meant as a reassurance to himself. "I'll tell her for you. Then I'll head back to town for the checkers. Mr. Bell and Mr. MacNamara will be there already."

A tiny, genuine smile touched his usually pensive expression. Miriam resisted the urge to rush over to him and hug him tightly. Too many of the patients at Blackburn hadn't ever shed their looks of worry.

"I like Doc's pa," he said. "It's sure easy to see where Doc gets his friendliness, isn't it?"

She set the basket of wash next to the fence post. "Mr. MacNamara is a nice man."

"Doc's ma, though. She scares me." He seemed to rethink that admission. "Not like I'm a child shaking with fright in the corner. She's just—She's not as personable as her husband."

"Savage Wells is unfamiliar to her. Everything about our lives here is different from what she is accustomed to." It wasn't a hard thing to piece together; Miriam simply pictured her own mother coming for a visit. "I would wager that if we were to meet Mrs. MacNamara in Washington, amongst her friends and the familiar surroundings of her home, she would be every bit as personable as her husband."

Andrew scuffed his toe against the dirt. "But then *we* would be uncomfortable."

He was quick, though most people likely didn't take the time to find that out.

"Thank you for checking on the Clarks, Andrew. You take good care of this town."

He left, heading for the moonshine shed. Paisley and Gideon both said that Andrew was much improved since he'd first returned from the war. She hoped he would continue to recover.

The Clarks were an easy distance from Tansy's home. Miriam arrived there quickly.

"Good morning." She smiled when Mrs. Clark opened the door. "Andrew said your girls were ill."

The poor woman looked bedraggled. "I ain't seen 'em this ill before. I'd rather Doc see to them."

"Dr. MacNamara will not be back for at least a week." Miriam would do well to act as confident in herself as she wanted the town to feel. "Where are the girls now?"

"Over here." Mrs. Clark ushered her over to a trundle in the corner where two small figures lay tucked under blankets.

Miriam knelt beside the low bed. "Do you have a lantern or candle I could use?" The corner was a bit too dim.

Mrs. Clark complied. What the light revealed made Miriam's breath catch. The girls were not, as Andrew had reported, flushed. The rosiness of their cheeks was a rash.

"When did the rash first appear?"

"It wasn't there last night, but it was this morning." Mrs. Clark understood that the rash did not portend anything good.

Miriam eyed it more closely, growing more convinced of what she was seeing. "Does it extend to their chests and bellies?"

"It does."

Miriam's mind spun fast and furious, wrapping itself around the potential enormity of this. "Your oldest. Is he unwell also?"

Mrs. Clark's lips pressed together, and her forehead wrinkled deeply. "He was dragging a bit this morning when he left for school. But he didn't have a fever. He also didn't have much of an appetite, now that I think on it. He hardly ate."

So the Clark boy might be infected as well. "Andrew said Georgette Abbott was ill. Do you know if she has developed the rash?"

"I don't know."

Miriam frowned. "Are any of the other Abbott children ill?"

"Georgette is the only one too young for school. All the other children walked with my Frank this morning."

"To school?"

Mrs. Clark nodded.

Goodness gracious. This may be at the school. "Mrs. Clark, may I have a word?"

They stepped across the room. Miriam wasn't entirely certain of everything that needed to be done, but her absolute first step had to be gathering more information.

"It doesn't look like measles," Mrs. Clark said.

"It isn't." Miriam wished it were.

Mrs. Clark took a shaky breath. "I kept hoping somehow it was. Measles is bad, but it's not as terrifying as what I'm afraid this is."

"I believe you already know what we're facing."

"Scarlet fever." Hers was a shaky, horrified whisper.

"Scarlet fever isn't only dangerous." Miriam held the woman's gaze. "It is also catchy. No one quite knows how it spreads, only that it does, and does so like wildfire. Your oldest has likely contracted it as well, which means it may be all over the school by now. I need to get to town, but I cannot abandon your children here when they are ill, especially if it has spread to your neighbors."

Mrs. Clark, to her credit, remained calm.

"Is your husband home?"

"He's in the fields."

"Fetch him so he can help get your children to town. Then I need you to go to the Abbotts' and see if they have thrown a rash yet. If they have, send them to Dr. MacNamara's home in town."

Mrs. Clark agreed. She gave her girls a forced smile and wave and hurried out of the house.

Miriam wiped all traces of worry from her expression. She kept herself calm while the wagon was hitched and the girls set in the wagon bed as they drove to town. She held silent despite her spinning thoughts.

Scarlet fever. Heaven have mercy on us.

She had only just tucked the girls into bed at Gideon's home when Cade arrived. She explained the situation to him in hushed tones near the top of the stairs.

"Am I needing to quarantine the town?"

"Not yet. But I need to see if it is at the school."

"You believe it is."

There was no keeping secrets from the man. "I am convinced of it. If I find even one child with this, especially one who is already throwing the rash, then we have to assume every child in the school is ill, even if he or she isn't exhibiting symptoms yet."

Cade gave a decisive nod. "That is where the quarantine has to be applied. To the children."

"Precisely. All the medicine they need is here, so bringing them here makes the most sense. Since we don't know where this illness is originating or precisely how it spreads, isolating those who are infected is our best option." She pushed through her growing worry. "The disease is known enough, and feared enough, that parents will understand the necessity, but I know they will worry, especially with Gideon gone. They'll want to be with their children, but there will not be room."

"Don't fret over the parents," Cade said firmly. "They can be kept calm. What else do you need?" He certainly had a cool head in a crisis.

"Someone should check on the families who live a little further afield," she said. "If this has reached that far out and they need medical attention—" She shook her head. "And we must warn those further away not to come to town until this has passed."

Cade straightened his hat. "Don't waste a single thought on anything other than doctorin'. You've a sheriff, a deputy, and two of the finest members of the marshal service in this town who'll see to the rest."

Hawk was quickly pressed into service, assigned to accompany Miriam to the schoolhouse. Cade headed to the jailhouse to update Andrew and Paisley and come up with a plan. Depending on what Miriam found, they might quickly be in a sticky situation.

"I lost two brothers to scarlet fever," Hawk said as he and Miriam turned toward the school. "It is a fearsome opponent to face down."

Miriam understood that well. She had acted as nurse for patients who'd contracted the deadly illness. She remembered all too vividly. The fever. The rash. Too many didn't survive.

"I keep telling myself I'm not going to find anything worrisome at the school," she said.

"But?"

She let out the tiniest of breaths. "I know I will. I know it."

They stopped at the bottom of the steps, looking up at the schoolhouse door. "We'd best put on our most casual expressions," Hawk said. "No use panicking the children the moment we walk in."

"Their parents will panic enough when they hear the words 'scarlet fever.' I can only hope Miss Dunkle is made of sterner stuff."

They climbed the steps and slipped inside the already open door.

Miss Dunkle, her hand on the back of a student whose head was laid on his desk, looked up as they entered. Not a moment's confusion or surprise crossed her features. She looked utterly relieved.

"I don't know how you knew," Miss Dunkle said, "but I'm glad you did."

That did not bode well. "How many children are ill?" Miriam asked.

"We're at five now, though a few of the others are beginning to pale."

Miriam did a quick visual inspection. A good number of children did, indeed, look less than well. "Who's the worst off?"

She indicated the student directly beside her. "Frank Clark." The boy kept his head on his desk.

Miriam caught Hawk's eye. If the boy was too weak, she might need Hawk's help examining him.

She knelt beside Frank. And there it was: the beginnings of the scarlet rash on his face. She undid the top button on his shirt and, as she'd feared, saw that the rash was on his chest as well.

A quick inspection of the other children who were feverish and sluggish revealed two more already showing the rash. Amongst the rest of the students, nearly all had sore throats or general feelings of being unwell. Some of that might have been worry manifesting itself as illness, but Miriam wasn't about to take chances.

Miss Dunkle pulled her aside. "I know what that rash is, Nurse Bricks. This is no small thing." She wrung her hands. "Why did Dr. MacNamara have to leave? Now, when we need him so much?"

"You aren't entirely without help," Miriam reminded her. "I have years of training and experience with this disease. I'll do all I can."

Miss Dunkle's expression grew more worried. "You cannot possibly replace the training and experience of an actual doctor."

"I didn't—"

"You cannot promise me all of these children are going to be fine. I know you cannot."

"Not even Dr. MacNamara could promise you that." Miriam told herself to be patient. Behind Miss Dunkle's critical words was an undeniable worry. She loved the children in her charge, and she was afraid for them. "Still, I have every intention of doing what I can to get word to him so he can decide what's best to be done. Until then, I am all you have. And these children need to feel your confidence."

Miss Dunkle nodded feebly.

"Now, rally the troops. We're going to walk them to Dr. MacNamara's house."

Miss Dunkle hesitated. "I don't know that Frank has the strength."

"Hawk will see to Frank." Miriam knew she could make that vow with surety. Hawk wouldn't leave a person suffering without doing all he could to help.

Miss Dunkle had the children organized and moving in orderly fashion down the street in no time. Miriam watched them all, noting which seemed healthiest and which were the most likely to throw spots soonest. At least half of them already had symptoms. How many more would by nightfall?

Chapter 26

"What do you mean he is not coming back?" Mrs. Mac-Namara's usually cultured voice had turned decidedly shrill.

"He can't leave Quarterville until he knows the patient he operated on is out of danger," Hawk explained again.

Miriam had felt the same drop of her heart that had no doubt inspired Mrs. MacNamara's outburst, but right on its heels had come the knowledge that Gideon was absolutely correct. He had to tend to his patient before he could come home.

She was sorely tempted to drop onto the sofa and allow herself some much-needed rest. But she firmly suspected if she permitted herself even a moment's respite, she would never convince herself to get up again.

The instructions Gideon had sent back with Hawk hadn't included anything she didn't already know, but holding the note brought her reassurance. It was proof she'd been doing the right things in treating the children. It was a link to him and the calm confidence he exuded. And it brought the increasingly familiar warmth of his affection. He had, after all, taken the time to remind her to think of her own health as well.

"People will die without a doctor here," Mrs. MacNamara insisted.

Miriam put Gideon's note in the pocket of her apron and squared her shoulders. "People die of this even with a doctor." It was the harsh reality of scarlet fever, and one they would all do well to accept. The coming days and weeks were going to be harrowing. "Gideon sent instructions, and they are exactly the things we have already been doing. The same treatments, the same approach."

"We have been taking that approach for four days," Mrs. MacNamara said. "The Clark children are growing worse almost by the minute."

Miriam kept her posture confident despite the worry clutching her heart. "We are doing everything possible."

Paisley and Cade were firmly on Miriam's side of things. Tansy had also fallen in line with what Miriam had asked of her the last few days. Hawk gave Miriam a nod of encouragement.

She took a deep breath and pressed ahead. Their work was far from done, and they couldn't waste more time on discussions. "We'll keep taking it in turns. Two people sleeping at a time, with the others split between here and the jailhouse. Either Paisley, Cade, or Hawk will be on duty so someone can patrol the town and enforce the quarantine."

Only Mrs. MacNamara shook her head in disagreement. "Marshal Hawking should go to Quarterville and tell Gideon to come home."

Miriam was exhausted and keeping calm was not easy. "If he leaves Quarterville, his patient will have no one."

Mrs. MacNamara tilted her chin upward. "*We* have no one."

"We have *me*. I will have to be enough for you and enough for this town." She was far too close to losing her temper. She dare not risk it. "Mr. MacNamara, I believe you and your wife are the next to be granted a few hours of sleep."

He seemed to understand the urgency in her suggestion and quickly ushered his wife upstairs.

"Pais and I will head back to the jailhouse," Cade offered.

So many were ill with the fever that they couldn't all be accommodated at Gideon's house.

"Tansy and Hawk, will you check on the patients here?" she asked once the O'Briens had left. "I will move between the two locations, helping where I'm most needed."

Neither of them left to follow her instructions.

"When do *you* sleep, Miriam?" Hawk asked.

It was concern, not distrust, that made them hesitate. "In two more rotations," she said. "Provided no new patients arrive, no new rashes appear, and no one—" Pain clutched at her heart. "And no one slips into convulsions." Not that she could actually help at that point, but she would not allow anyone to suffer those final moments alone.

"I'll check in on the first room." Hawk slowly climbed the stairs.

Tansy remained behind. "How're you holding up, Miss Miriam? No signs of an upcoming episode?"

"None," Miriam said, grateful that Tansy had waited until they were alone to ask. "Though that is no guarantee."

"Don't work yourself into illness," Tansy said. "That'd help no one, least of all you."

Between Tansy and Gideon, she was being fretted over endlessly. She ought to have been annoyed, but instead found it touching.

She wandered into the kitchen, needing a moment to collect

her thoughts and rally her courage. The coming hours and days would be brutal.

She pulled her sketchbook from its shelf and clutched it a moment. Could she allow herself a moment, even a brief one, to draw, to calm herself, to focus her mind once more? Could she afford not to?

Her eyes closed, she lowered herself to the floor, sitting with her knees up, the same pose she'd assumed so many times in her cell at Blackburn.

With a deep breath, she opened her eyes, untied the leather strap of her book, and turned to a new page. Quick strokes soon formed the familiar shape of Rupert's face, his eyes not worried as they'd been in her first sketch of him. This time, they were feverish, cloudy. A lump formed in her throat as she shaded in the rash that had appeared on his face that morning. The horrid, terrifying rash.

She loved that sweet boy. What if she couldn't save him?

Miriam hadn't slept more than a few minutes in the past forty-eight hours. The Clark children were approaching the crisis point. She expected it to happen any moment. They needed her. She was all they had. The parents of her dozens of young patients were gathered at the reverend's home, praying and hoping.

She pulled a length of bandaging from the armoire in Gideon's room as Mrs. MacNamara stepped inside. Much of the woman's blustering had dissipated, and now she looked at the children with true compassion and even spared a concerned glance for Miriam.

"I've been sent to tell you that you are overdue for a rest," Mrs. MacNamara said.

"I can't." Miriam set the bandaging on the end table and worked to get the sling off her own arm. "The situation has grown dire. I might be able to save these children, but only if I'm awake."

She bit back a groan of pain when her arm dropped from its position. If she could keep her upper arm near her side, it would hurt less, but the task would require another set of hands.

"I need your help," she told Mrs. MacNamara. "I need to use this"—she held up the bandaging—"to secure my upper left arm to my side by wrapping the cloth around me, under my right armpit. I need help tying the knot."

Mrs. MacNamara shook her head. "I've never tied any kind of important knot."

Miriam had always found Mrs. MacNamara unsympathetic, above her company, uncooperative. But now she heard something new in the woman's objections—an almost crippling lack of confidence. That was something she could relate to.

"Even a bow will do. It only needs to keep my arm still."

"Wasn't that the reason for the sling?"

"I need more use of my hand than the sling allows." Miriam wrapped the bandage around herself, wincing with each stab of pain. She clutched the two ends of the bandage in her hand. "Will you tie it for me, please? There isn't a particularly right or wrong way, I promise."

Mrs. MacNamara's fingers shook as she worked. "Do you need it tight?"

"Yes, as tight as possible."

Another nod. More finger shaking. Was all of her blustering an attempt to hide her uncertainty? How many people hid behind such things?

"Will that do?"

Miriam tried moving her arm. It held fairly still. That would do for now. "Thank you."

She stepped out and made her way swiftly down the corridor to the room where the Clark children rested. Hawk bent over their forms, dabbing their foreheads with damp cloths.

"Any change?" she asked as she crossed to them.

"They ain't moving around as much."

"*How* have they been moving?" Surely she would have been sent for if they'd begun convulsing. With scarlet fever, once that started, there was no saving them. It was the violent throes of unavoidable death.

"Like they're uncomfortable. Moaning and such." Hawk's brow pulled in worry, but he was calm, as always. She needed that from him.

The Clarks looked bad off. All three had been shaved that morning, cool cloths kept on their bare heads at all times, but it wasn't helping. They weren't breathing well, and their fevers were raging. They'd stopped vomiting, but likely because they had nothing left in their stomachs.

Miriam turned back to the doorway where Mrs. MacNamara stood. "I need ice. Their fevers have to come down."

She rushed off. The trip to the town ice cellar was one made often these past days. The task, in fact, had been given to the anxious parents waiting for word of their children. A shout was issued from Gideon's porch, and people rushed to the cellar, returning and leaving the ice on the steps.

Miriam would have more as quickly as the town could manage. She only hoped it would be enough, and that it would arrive in time.

Andrew appeared in the doorway next.

"Pour cups of water," she said. Her arm wasn't reliable enough for making the attempt. "If we can get them to drink, it'll cool them from the inside."

Andrew did as instructed without question or hesitation.

Miriam grabbed one of the damp rags and began sponging water on the children's limbs.

She paused her ministrations long enough to check the chart on the bureau where she'd kept a record of the medicine she'd given. It wasn't time for more. She prayed that what medicine she had been able to deliver was doing its job inside the children's fever-ravaged bodies.

The sound of footsteps, heavy and quick, on the stairs pulled her attention to the door. Cade appeared with Rupert Fletcher in his arms, inert and unresponsive.

"We don't know what happened," Cade said. "He just went limp."

There wasn't room on the bed beside the Clark children, but she couldn't divide her time between rooms. She snatched an extra blanket off the end of the bed and flicked it onto the floor, pain shooting through her unhealed arm at the movement.

"Lay him down," she said, dropping to the ground beside the blanket. He was so pale, so still. He struggled to breathe. She touched his cheek. He was burning up. "Get his shirt off." She struggled to her feet, then moved to the washbasin and the rags there. "When did Rupert last get silver nitrate?"

Cade handed her a paper covered with her own frantic writing: the chart from the room Rupert had been in. She let loose a breath she hadn't known she'd been holding. He was ready for more.

"Cool him," she said, handing Cade the cloth. She pulled the bottle of medicine from her apron pocket.

Rupert's eyes opened, though she didn't think he saw anything.

"You hang on, Rupert," she said. "You be strong and fight."

She couldn't get the lid off the bottle. The pain in her shoulder was too intense. *If Rupert can fight through this, so can I.* She tried again, but without success.

Someone knelt beside her and covered her hands with his. Familiar hands.

Gideon. Thank the heavens. She could have cried with relief.

"I'll give him the medicine," he said. "You help shave his head."

She set the bottle in his hand. He held her gaze for the length of a breath. No words were exchanged. They weren't necessary. He silently offered his strength and reassurance. She nodded in gratitude.

She pulled a camel-hair brush from her apron pocket and gave it to him. Hawk had replaced the damp cloths on the Clarks' bare heads with fresh ones. They'd need to do the same once Rupert's hair was gone.

Gideon's father arrived with a bowl of chipped ice. Not a word was spared greeting his newly returned son. Everyone understood the danger they were facing.

Rupert gagged as Gideon brushed the silver solution over the sores in his throat. His body was racked with the fruitless heaving of a stomach that was already empty.

Miriam set the boy's head on her lap, trying to soothe him while they waited for his stomach to settle. At least there were no convulsions. There was still hope.

"Father, will you and Mother do the shaving?" Gideon asked. "I need to get an accounting from Miriam or I'll be no help at all."

She couldn't bring herself to move. Every fiber of her being begged her to stay with this child who had been the first in Savage Wells to show her acceptance and kindness. He was dear to her, and she couldn't bear to lose him.

Mrs. MacNamara set a gentle hand on her good shoulder. "Let us see to the boy. Gideon needs your help."

She nodded and, with a heavy heart, relinquished her position. "Be careful not to nick him. He had a sore turn putrid a few weeks ago. He might be prone to infection."

Mrs. MacNamara took Miriam's place. Though she was a bit stiff in her ministrations, she was gentle. Mr. MacNamara had taken up the razor. Miriam hesitated, unable to look away from Rupert.

Gideon's hand rested gently against the small of her back. He nudged her the few steps into the hallway. He turned to face her.

"Have we lost any yet?" The gravity of the situation required they be efficient and focused, but her heart ached for a word of reassurance, a momentary embrace.

"No," she said. "The Clarks were ill first; they're the furthest along. The Abbott children grew ill about the same time, but they are doing better. Rupert—" Emotion clogged her words.

"Hold yourself together, Miriam."

She breathed and pushed ahead. "Rupert's rash was new last night. He began vomiting only this morning. He is growing worse faster than any of the others."

"How many are ill?" he asked.

"Twenty-three children. Two adults."

Daunting numbers, but he simply nodded. "How many are receiving silver nitrate?"

"Both of the adults and ten of the children—the ten who are in the worst condition."

"Epson salts for the others?"

She nodded, feeling calmer. "Even those who haven't shown symptoms. There's no danger in having them gargle, and it might give us a head start on any new cases." She looked up at him. "I've wished you were here so many times the past few days. I never could be sure I was doing the right things."

"As near as I can tell, you have been doing everything I would have done."

"Then why do I feel so defeated?" she whispered.

"Because you are exhausted." He spoke matter-of-factly, with none of his jesting tone she knew so well. "Have you been tracking their doses?"

She nodded and pulled the paper Cade had given her out of her apron pocket. "This is the chart from the room just above us, where Rupert was. This one"—she motioned to the room behind them—"is where we keep the sickest children. Every room has a chart."

He took the paper and put it in his own pocket. "Is there a room the patients aren't using?"

"Yours. Those of us treating the ill have taken it in turns to lie down and rest."

"Is anyone in there now?" he asked.

She shook her head. "We needed everyone working."

"Your next assignment, Miriam, is to go into my room and rest."

"I can't. Not with these children so near the point of—"

"A quarter hour, Miriam. Only fifteen minutes. You don't have to lie down. You don't have to close your eyes. Just breathe for fifteen minutes, away from the worry and the panic and the weight you have shouldered." His expression was sterner than she'd ever seen it. "If you don't, you will fall to pieces, and I need you to be strong if we are going to get the children through this."

She suspected he was being firm with her, not out of a lack of empathy for all she'd been through, but as a means of keeping her calm.

"Fifteen minutes," she repeated.

"Then come back here. I'll need you."

She held his gaze. "I did my best." It was important he know that.

"I have no doubt you worked miracles, Miriam."

"You're not disappointed?"

He shook his head. "Not in the least."

His praise, offered quickly in the moment before he returned to the sickroom, quieted many of her doubts. She had done her best, and she had done well. She would allow herself to rest for the prescribed fifteen minutes, then together she and Gideon would do everything in their power to save this town.

Chapter 27

Gideon sat in the hallway, his back pressed against the wall outside the bedroom where the sickest of the children were being tended. Miriam slumped against him, deeply asleep. Hawk sat opposite them, leaning against the spindled bannister surrounding the staircase.

"We should have been burying children today," Gideon said. "As sick as they were when I arrived last night, I was certain they wouldn't all survive. I don't know how they pulled through."

"The answer to that question is asleep on your shoulder." Hawk motioned with his chin. "Ran herself to tatters, rushing from one child to the next, between this house and the jailhouse, seeing to patients. I think this is the first time she's truly slept in days."

Gideon gazed down at her. Dark circles of exhaustion marred the skin under her eyes. "I should have come back sooner. She's still recovering herself."

Hawk tugged his hat lower, covering his eyes. "I don't know many people who would pull their arm out of a sling and endure the kind of pain she did all to help another person. She has grit—there's no denying that."

"You're fond of grit, if I'm not mistaken."

Beneath the brim of his hat, Hawk grinned. "We've a friendship between us, but nothing beyond. She'd tell you the same."

"Let's not wake her up to ask. We might yet have more children pass through the crisis phase. She'll need her strength to endure another night like last night."

Someone was coming up the stairs.

"What are the chances that's good news?" Hawk wondered out loud.

"I'd say about zero."

Cade stopped a few stairs short of the landing and talked to them over the bannister. "The stage let down two passengers."

"Did you warn them we have scarlet fever in town?" Gideon asked.

Cade nodded. "One of them's a doctor. You have an offer of help."

Hawk sat up straighter and tipped his hat back, eyeing Gideon. "Good news, after all."

"Where is this doctor now?" he asked Cade.

"Over at the jailhouse, looking in on the patients there. He said he'd come over this way if all was well with them."

This was a bit of desperately needed good news. Miriam would at last get some real sleep, and Gideon would have the medical help he required.

"Send him over right away. I'm going to see to it Miriam lies down."

He adjusted his position, slipping an arm behind her. When he jostled her injured arm, she groaned in her sleep, her features turning in pain. He'd need to slip her arm back in its sling before she lay down. She didn't awaken enough to stay upright.

"Best carry her, Doc," Hawk said. "She's dead on her feet."

He managed, with Hawk's help, to get her in his arms and safely situated. He carried her into his room. She winced with every step he took.

He laid her down on the bed. She didn't even wake as he slipped a sling around her neck and tucked her arm into it. He retied the bandage holding her arm against her side. If her arm kept still, it wouldn't hurt her as much, and she'd sleep better.

He pulled the blanket over her. "You can rest now, dear. We have help."

Her health concerns could not be hidden forever; eventually the people of Savage Wells would become aware of the full situation. But after this past week, they had reason to trust her, to have faith in her ability to help them. She had saved their children. He knew it, and he would make absolutely certain the town knew it. They needed her. And so did he.

He pulled the door closed. Hawk had disappeared, no doubt checking on a patient or heading back to his office. He'd been helpful during the crisis, but he still had a territory to protect.

Gideon peeked into the room where the Clark children and Rupert slept. They were still not truly well and wouldn't be for some time yet. Father sat beside the bed, watching over them.

"Are you in need of anything?" Gideon asked.

He shook his head. "But fevers are climbing in the room above us."

Gideon moved swiftly down the stairs and out onto the porch. As always, someone was watching. Reverend Endecott arrived almost immediately, ready to help.

"We need ice." Gideon was careful to sound calm. There was no immediate, looming crisis. He didn't mean to keep the worried parents in a constant state of terror.

The preacher turned and waved Mr. Abbott in the direction

of the ice cellar before returning his attention to Gideon. "How are the children?"

"Some are on the mend, thanks to Nurse Bricks. We have a few who are still in difficult straits, but they've been expertly tended, which gives them a far better chance than they would have had otherwise."

"Thank heaven for Miss Bricks," the preacher said. "What would we have done without her?"

"If I can be frank, Reverend: without her, you would be overseeing funerals today, not gathering ice."

Mr. Abbott, who had three children in quarantine, arrived in that moment with ice. He paled at the bold pronouncement but didn't speak. He set the ice block on the porch and took a step back.

"Will you thank her for us?" he said after a moment. "We'll be forever grateful to her."

"I will," Gideon promised.

He took up the ice, wrapped in burlap to protect his hands, and lugged it to the kitchen. Andrew was inside, finishing a sandwich.

"I can chip that," he offered, nodding to the ice.

Gideon hadn't needed to issue instructions since returning. Everyone knew what to do; Miriam had seen to that.

He returned to the entryway just as a man came through the front door.

Gideon stepped closer. "You're the doctor who has just arrived in town?"

The man nodded and hung his bowler hat on the hatstand near the door. "I am at your disposal, Dr.—"

"MacNamara." Gideon held out a hand in greeting.

"A pleasure to meet you. I am Dr. Blackburn."

Chapter 28

Blackburn clearly thought Gideon was odd for insisting on repeated handwashing and clean instruments. He asked several times if doing so was truly necessary and whether or not it wasted valuable time. He did not, however, refuse, for which Gideon was grateful.

Gideon gave strict orders to his parents, Cade and Paisley, Andrew, Tansy, and Hawk that Miriam was not to be disturbed—for days, if necessary. They would sleep in the vacant room beside the marshal's office in turns. Even Gideon would be afforded sleep now that there was another doctor in town. His optimism grew by the moment.

He and Blackburn sat in the room with the sickest children. Their efforts to cool the children's fevered skin was proving beneficial thus far.

"I am hopeful that these are the last who will grow dangerously ill." Gideon replaced the cool cloth on Daniel Staheli's shaven head. "Even those who have the rash are doing better than these children were at that same stage."

"They were likely already in your care when their symptoms began. Early treatment significantly improves outcomes."

Gideon nodded. Miriam had directed all the children gargle with Epson salts as soon as they arrived at the house. That had likely staved off some of the infection, giving the remaining children a better chance.

There was nothing to do at this point for these children except keep their fevers down and apply the silver nitrate. That meant the rare opportunity to converse with another doctor, something he hadn't done in years.

"Were you on your way to or from your place of practice when you arrived here?" Gideon asked. Maybe Blackburn worked near enough for a correspondence.

"Neither, actually. I've been traveling with a friend of mine on our way to visit a family member of his who is in dire need of medical care. Carlton is very concerned—as am I."

"And I am keeping you from reaching your destination."

Gideon dabbed a damp cloth along Daniel's thin arms. Blackburn tended to Freddy Canton nearby.

"Our undertaking is not a matter of immediate life or death," Blackburn said. "We have time enough to help you see your town through this crisis."

"Your timing could not have been better," Gideon said. "We were stretched to our limit. I only just returned from calls in a town quite far from here. My nurse managed without me, but I don't know how much longer she could have stayed on her feet."

"I don't believe I have met your nurse yet." Blackburn shifted to another bed in the room.

"She's been sleeping today." Gideon moved to another child, a cool cloth in his hand.

"Once she is awake, I will make certain to greet her." There was something odd in his tone, but Gideon couldn't quite put his finger on what. Blackburn was focusing on his efforts—that likely had rendered his words a little tight, a little muttered.

"How are those two?" Gideon asked, indicating the Patterson children Blackburn was tending.

"Their fevers have spiked," he said. "I'm growing concerned."

Gideon snatched up his stethoscope and listened to the breathing and pulse of the children. Neither sound set his mind at ease. He stepped to the doorway and into the hallway. Father was just stepping out of another room.

"We're going to need help in here," Gideon said. "Who else is up and about?"

"Your mother."

"Send her for ice. I'll need you in here."

A moment later, Gideon and Blackburn were at the bedside, and Father stood nearby, waiting for instructions.

"Check the chart," Gideon said. "When did these two last have the silver?"

Father glanced at the paper on the bureau. "About four o'clock."

"No 'abouts,' Father. I need the exact time."

"Three forty-seven."

It was still too soon. "What about fever powders?"

"Last dose was at five past three."

That would do. "Fetch them for me."

"Which ones are they?" Father asked. No matter that they'd been at this for a few days, the bottles and vials could be easily confused.

Before Gideon could answer, another voice responded.

"I will get them for you." Miriam crossed with determined stride to the tray of medicines set atop the lowboy. Her hair was a mess, with curls jutting out in all directions, and her dress was wrinkled. She must have come directly from bed.

Gideon ought to have sent her back to rest, but an extra pair of trained hands during the coming hours of danger could make all the difference. "They're on the table beside the other bed."

He could hear her moving, but neither he nor Blackburn abandoned their efforts long enough to look. Her footsteps brought her to him.

She set the jar in his hand. "Is there anything else I can—"

She stared at Dr. Blackburn, her expression one of shock, disbelief. Every ounce of color drained from her face.

Blackburn looked up at her. "Hello, Miriam."

Hello, Miriam?

She took a step backward. Her breaths came shallow and quick. She didn't say a word. Blackburn returned his attention to treating his patient.

They knew each other, that was clear. Miriam was unhappy to see Blackburn. Blackburn seemed relatively unconcerned.

She blinked a few times and turned woodenly toward Gideon. "What can—" A quick breath. "What can I do to help?" Her voice hardly rose above a strangled whisper.

"Keep cooling the Staheli children. We might be able to keep them from reaching the critical point." He unscrewed the lid of the fever powders and waved his father over. "Two glasses of water."

The room remained nearly silent as they attended to the children's fevers, cooled limbs and heads. Gideon administered the silver nitrate when the time arrived. The Patterson children didn't worsen. The Staheli children didn't either.

Reports from the other rooms were encouraging. Conditions

were holding steady, though if one thing could be counted on with scarlet fever, it was that things could change quickly.

"Blackburn, can you look after these children for a moment?"

Blackburn nodded.

Gideon rose. "Miriam, may I talk to you in the corridor?"

He hadn't expected her to hesitate. But she stayed where she was, eyes darting between Dr. Blackburn and the children. "I would rather stay with the children."

"Dr. Blackburn has agreed to look after them," Gideon reminded her.

Her chin tipped upward. Her gaze hardened. "Thus, I would rather stay with the children."

Blackburn looked at her, a patient sadness in his eyes. "Oh, Miriam. Do not try this tack again. When has it ever worked?"

"I will not be intimidated by your falsehoods."

His expression didn't change. "I have tried to help you make the best of your situation, but you keep making things worse for yourself. Heaping accusations upon me, growing paranoid, hiding behind lies."

She shook her head. "I haven't done any of those things."

Blackburn's gaze darted to Gideon. "She hasn't told you any lies?" he asked doubtfully.

Gideon couldn't honestly deny that she had.

Blackburn nodded knowingly. "I've had to endure this almost daily for two years."

Two years? They had known each other that long?

"*You* have endured?" Miriam tossed back. "No. *I* have—"

"Please," Blackburn interrupted, motioning at the children. "This is hardly the time or place for more of your accusations."

She stood rooted to the spot, watching Blackburn silently.

Gideon needed to sort this out, but he also needed to let

the children rest. "Please, Miriam. A moment in the corridor. Blackburn, keep an eye on the children."

"Of course," Blackburn said, and returned to his efforts.

Gideon stepped into the hallway, waiting. Miriam joined him after a drawn-out moment. He pulled the door closed.

Her paralysis evaporated, giving way to tight pacing. "How did he find me? How did he know?"

The question was clearly directed at herself, but he felt compelled to answer.

"He said he was only passing through on his way to see a friend's family member. He stayed to help with the epidemic."

She shook her head. "He hasn't an ounce of compassion. The illness was an excuse."

"He didn't know you were here when he heard about the fever."

"He knew," she said, facing him. "He knew I was here. I know he did."

Lashing out. Growing paranoid. Blackburn had spoken of exactly that. Yet, it didn't sound like Miriam.

"I think you had best tell me how you know Dr. Blackburn," Gideon said.

"I told you I spent two years at an asylum."

He nodded; he remembered that very well.

"It was Blackburn Asylum in Nebraska."

He motioned to the closed door beside them. "*His* asylum?"

"Yes. And it was as horrible as I told you. *More* even."

The doctor he had been working with the past few hours did not match the monster she had described. How did he reconcile that? "If it was so terrible, why did you keep working there for so long?"

Her brows drooped in misery. Her voice fell. "I didn't work there."

"I don't understand."

She rubbed at her face. Took a deep breath. "Unexplained seizures in a woman is considered a sign of madness. Too many doctors believed that, and they convinced my parents to believe it. There have been moments when they have nearly convinced me of it."

The truth of what she was saying hit him in an instant. "You were a patient."

"I was an inmate," she said through tight teeth. "We were all prisoners. I had nursing skills and knowledge, so Dr. Blackburn put me to work. I watched him torture people, Gideon. I watched him destroy his patients out of everything from frustration to curiosity."

He had watched Blackburn competently and compassionately care for the children these past hours. He couldn't reconcile such drastically different images.

"When I couldn't endure it any longer, I escaped and ran," she said. "I managed to get to St. Louis. I told the Western Women's Bureau that I was looking for employment out West, preferably in a small, isolated town. I thought it less likely he would find me in someplace quiet."

"You didn't tell me any of this." He'd actually started to believe they had built a relationship of trust between them.

"He will take me back there, Gideon," she said. "I cannot go back there. I won't."

He was utterly unprepared for all of this. The lies she had told him, it turned out, were but a drop of rain compared to the ocean of what she'd not admitted to.

She looked at him. "You said yourself that a single symptom

is not enough for a diagnosis of madness. Does anything about me these past two months, outside of my seizures, make you think I am mad?"

His mind spun over every encounter, every conversation. He had, in his study of her condition, come across information about the suspected role of madness in seizures, but he had dismissed that possibility out of hand. *One symptom is not enough for a diagnosis of madness.* Nothing about her spoke of a failing or struggling mind. Nothing.

"No," he said. "I've worried about your health, your endurance. But I haven't for a moment doubted your sanity."

She stood so still, he wasn't even certain she was breathing. "Then, please, help me. He will take me back, and I know I will never be able to leave again."

"Perhaps if I spoke with Blackburn and explained why I'm certain your diagnosis was made in error."

She shook her head. "He cannot be reasoned with."

"I've spent hours with him today. He seems entirely reasonable."

"And I've lived two years in his prison, Gideon. I have seen him ply people with poisons. I have watched him callously end lives. And I have seen him turn amiable and friendly and pleasant when donors and important people came by. He can be whatever he needs to be in any given moment, but I am telling you, he is dangerous, and he has come here for *me*."

She had lied to him before. She'd still been lying to him by omission right up until the moment she saw Dr. Blackburn in the sickroom. He couldn't entirely overlook that, yet neither could he doubt her sincerity. The fear in her eyes was unmistakable.

"Why didn't you tell me any of this?"

"I told you more than I've told anyone else," she said. "I

told you about George and his apple. I told you I ran away from home. I told you I was at an asylum in Nebraska."

"You told me *at*," he emphasized. "Not *in*."

Her gaze dropped away. "Do you have any idea what it's like to fear for your life? To be willing to run into the unknown and hide everything about yourself because it is the only chance you have of surviving?"

"You truly believe you are in that much danger?"

Her next breath shuddered. "I know I am."

The anguish in her face tugged at his heart. He wouldn't abandon her. He wouldn't turn his back on her.

"I wish you had told me about this *before* Blackburn's arrival forced you to. That is a breach of trust that I cannot overlook easily."

She nodded and sighed.

"We have to tell Hawk, Cade, and Paisley. I don't know the legalities here, but they will."

"You're going to help me?" Both hope and doubt lay in her question.

"I'm a doctor." He set his hand on the door handle. "It's what I do." He pushed the door open and stepped inside the sickroom, his mind spinning, his heart heavy, and every inch of him exhausted.

Chapter 29

The highest of the fevers broke in the early evening hours. No other children showed signs of immediate worsening. Miriam slipped from the room where the Staheli, Canton, and Patterson children were resting and moved quickly downstairs to look in on Rupert.

He smiled at her as she stepped inside. "Howdy, Miss Bricks," he said weakly.

Hearing his voice brought a wave of relief. He'd been at death's door two days earlier, but he was alive. He was recovering.

Miriam knelt on the floor beside his cot. "How are you feeling, Rupert?"

"Tired." He turned onto his side, looking at her. "I miss my ma."

"You could write her a letter," Miriam suggested. "I'd bet Tansy or Dr. MacNamara's parents would set it out on the porch the next time someone brings ice."

Rupert's brow tugged in thought. "I don't write good."

She took one of his hands in her good one. "She will love whatever you can do. You could write something. Draw something. If you aren't feeling well enough, I will happily write your message for you."

"Would you write something for *my* ma?" Frank Clark asked from the bed nearby. "My sisters can't write yet." They were sleeping in the room as well.

"Of course," Miriam said. "And Miss Dunkle would help, I'm sure."

Why hadn't she thought of this sooner? Nearly all the town's children had been quarantined for more than a week, separated from their families. What a difference a single word of greeting and love could make. During her long years at Blackburn, she had ached for any indication that someone remembered her and loved her.

"Think about what you would like to send to your parents," she said. "I will be back in just a moment."

She moved to the bedroom door just as Mr. MacNamara stepped out of an adjacent room. "May I ask a favor?"

"Of course, sweetheart." He had begun calling her that during the past week in a tone she wished she had been able to hear from her own father. In that moment, nearly broken by the weight of worry—for the children, for the town, for herself—his fatherly fondness brought a tear to her eye. For a moment, she couldn't speak.

He set his hand lightly against her back and led her away from the door. "Oh, Miriam. Don't cry. I know it's been difficult, but the ill children are on the mend. There have been no new rashes or sore throats for two days. You're nearing the end of it."

"I am nearing the end, yes." She most certainly was. Dr. Blackburn was in this town, the place she'd begun to think of as home. He wouldn't leave her here in peace.

"How is your arm?" he asked. "Gideon was worried for you

at breakfast. I hope you didn't injure it more pulling it from the sling earlier."

"I likely did," she admitted. "But it was, as they say, all hands on deck—even injured hands."

"Even fine, high-society hands." Mr. MacNamara grinned. "I nearly had a stroke seeing my wife carry dirty linens around the house."

"What I have asked of her has fallen far outside her purview," Miriam said. "I have been so grateful for her help."

Mr. MacNamara smiled. "It is little wonder Gideon treasures you so much, sweetheart."

"I don't know about that."

"Well, I do. And I am his father, so I know these things."

His teasing tone lightened her heart, something she had needed the past few days—years, really.

"What was the favor you needed to ask?" he asked.

They *had* veered from the topic. "I think the children would enjoy sending messages to their family members—little notes or drawings, things like that. Would you ask Gideon if he has any extra paper and pencils? And perhaps Miss Dunkle could help her charges craft their offerings? The notes can be left on the porch for one of the parents to collect."

"A fine idea," he said. "And, with a bit of notice, the parents could prepare something to leave for their children as well. You leave it to me, Miriam. I'll see to it." He stepped toward the head of the stairs.

"And when you see Gideon, would you tell him—" She thought better of it.

"What would you like me to tell him?"

She shook her head.

"Go ahead," he said gently.

"Tell him that I'm sorry, but I didn't know what else to do."

His gaze was kind, but confused. Clearly Gideon hadn't shared the newly revealed details of her situation. "I will give him the message."

He started down the steps. She returned to Rupert and the Clark children. They watched her arrival with hopeful gazes. She would not disappoint them.

She carefully tore a page from her book and brought it to Frank Clark.

"Thank you, Miss Bricks," he said.

She pulled one of her extra pencils from her apron pocket and gave it to him. "Write something on behalf of your sisters, as well. I'm certain your mother and father will appreciate that."

Rupert wasn't sitting up when she reached his cot, but he was alert. The sight of his shaven head broke her heart. She sat beside his cot as she'd done many times over the past days.

"I'm not good at writing," he said. "I can only write my name."

She tore another sheet from her sketchbook and set it on the cot along with a pencil. "Draw a picture," she said. "Then write your name. I promise your ma will love it."

"Can I draw a picture of you?" he asked.

Sweet boy. "You can draw whatever you want."

He adjusted his position so he was lying on his stomach, propped up on his elbows, with the sheet of paper in front of him. He popped the back of the pencil in his mouth, thinking.

"Take your time," she told him.

He nodded but didn't wait another minute before beginning his drawing.

Miriam stood and walked to the bureau. She checked the chart of medication doses. The children only required gargling

Epsom salts now. And only Rupert had needed fever powders in the last twelve hours. That was a good sign.

"Miriam." The voice sent ice through her veins. Dr. Blackburn.

She didn't turn around, but she knew he was in the doorway. She had become an expert over the past two years at hiding every emotion when he was near. Nothing motivated him more quickly than realizing he could make someone afraid or unhappy.

When she turned around, head held high, her expression remained neutral. "Dr. Blackburn. Did you need something?"

The corners of his mouth turned downward. He eyed her with annoyance. "What could I possibly want?" he asked dryly.

"I have patients to see to," she insisted.

He eyed the boys a minute before returning his increasingly impatient gaze to her. "They are occupied and in no danger. I believe they can survive without you for a few minutes."

She shook her head. "I won't abandon them."

His eyes hardened. "You would rather *alarm* them?"

She came a few steps closer, lowering her voice. "That's not what I said."

"You know perfectly well that if I wish to speak to you, I will." He reached out and snatched her arm, sling and all. "Why would you choose to distress them by subjecting them to a scene?"

"That isn't what—"

"These children have been through enough," he said. "Be considerate of them and stop objecting to something as simple as a brief, private conversation."

She knew it wouldn't be anything nearly that simple and that he wouldn't hesitate to distress the children if it served his ends.

"In the corridor," she said.

He yanked her arm. Pain shot through her shoulder, but she refused to give him the slightest reaction.

He released her arm once they were out of the room. She stepped away from him, keeping enough distance to stay out of reach. He laughed, shaking his head as if her desire for safety was ludicrous.

"I told MacNamara to watch for signs of your paranoia. I didn't realize it had reached these levels."

She shook her head. "I am more than justified—"

"Being away from the asylum has clearly exacerbated your condition." He eyed her more closely, sending shivers of apprehension over her. "You have probably had more of your fits."

"They are not 'fits,'" she said in a low, tight voice.

"You know irritability is one of your symptoms." He was disturbingly good at sounding empathetic when he was anything but. "Once this epidemic has passed—which will be soon—I will see to it that you are returned where you are meant to be. Everything will be as it should. Everything."

The last word rang with a promise that Miriam couldn't let herself contemplate.

"A few more days," he said, moving to the staircase. "I doubt there will be any objections to your departure."

"I am not alone this time," she said. "There are people on my side now."

He looked up from the step he stood on. His smile clutched at her throat. "I am not alone either, Miriam."

Chapter 30

The children had eagerly taken to the task of writing notes for their parents. Miriam stepped out onto the porch with an entire stack. She set it on the swing and placed a large rock atop it in case the Wyoming wind decided to cause trouble.

She waved to the families, standing across the road. "Likely only a couple more days," she called out to them.

They cheered in response. It warmed her heart to see such love amongst these families. She missed that about her own family. So much had changed when her health had changed. Embarrassment replaced tenderness. Eventually all she felt from them was resentment and disappointment.

She returned to the house, closing the door behind it. Long, slow breaths didn't restore her energy. Too much weighed her down. She tried to will herself to keep moving, to face the re-mainder of her day, to endure another moment in the same house as Dr. Blackburn.

"I am so tired," she whispered, leaning against the front door.

Once Gideon was awake, in another hour or so, she would

have her turn to rest. She knew she wouldn't sleep, but at least she'd be alone for a brief, fleeting time.

If only I can stay on my feet until then. Exhaustion didn't merely make things more difficult, it frightened her. She couldn't be certain there was a connection, but she often had seizures when she was overly tired. The possibility that one might lead to the other was enough to give her tremendous pause.

Gideon came down the stairs in that moment.

"You are supposed to sleep for another hour, Gideon."

"I'm more than ready to be up. What do you need?" he asked.

What did she really need from him? The answers rushed quickly over her. She needed more than his confidence in her as a nurse, more than his lukewarm support in the face of Dr. Blackburn's arrival, certainly more than his friendship. She needed the devotion his words and gestures seemed to have been hinting at before her past had been laid bare.

She needed his heart in a way he had never fully offered.

None of those words would ever be permitted to pass her lips, not when everything was still so uncertain. The thought of opening herself up to more pain and misery was unendurable. And yet, she was falling apart.

"I need a hug." She knew it was a dangerous request, but "need" was the right word. Despite her confident words to Dr. Blackburn, she'd felt so alone in the twenty-four hours since she'd confessed to Gideon all that had happened before her arrival in Savage Wells. She needed a moment of his affectionate touch.

He crossed directly to her. "I am quite good at hugs, dear."

Dear. "Does this mean you're not angry with me anymore?"

"I was never angry." He set his hand gently on her unslung arm. "Surprised. A little frustrated. Mostly worried." His other arm slipped around her waist, and he pulled her gently into his embrace.

She laid her head against his shoulder and pressed her open palm to his chest. "Much better," she whispered.

His shoulders moved with his rumbling laugh. "This was easy enough. What else can I do for you?"

Oh, how she needed him. She couldn't remember the last time she'd felt so warm and protected. For that one moment, safe in his arms, she could forget about everything else waiting for her in the outside world.

"Will you play your cello again? Your 'Gentle Annie' is the most peaceful sound on earth."

Was it selfish of her to wish they could stay precisely as they were and not go back to work?

"Once you've rested and the house is empty again, I will play it for you," he said.

How tempting it was to lean all of her weight against him and allow herself to drift away.

The door opened behind them, and Paisley peeked inside.

"Enough sparkin', you two. Mr. Larsen needs to talk to Miriam."

"Who is Mr. Larsen?" Miriam asked.

"Attorney. Hermit. Man of mystery." Gideon made no move to release her. "Do you know what he needs to discuss?"

"I'd wager something to do with Blackburn," Paisley answered. "He talked to the doctor for nearly an hour."

This was the moment of truth, then. Mr. Larsen, an attorney, meant to tell her what her legal options were, assuming there were any. Miriam knew she had to face the reality of it, but she couldn't force herself to step away from Gideon's embrace.

"What if he has bad news?" she quietly asked.

"Even terrible news is worse when heard too late." His hand rubbed her back. Up and down. An unwavering, steady rhythm. He bent close enough to speak softly and still be heard. "You are strong enough for this."

After one last, fleeting moment to relish Gideon's attentions, she stepped back, head held high, and pretended that she was equal to the task before her. "We had best go talk with Mr. Larsen."

Gideon and Paisley walked with her out the door and across the side yard to the jailhouse. Mr. Larsen meant to meet with her there, it seemed.

Gideon held her hand as they stepped into the jailhouse. Mr. Oliver and Eben, the local blacksmith, were playing a game of cards. They were the only two adults who had contracted the fever, and both were nearly restored to full health. Another few days of rest and they could return to their homes and jobs.

"Mr. Larsen is in the back room," Paisley said.

The room was small, not much larger than the recovery room at Gideon's house. A man Miriam didn't recognize sat at the narrow table in the corner. Hawk leaned against the wall. Cade sat on a cot against the opposite wall.

Gideon led Miriam to the table, where she took the only other chair in the room. Paisley sat beside Cade. Gideon closed the door and leaned against it. They would have been hard-pressed to fit another person in the tiny space.

The man at the table had the bearing of an attorney: confident, no-nonsense, with eyes that studied and evaluated, and an aura of logic rather than emotion. He was younger than she expected, perhaps only a few years older than Gideon.

"You are Miss Bricks?" he asked.

"I am."

"I am Thomas Larsen. Sheriff O'Brien asked me to evaluate your situation."

Miriam nodded, feeling the tension building in her neck.

"Dr. Blackburn has all of the required paperwork proving that you are a patient in his asylum. Insisting on verification of authenticity might delay a decision; however, I do believe the law is on his side in this matter."

With a heavy heart, she admitted, "I know."

"What if another doctor disputed his claim that she is mad?" Hawk asked.

Mr. Larsen motioned toward Gideon. "Dr. MacNamara, you mean?" He shook his head. "He is not neutral in this matter. His viewpoint would be dismissed as biased."

"To my knowledge," Miriam said, "only the doctor who ordered the person committed can authorize the patient's release. Dr. Blackburn would never agree to that."

Mr. Larsen folded his hands in front of him. "Dr. Blackburn only signed your commitment papers as the receiving physician. He was not the one who ordered you to be institutionalized."

Miriam nodded. "Dr. Parnell handed me over. Do we need to contact him?"

Mr. Larsen shook his head once more. "According to the paperwork provided by Dr. Blackburn, you were officially committed by Carlton Bricks."

Goodness gracious. "He is my father. But he lives in New York, nowhere near Blackburn Asylum."

Mr. Larsen tapped his fingers on the tabletop. "The authorization likely came by way of telegram with the signed papers following in the mail. From what Dr. Blackburn told me, you were given the same diagnosis and ordered committed while in your family's care many years earlier."

"That is true." Her family had meant to deliver her to the New York State Lunatic Asylum, which had necessitated her initial flight. "Dr. Blackburn must have sent word to them, though Dr. Parnell's orders should have been enough."

"I do not know his reasons for going to the extra trouble," Mr. Larsen said, "but he strikes me as a methodical person, one who would not act without reason. That, of course, begs the question of why bringing you back to his institution was important enough to come all this way."

"Or," she added, "how he found me here to begin with."

"I do know the answer to that. He received a telegram from Dr. Parnell, who received a telegram from Dr. MacNamara."

She looked at Gideon, but he was clearly confused by the assertion.

"I don't know a Dr. Parnell," Gideon insisted. "I certainly didn't send him a telegram."

"Actually, Doc, you did." Hawk spoke with an odd mixture of confidence and hesitancy. "You had me send them on your behalf when you were trying to sort out the mess with the marriage bureau."

What did the Western Women's Bureau have to do with this? She hadn't told the bureau about her time at Blackburn. "Why would our troubles with the bureau have anything to do with my medical history?"

Gideon cleared his throat. Miriam didn't like the guilt that crept into his expression. "I was—I could tell you weren't being forthright about something, about a number of things, and I wanted to find the answers."

How clever she thought she'd been, tucking herself into an isolated corner of the world. If only the Western Women's Bureau had been honest with her and Gideon. Had she come to claim the job she thought she'd been offered rather than a marriage, no one's suspicions would have been raised. Gideon would not have begun questioning her background.

"Who else did you contact?" she asked, but the answer came to her in the next instant. "The other doctors I worked for." Weight settled on her, pulling down on her body and mind and heart.

"Miriam, I didn't mean for—"

She turned her gaze back to the tabletop. "I am never going to be able to work again, am I? My past will always catch up with me." She leaned her elbow on the table and dropped her head into her upturned hand. To Mr. Larsen, she asked, "What options do I have?"

"Not many, I'm afraid. As a woman committed by a male relation, only he can authorize your release. Unless you have a closer male relative than the one who signed the papers."

"What relative could possibly be closer than a father?"

Mr. Larsen steepled his fingers. "A husband, but it is my understanding that you are not married."

"I am not."

"What if she were to marry?" Paisley asked. "Could her husband then authorize her release?"

"A person who has been declared insane cannot marry," Mr. Larsen said. "In the eyes of the law, he or she is not considered capable of making that decision."

Of course not. "So not only will I likely never be able to work again, but I can never marry, never have a family. I cannot stay here. I cannot go home." She rubbed her hand over her face. "But I know what awaits me at Blackburn Asylum, and I will not go back there."

Gideon approached and set his hand on her shoulder. "We'll think of something."

His touch didn't bring much comfort. She kept her focus on Mr. Larsen. "How long do I have before I can no longer refuse to go with Dr. Blackburn?"

"According to the law, you are not permitted to refuse now," he said. "And though Marshal Hawking has been unwilling to take you into custody, he is not legally permitted to refuse either."

"I don't have an extradition order," Hawk said.

"One is not required. As a US Marshal, you have jurisdiction across all territories."

Tears stung the back of Miriam's eyes as the hopelessness of the situation settled over her. Dr. Blackburn could take her back at any moment.

"What if we won't hand her over?" Hawk asked. "Cade and Paisley and I are all agreed that the law is wrong about this one."

"You'd likely all lose your jobs. You could be brought up on charges of obstruction of justice as well as harboring and abetting a fugitive."

Miriam wasn't going to allow that to happen to these people who had stood as her friends. There had to be an answer. "Only my father can authorize my release?"

Mr. Larsen nodded.

"Could he be convinced?" Gideon asked. "My family knows a great many influential people in New York. We could put some pressure on him."

"He might." Then she shook her head. "The possibility is slim, though."

"Still, it is a possibility." Gideon sounded hopeful.

"He is in New York, and Blackburn's asylum is in Nebraska. The doctor's influence over him is likely to be minimal," Mr.

Larsen said. "Working to convince Mr. Bricks to allow Miss Bricks to be released is your best chance for success. In the meantime, I will study this area of the law more closely and see if I can learn more."

"Thank you, Mr. Larsen, for your assistance in this matter," Miriam said. "Please let me know if you find anything that might be helpful."

"I will." He hadn't looked her in the eye once since her arrival, and though he spoke with authority and eloquence, he seemed remarkably uncomfortable with conversation.

"I am sorry we haven't met before," she said. "I feel rather like I am taking advantage of a stranger."

She actually heard his thick swallow. "That is my fault. I don't come into town often."

"Well, next time you do—if I have not been taken to Nebraska—please come say hello, even if you don't have any good news for me."

His ears turned red, but his expression didn't change. He stood and offered a nod to the room in general before leaving with calm but swift strides.

Finding no better way to make her own exit, Miriam borrowed a page from Mr. Larsen's book: a quick, general nod and an even quicker departure.

Gideon stopped her at the door with a hand on her arm. "Miriam, I—"

This time she pulled free. She wasn't ready to talk. Every fear she'd had—that the law would force her back, that anyone who tried to help her would be punished, that her fate rested in the hands of her distant and uncaring father—had been confirmed in a matter of minutes.

She couldn't bear to think about the future she faced, let

alone speak of it. Without a word, she rushed from the jailhouse and across the side yard. Though the pull of her quiet room at the hotel was strong, the children of Savage Wells still needed her, and they were at Gideon's house. She wouldn't abandon them, no matter her current worries.

One room would be vacant and peaceful.

She pulled open the door to the tiny under-stairs recovery room and plunged into the darkness. She rested her head against the closed door and tried to breathe.

Chapter 31

Gideon stepped inside his house and came face-to-face with his father.

"I assume the attorney didn't have good news?" Father said.

"How did you know about the meeting?"

Father smiled briefly. "Paisley told me. I mean to send a telegram to Ian and see what he thinks. Perhaps he's aware of some legal precedent your local attorney is not."

"Perhaps." But Gideon didn't imagine that was the case. Mr. Larsen lived in the middle of nowhere, but he was as dedicated to his profession as Gideon was to his own.

"Miriam has taken possession of your recovery room below the stairs. She wouldn't allow Hawk in, or Paisley. Even I received nothing more than a request that she be left in peace." Father glanced toward the closed door.

"I doubt I'll have any more luck than you did," Gideon said. "She doesn't trust easily, and all her defenses are up right now. I don't know how to bridge that gap."

"When your mother is angry with me, flowers and a tin of

Booth's butterscotches are the only thing that saves me from her black books."

Gideon had so desperately wanted to avoid the anxiety he'd seen his own father carry around all his life, but there he was in the same situation: trying to prove himself to a woman he cared for deeply. There was, however, a key difference. Mother often grew upset with her husband over petty, unimportant things, and Miriam had turned away from Gideon for a real, legitimate reason.

"What does Miriam like in particular?" Father asked. "Perhaps you could approach her with a token of your affection."

"I can't recall her ever longing for anything in particular."

Except that wasn't exactly true. She had wanted to hear him play his cello. He'd meant to oblige her once the house was empty again. He had lived in Savage Wells for nearly four years and hadn't once played it within anyone's hearing. He'd told her his reasons were to prevent the townspeople from thinking him too odd or refined to be considered one of them. But it was more than that. Music was a personal experience, a deeply vulnerable part of himself. Opening that up to possible ridicule unnerved him.

What else has she ever asked of me?

She had called his playing "heavenly." The very antithesis of what she must be feeling. She needed it. His discomfort, his privacy all paled in comparison to that simple truth: she needed the music.

He started up the stairs.

"Where are you headed, son?" Father asked from the entryway.

"To fetch flowers and butterscotches."

"You keep those in your bedroom?"

"The equivalent." A moment later, he stood in the corner

of his room, staring at his cello case. The house was filled with the town's children, as well as Miss Dunkle, Paisley, Hawk, Tansy. Word of this would spread far and wide.

As the doctor, his life was open to everyone. His patients came by at all hours. They interrupted meals, pulled him from Sunday services, interrupted every social event he attended. Nothing in his life was his and his alone, other than this. Playing with so many people in the house meant losing the last shred of himself that he'd managed to keep private.

But Miriam was suffering, and she'd told him exactly what she needed. "The most peaceful sound on earth."

She deserves a measure of peace.

He grabbed the handle of his cello case and quickly returned downstairs. If he didn't give himself time to think, he wouldn't change his mind.

Father hadn't left the entryway. "I thought you said you don't play when other people are around."

"I don't. But Miriam finds comfort in it."

"Ah." Father nodded. "Your 'flowers and butterscotches.'"

Gideon propped the case up against the wall beside the recovery room door. He pulled a chair from the dining room and set it in place. He hesitated. "Do your offerings ever do what you hope they will?"

"Yes." Father's tone was empathetic. "At least, temporarily."

Gideon carefully lifted out the cello. He sat in the chair and rested the instrument against his legs and shoulder. He pulled his bow from the case and tightened its hairs. One deep breath proved insufficient, so he took another.

He pulled the bow across the strings. A few curious heads peered around the parlor doorframe. He paused to quickly tune the instrument, then drew the bow across the strings again. Tansy and Paisley both stepped out of the kitchen. Some children stepped into the entryway.

Please let this be worth it. He slowly, carefully, played "Gentle Annie," the song Miriam had specifically requested. Though he played it to offer her peace and reassurance, he found it worked its magic on him as well. He could almost forget his growing audience, his concerns over his parents, the uncertainty of Miriam's situation. The music soothed him.

He had finished his second Stephen Foster tune when the recovery room door inched open—not enough to see Miriam on the other side, but enough to know she was listening.

Quick as that, his enthusiasm grew.

A small hand tugged on the leg of his pants. Ginny Cooper looked up at him with wide, hopeful eyes. "Can you play 'Dan Tucker' on your giant fiddle?"

Giant fiddle. Wouldn't Mother be horrified by that? She had approved of the cello because it was dignified. How quickly this six-year-old girl had found something familiar and safe in something so new and unknown.

"I'm afraid I don't play that tune well, Ginny."

Her gap-toothed smile only grew. "It don't have to be pretty. We just want to dance."

Eagerness spread over all the children's faces. They had been stuck indoors too long, unable to run and jump and release their pent-up energy.

He bumbled his way through the requested tune and a great many others suitable for spinning and hopping and whatever dance steps the children chose to concoct. Father even joined in the revelry, spinning children up in the air to great squeals and pleadings for another turn.

The entryway and the doorways of the dining room and

kitchen were filled with children's laughter and enthusiastic sing-
ing along as more adults joined in.

He'd tucked this instrument away for years, thinking it a li-
ability, but it was quickly proving one of the most useful tools
at his disposal. In a mere thirty minutes, his houseful of dreary,
frustrated patients had transformed into smiling, laughing children again.

But had it helped Miriam? She hadn't emerged from the
room, but neither had she closed the door again. He wanted to
ask her how she was holding up, but it was not something he dare
do with so many little ears listening in.

He let his cello rest against his shoulder and his arms hang
down at his sides. "You have worn me out, children."

A general moan of disappointment rippled through the room.

"Perhaps if you are good and do what Miss Dunkle asks, I'll
play some quieter tunes for you before bed tonight."

Miss Dunkle called their attention to her. "You heard Dr.
MacNamara. Everyone back into the room you've been assigned,
whether that is the parlor or the dining room."

The children dragged their feet back to their rooms.

Ginny stepped up to him, smiling brightly. She clasped her
hands together and spun in a circle. "I love your giant fiddle,
Doc."

"I've always been fond of it myself."

"Will you really play it for us again?"

"I promise."

She skipped back to the parlor, energy and happiness in her
every step.

"I love your giant fiddle as well." Miriam's quiet voice tiptoed across the short distance between her door and his chair. "I
thought you didn't play for the town."

SARAH M. EDEN

"I don't." He set the cello carefully in its case.

"Then why the concert?"

He loosened the hairs of his bow. "I was playing for you. They happened to overhear."

"But you didn't want anyone to know about your cello. You swore me to secrecy."

"You needed the music today, Miriam." He set the bow in the case. "There was no other means of giving it to you."

The door opened further, enough for him to see her silhouette. He still couldn't see her face, couldn't gauge her feelings.

He latched the cello case, then turned to face her.

She took a small step past the door. "Everyone will know about your music now."

"I know." He moved closer to her. The thread between them felt so fragile, he feared it would snap and she would slip away again. "I had no idea my telegram to Dr. Parnell would cause all of this. I swear I didn't."

Her gaze dropped, as did her voice. "I know."

They stood near enough for him to reach out and brush his fingers along her cheek. The moisture he found there made his heart ache. "I don't know that I can make any of this right again."

"I don't think it can be made right."

He let his hand drop to hers. "I can play again if you would like."

She shook her head.

"Are you hungry? I'll get something for you to eat. Or tired? I'll make certain you're left in peace so you can rest."

Again, she shook her head.

"What can I do? Please, Miriam. I cannot bear to see you so unhappy without doing something to help you."

She leaned against the doorframe. "Everything rests on

240

convincing my father to care what happens to me, something I've never managed."

"We'll all help." He rested his shoulder against the wall next to her. "You aren't alone in this."

"Dr. Blackburn said he isn't either. I haven't sorted that bit out." She sighed and closed her eyes. "It worries me, though."

Gideon slid his arm around her waist. She leaned into the one-armed embrace.

"He has this way of making me wonder if . . . I know I'm not mad. I know I'm not. But, somehow, he makes me question myself."

"I have medical training too, Miriam, and I know he's wrong. The man I worked for at St. Elizabeth's, whose specialty lay in this area, would have denounced his diagnosis as well. Every other doctor who worked with him would too. We all would. I will remind you of that any time you find yourself doubting."

"Do you promise?"

He kissed her forehead just above the eyebrow, then on the bridge of her nose. She turned into his embrace and pressed her open hand directly over his heart. She'd done it before, and it never failed to send his pulse racing. He placed his other hand over hers, keeping the connection between them.

Their lips hovered not even a breath apart. It was a torturous, wonderful sort of agony. An uncertain promise. A fragile hope.

Then she—*she*—closed the minuscule distance. *She* kissed *him*.

He wrapped his arms fully around her, reveling in her warmth and the feel of her in his embrace. He returned her kiss with fervor, and she melted against him. He rained kisses along her cheek and her jaw, before returning once more to her lips.

But something changed in the next instant. She stiffened. She backed the tiniest bit away.

"Miriam?"

She shook her head and slipped further back. "This will only make things more difficult if my father doesn't side with us—with *me*." Tears filled her eyes.

He wished he could promise her everything would be well in the end, but there was only one reassurance he could fully offer. "I won't give up, Miriam."

He raised her hand to his lips and gently kissed her fingers.

Outside the recovery room, the front door opened. Gideon knew the squeak of those hinges. "Who wants notes from their families?" Father's voice called out.

Chaos erupted. Dozens of little voices cheered and shouted.

Miriam's eyes turned away, and a gentle smile tugged at her lips.

"That was a bit of genius, you know," he said to her.

"I hoped it would lift their spirits. They've been tucked in here for so long."

"Most of them can probably leave tomorrow," he said. "These notes will help see them through the night."

"I hope there's one for Rupert."

"I'm certain the Fletchers would not have passed up the opportunity."

Father appeared in the doorway. He grinned at Miriam. "You have one as well, sweetheart."

"Really?" Her suddenly excited gaze jumped from Father to him and back. "Who would be sending me a note?"

"It appears that you have, during this epidemic, won the hearts of this entire town," Gideon said. "I have no doubt any number of families would happily send you all the notes you could possibly read."

Father handed her the note. "Miriam" was written across the front of the folded piece of paper.

"It really is for me." She bit back a smile, but her eyes danced.

"Read it," Gideon said with a laugh.

Father met his eye. A quick nod of understanding passed between them. He stepped out to distribute the rest of the notes.

Gideon returned his attention to Miriam. Rather than the joy he expected, she was pale and shaking. Her eyes registered shock. Fear.

"Miriam?"

The paper trembled in her hand. "It's from my father."

"Your father?" How was that even possible?

"He is here." She took a quavering breath. "He came with Dr. Blackburn."

Blackburn's unidentified companion.

"We're too late," she whispered. "We're too late."

Chapter 32

Gideon hadn't ever sat on a war council, but seeing the grim faces at his dining room table, he felt he could imagine what one might have looked like. Those children who had not grown ill, or had experienced only minor symptoms, had been released to rejoin their families that morning. The house was quieter than it had been in a very long time. Miriam was as well.

"'Dr. Blackburn and I are very concerned,'" Paisley read Mr. Bricks's note aloud. She stood near the door, Cade beside her with his arms tucked affectionately around her. "'Someone with your condition should not be away from the help you require. You should not be imposing upon these good people. It is time you returned with him where you belong. His patience is holding, but mine is growing thin.' It is signed 'Carlton Bricks.'"

"Not 'Father' or 'Papa' or something like that?" Gideon asked.

"I suspect he doesn't like the reminder that he is related to me," Miriam said quietly. Hers was not a tone of defeat, but one of absolute weariness.

Father set his hand on hers. "You are a joy, sweetheart. Do not let him convince you otherwise."

"It is not *my* convictions that matter at the moment," she said. "Everything depends upon him."

"Unless Ian had some miraculous information," Gideon said, turning to his father.

"He agrees that her legal options are limited." Father quickly perused the telegram that had arrived that morning from Gideon's oldest brother. "He suggests Gideon gather testimony to contradict Blackburn's diagnosis. But he warns that casting doubt about her madness may not be enough to prevent her from being confined to the asylum."

Mother looked horrified. "She can be kept there even if multiple doctors believe she is not mad?"

Father nodded. "Ian says that a man can commit any of his female relatives for nearly any reason. If Miriam's father believes she belongs in an asylum, he can send her there. And only he can authorize her release."

Mr. Larsen had said the same thing. Gideon didn't like hearing it confirmed. He couldn't sit still any longer. Pacing seemed his only viable option.

"How do we best press the man?" Cade was always one for cutting to the heart of a matter.

Everyone looked at Miriam. "Few things are as crucial to my father as his sense of importance, and how he is perceived. He has worked very hard to improve his standing among people of status. He wants nothing more than to be admired and revered in the way he admires and reveres those he views as his superiors."

Mother casually entered the conversation. "I believe your eldest brother's upcoming run for a seat in the state legislature is also of particular concern to him. And your younger sister is on the verge of a very advantageous match."

"I didn't know about either of those," Miriam said. "I haven't spoken to my family in years."

"Your older sister's husband is in line for a promotion at the bank where he works," Mother added. "Your mother is angling to be made a matron of the women's opera society."

"She has always wanted to be," Miriam said.

"My friend, Julia Cockling, suspects she will achieve it soon, provided nothing untoward occurs."

Gideon, who'd been rendered mute by shock, found his voice at last. "How in the world do you know all of that?"

Mother gave him an exasperated look. "I arrived here to find that my son had attempted to marry a stranger, one who had refused him but still managed to get a position working for him, and who was clearly from a background of some affluence in, as she told me herself, New York City. There were a great many gaps in what I knew. I sent some telegrams."

"Telegrams?" Cade repeated dryly. "So Gid gets that talent from his mother."

"Hush, Cade," Paisley said, though she smiled unrepentantly.

Gideon rubbed the back of his neck. "A family with aspirations in politics and society would be very keen to avoid anything they might find . . . embarrassing." How he hated using the word, but could think of no other way to accurately describe how the Brickses seemed to view their daughter.

"Precisely," she said.

Father squeezed her fingers before speaking. "We could press the point that, this far West, you would have no impact on their social aspirations whatsoever. I can't imagine you have any plans to rejoin them in New York."

"None, whatsoever," she said firmly. "They showed me years

ago that I don't have a place among them. I won't go begging for one."

Gideon nodded as he paced back to the table. "If we all go to the restaurant tonight and, over dinner, confront him about—"

"Won't fadge," Cade said. "A man who'd lock up his daughter so she won't make him look bad—his view of things, not mine, Miriam—will only feel more justified in that choice if a group comes down on him all at once because of her."

"And I would guess threats would make him defensive, as well," Paisley tossed in.

Miriam nodded, her shoulders drooping. Gideon hadn't always been on the best terms with his parents, and he had known the misery of feeling like a disappointment in his mother's eyes. This, however, was an agony he could only begin to understand.

The conversation wasn't proving reassuring. "If threats and logical arguments won't sway him, what else do we have?"

"You have me," Mother said. Her chin tipped at a confident angle. "I know I've been rather useless since my arrival here. I will admit I am out of my element. But, swaying people who place more importance on how they are perceived in the eyes of those with influence and standing than on almost anything else . . . Well, that is something for which I have a decided knack."

Father met Gideon's eye. "She's not wrong."

Mother clasped her hands on the tabletop in front of her. She looked to Miriam, then Gideon. "The four of us will have our supper at the restaurant tonight, where Mr. Cooper tells me Mr. Bricks can be found every evening. Dress sharply, Gideon. It is crucial that he understand our own family's position." Her attention returned to Miriam. "Have you a dress other than the gray ones you've worn these past couple of weeks?"

Miriam shook her head.

Mother made a sound of pondering. "I do believe it is important that you look the part of a society miss, no matter that he has placed you in the position you are in. He must be able to imagine you as part of the world he aspires to."

Paisley jumped in. "You can borrow the blue one of mine that you wore to the social. You looked beautiful."

Mother met Gideon's eye. He nodded emphatically.

"Perfect," Mother said. "We will all assume our best manners, dress to the nines, and put on airs so thick and unmistakable that he will think he has somehow returned to the bosom of Eastern society without realizing it. Then we will make absolutely certain he knows that we firmly consider Miriam as worthy of that society but aren't entirely sure about him yet."

"The idea is a little distasteful," Gideon said.

"I know." Mother appeared empathetic, yet she did not back down. "But these are the things that are important to him. We must play his game, Gideon, but we will play it better."

"What do *we* do?" Cade never had been one to endure veering topics.

Mother had a ready answer. "You keep an eye on Dr. Blackburn. He is a little too . . . disarming. I do not trust anyone who can so easily be whatever is best in a given situation."

"I've worried that he'll simply snatch Miriam away when no one is looking," Paisley said. "We'll track every move he makes in this town."

"It is a shame Marshal Hawking was called away," Mother said. "I suspect he has some influence with the judge in Laramie whom Dr. Blackburn contacted."

"I'll wire Hawk over in Garriotville," Paisley said. "If he'll send word to Judge Irwin, that might buy us a little time."

"Let us hope so," Miriam said on a sigh.

Mother met Gideon's eye again. "Do you still have the tapestry waistcoat I sent you for your last birthday? Pairing that with your black cutaway sack coat and the pinstriped trousers you wore on Sunday would give exactly the impression we need."

"Wealth and influence?"

Mother smiled. "You have to convince him to put more store in your word than in Dr. Blackburn's. Your appearance is crucial in that."

"Have faith, son," Father said. "None of us are abandoning this fight."

Gideon smoothed the pointed edges of his narrow, silk bow tie. When Mother had sent it a few months earlier, he'd assumed he'd never wear it. The look might be the height of fashion in the East, but appearances were kept simpler in the West.

He made a quick check for lint or stray threads. Everything was impeccably turned out. Before coming to Savage Wells, Gideon would have been quite pleased. Now he mostly felt absurd.

Miriam had grown up in much the same circles he had; she might actually appreciate the touch of elegance. She might be impressed. Or, she might find him as ridiculous as he felt.

Mother and Father stood in the entryway when Gideon arrived. A flood of memories washed over him at the sight of them dressed in their finery. He'd attended more balls and soirees and society gatherings with them than he could count.

"Oh, Gideon." Mother clasped her hands. "Don't you look a sight."

"I feel a fool," he admitted. "This"—he motioned to his appearance—"isn't who I am anymore."

"What you wear has never been 'who you are,' son." She patted his cheek, something she hadn't done since he was young.

Father set a hand on his shoulder. "You aren't the only one feeling overwhelmed." He motioned with his head toward the door of the recovery room.

"Miriam?"

Father and Mother nodded in unison. They weren't often united in anything. Seeing them this past week working together without their usual disagreements or tension had been shocking, to say the least.

"Go to her," Father suggested. "This will be a harrowing evening for her."

Gideon had seen for himself how nervous she was at the prospect of confronting her father. But there was nothing else to be done. The only way to guarantee that she would be free was to convince Mr. Bricks to release her.

Gideon gave a light rap on the door of the recovery room. "Miriam?"

A quiet "Come in" answered.

He stepped inside. She sat on the edge of the bed, her head lowered. Her shoulders rose and fell with each breath. It was steady, which was reassuring.

He leaned against the doorframe. "Mr. Cooper tells Mother he will have chocolate cake tonight," Gideon said. "I, for one, am looking forward to that."

"Do you like chocolate—" Her question trailed off when she looked up at him. "You've never worn that before."

"I look ridiculous."

She shook her head. "You look very handsome."

He twitched an eyebrow upward. "Are you saying I haven't ever looked handsome before?"

One corner of her mouth tipped the tiniest bit. "That is not at all what I'm saying." Another fortifying breath filled her frame. "I'm not certain my father will think any better of me in this borrowed dress. It isn't the height of fashion like your mother's gowns. The fit is just wrong enough that he will know it isn't mine."

He hated seeing her struggle. She'd been strong through so many things, too many things.

He crossed to sit beside her on the edge of the bed. "My mother once told me that confidence is the currency of high society. No matter what you profess to be, what you are *perceived* to be depends entirely on how well you wear your claim."

She rested her head on his shoulder. "He knows who I am and where I've been these past years. Your family can pretend I'm part of your world, but my father will know it is a lie."

He slipped his hand around hers. "My darling Miriam, we will not be pretending. My parents have voluntarily joined forces in this effort, something I have only seen them do once before."

"When was the last time?" She set her free hand on his arm, leaning more fully against him.

"When I decided to attend medical school. My mother was not happy about it at first, but when she realized I meant to pursue it regardless, she began coming around. By the time I was making formal arrangements to leave, she was on my side. She and Father pulled every string at their disposal, called on every favor owed them, and before I knew it, I had comfortable accommodations and a position working as a political secretary to a very influential man so I could support myself. That they are doing so much now for you, and doing it together, willingly, tells me everything I need to know about whether or not they consider you 'part of their world.' They care about you, Miriam."

"Do you?" The question was so tentative, so uncertain. The arrival of two men who questioned her value had left her doubting her worth.

"I love you, Miriam Bricks," he said without hesitation. "So much so, in fact, that I find myself torn between raining misery upon the Western Women's Bureau for the trick they played on us and sending them my profound gratitude."

"Go with 'misery,' Gideon. It will be far more fun."

Hearing her jest, however briefly and quietly, eased some of his worry.

"Are you ready to slay this dragon, Miriam?"

"I'd feel more ready if I truly looked the part. I have only a secondhand dress."

"That is not entirely true." He had almost forgotten. "I've brought you something."

She sat up enough to look into his eyes. "You have?"

"Now, don't get your hopes too high. It isn't anything truly fine or fancy." He reached into his pocket. "I meant to give this to you before the social a few weeks ago, but I didn't have the chance." He pulled out the length of blue ribbon. "I heard you tell Hawk you wished you had a ribbon for your hair."

Miriam accepted it with all the care one generally reserved for fine jewelry and gemstones. "I've dreamed about hair ribbons." She ran a finger down the length of it. "We were permitted so little at the asylum. I had to hide my sketchbook or Dr. Blackburn would have taken it. I found myself longing for the oddest things.

A dress that wasn't gray—I didn't even care what color. Candy, which is even sillier than a hair ribbon."

"You were longing for simple joys, Miriam, and clinging to hope. That is a show of strength."

She squared her shoulders. "Dr. Blackburn did not manage to crush me after two years of trying. I can certainly survive a single dinner with my father."

"I know you can."

"Will you tie this in my hair?" She indicated the ribbon.

"I can't promise to do so with any degree of expertise."

She smiled at him. Heavens, that smile melted his heart every time. "I'm certain your mother will fix it if you do too terribly."

He laughed. "I am certain you are correct."

She set the ribbon in his hand, then turned her back to him. "A bow around the knot of hair, please."

The undertaking was more complicated than he'd antici-pated, but not because of the ribbon or his ability to tie a decent bow. There was something intimate in touching her hair the way he had to in order to secure the ribbon. Loose curls flowed from the knot of hair, hanging in auburn tendrils. Her hair was soft beneath his fingers and smelled of flowers.

"Have I ever told you that you have beautiful hair?" His hands shook as he worked at the bow.

"*No one* has ever told me that."

He dropped his hands away. The bow was lopsided, but he didn't know that he could keep fussing with it. This closeness had his pulse pounding and his thoughts spinning in too many direc-tions.

"We had best be on our way." He stood and breathed.

She looked up at him with nervous anticipation.

He offered her his arm. He'd employed that gesture often

enough during his society years for it to feel normal. She slipped her arm through his, and he walked with her toward the front door.

Mother gave them both a quick perusal, then a crisp nod. "Screw your courage to the sticking place. It is time to beard the lion."

Chapter 33

Miriam had been beaten down by her father's indifference before. Facing it again dredged up so many worries and opened anew far too many wounds. But walking into the restaurant on Gideon's arm in the wake of his parents in their finery and unmistakably regal bearing, she could almost believe that this plan could work. If confidence was indeed the currency of high society, Mr. and Mrs. MacNamara were the wealthiest people Miriam had ever known.

Only a few people were in the restaurant when they stepped inside. Mr. Cooper, the mayor and his wife, the man who ran the bank—Miriam didn't know his name—and the person they'd come to see. Her father was facing away from the door, but she knew him without seeing his face.

Her mind screamed for her to run, to leave him and the danger he posed far behind. Her heart cried out for him to love her as he'd once done, to be her father again, to care about what happened to her.

Mr. Cooper approached. He bowed deeply, something Miriam hadn't seen anyone do in Savage Wells in the months since her arrival. "Welcome to our establishment." His adopted accent had never made sense to Miriam. It was clearly intended to be British, but it just as clearly wasn't real. No one in town ever commented on it, though.

"A table for four, my good man." Mr. MacNamara spoke with that hint of impatience all men of wealth and standing seemed to use. If she hadn't come to know him so well in the weeks he'd been in town, she would have been intimidated.

Mr. Cooper led them through the small collection of tables to one directly in the middle of the room. He eyed his other customers with a barely concealed look of triumph.

"Have you nothing by a window?" Mrs. MacNamara asked. "I would so enjoy a window." It was a demand to be reseated, but not phrased as such.

"Of course. Of course." Mr. Cooper jumped to accommodate them.

Oh, yes. Gideon's mother was quite good at this game.

They were seated and told the offerings for the evening. Their orders were placed, and Mr. Cooper hurried off to see to their meal.

After a moment, Gideon rose. He gave her a quick wink, then walked in the direction of the nearby table where Miriam's father sat alone.

"Begging your pardon, but it has been brought to our attention that you are connected to Miss Bricks." Gideon used the same slightly superior tone as his father had. It was not offputting, simply an unmistakable reminder that he came from a position of influence and importance.

"Well, I—"

"We would be pleased if you would join us. Any connection of hers is always welcome."

That might have been laying it on a bit thick. Still, Father agreed. The sound of his footsteps sent waves of apprehension over her. Their last years together had been miserable. And so much depended upon this.

Father was given a seat between Gideon and Mrs. Mac-Namara. Though she appreciated not being required to sit beside her father, the arrangement placed him almost directly across from her, where she couldn't avoid meeting his eye.

Confidence. Wear your claim.

She looked at him. She dipped her head, smiled a little. "It has been a long time, Father."

He was not cowed, but neither did he balk. "I trust you received my note yesterday."

"I did."

His eyes darted to each of the MacNamaras in turn before resting once more on her. "I was very specific in my instructions."

She hadn't anticipated him broaching the subject so directly. "I am a nurse with patients who need me."

"Most of the children went home today," he answered back. "And Dr. Blackburn is anxious to have you back under his care."

"I have met Dr. Blackburn," Gideon said. "Helpful during an epidemic. I was surprised that he was so unfamiliar with the writings of Semmelweis, though. If one hopes to be regarded as anything more than merely 'competent' as a physician, one must keep abreast of all the newest developments in medical science."

"Does he not subscribe to the journals?" Mr. MacNamara managed to look shocked but somehow also not surprised.

"I suspect not." Gideon gave his parents a look of sorely tried patience.

"He seemed very knowledgeable to me," Father insisted.

"He is not *un*knowledgeable," Gideon said. It was not the most flattering of praise.

Father's brow drew in confused thought. That was a good sign. He needed to doubt Dr. Blackburn. He looked at Miriam. "Do you know about this Semmelweis?"

"Of course," she answered, trying not to smile. Gideon himself had told her about the doctor and his theories of regular handwashing. "He is the foremost expert on the emerging field of instrument sterilization as a means of forestalling infection. This is part of the future of medicine. No one who hopes to successfully treat patients would ignore emerging ideas and discoveries."

"Hear, hear," Mr. MacNamara said.

Father's expression grew more pensive.

Mr. Cooper arrived, carrying a tray of food. He set it out on the table, with nods and smiles and repeated expressions of hope that they would be pleased with the comparatively simple fare. Mrs. MacNamara's insistence that they look and act the part of high society gentlemen and ladies had worked as far as the restaurant owner was concerned. Mr. Cooper also owned and ran the hotel, and Miriam had interacted with him on any number of occasions, but he had never scraped and bowed this much.

"Would you bring Mr. Bricks's meal to our table as well?" Gideon requested. "We've invited him to join us."

"Of course, of course."

"And please make certain there is a slice of chocolate cake for Nurse Bricks when she has finished her supper," Gideon added. "She seemed particularly hopeful for a slice. I do not wish for her to be disappointed."

"None of us would want that," Mr. Cooper said. "After all she did for my Ginny." He faced her directly. "Anytime you want a slice of cake, you simply come ask. You can have all you want, free of charge. It's the least I can do."

"Thank you." She was genuinely touched by the offer.

The briefest twinkle of triumph filled Mrs. MacNamara's eyes before being tucked away again. The praise Mr. Cooper had offered hadn't been solicited, but it was helpful to Miriam's cause.

"I didn't realize you did so much here," Father said once the proprietor had disappeared into the kitchen.

"She is invaluable." Gideon spoke firmly, insistently.

Something like a warning crossed both his parents' faces. Apparently, subtlety was best.

"Tell us about your family, Mr. Bricks," Mrs. MacNamara said. "I seem to remember my dear friend Julia Cockling mentioning a Bricks who was making some inroads into political circles in New York."

"Cockling?" Father sputtered. "Senator Cockling's wife?"

Heavens. Miriam hadn't realized Mrs. MacNamara's casually mentioned friend was a senator's wife.

"Indeed," Mrs. MacNamara said. "Is the young Mr. Bricks she spoke of connected to you?"

"My son," he said. "My eldest."

"You must be proud of him," she said.

"I am."

Miriam tried not to let those two words pierce her, but they did. He had not once said he was proud of *her*.

Mrs. MacNamara continued. "Are the rest of your children as accomplished as your eldest and your daughter here?"

He hadn't a ready answer. If they were truly fortunate, he was at least beginning to think of Miriam in the same terms as her older brother: accomplishment, pride, worth.

Just as Miriam began to let herself feel hopeful, Dr. Blackburn arrived. Cold tiptoed down her spine. She tried to hide her reaction but didn't have faith in her ability.

He crossed directly to them. "Good evening," he said quite pleasantly.

The MacNamaras returned the greeting with their impeccable manners. Miriam couldn't manage a single word.

Dr. Blackburn addressed her father next. "My apologies for being late. I was hoping to receive an answer to my telegram, but, alas, things move slowly in these territories."

Father nodded. "I was invited to join the MacNamaras and . . . Miriam."

Why was even her name difficult for him to say? Was he so uncomfortable with her? Embarrassed?

Dr. Blackburn looked to her with an expression of mingled worry and pity. "I hope you aren't overtaxing yourself. With all you have pushed yourself to do lately, your strength will soon be nonexistent."

"My strength is sufficient," she insisted.

He held his hands up in a show of innocence. "No need to grow defensive. I was merely concerned. I know well the limits faced by one with your condition."

"My only relevant 'condition' is hunger. Something I mean to reconcile momentarily."

Dr. Blackburn sighed sadly. He turned his gaze to the others at the table. "Many never move past denying their limits. It is, perhaps, the most tragic part of my area of specialty: helping people who are too far gone to realize they need help."

Father nodded minutely.

"I am not certain to what you refer," Gideon said. "Miss Bricks spent unending, grueling hours of effort calling upon a deep store of expertise and ability to save dozens of lives, but she certainly understands that every person has limits to their endurance under such conditions. She has rested as needed and as able."

Dr. Blackburn's lips pulled tight. "I am not unaware of your fondness for her. I haven't the luxury of letting my judgment be colored by such things. Too much depends upon my willingness to do what must be done."

Another nod from Father.

"One must wonder how much of what you do *must* be done and how much you simply *enjoy* doing," Miriam inserted. "That is an error no doctor can afford, but too many allow."

"Do not grow hysterical, Miriam," he answered with slow emphasis.

How she hated that word. Only female patients were ever labeled "hysterical," and only when they objected to his inhumane treatments and biting rebukes.

"He knows what he is about," Father said, motioning to Dr. Blackburn. "Not many doctors have dedicated their lives to tending those who . . . who are like you, whose minds are a danger."

"My mind is not—"

"He said you would deny it." Father rose. "Those most in need of treatments for the mind don't know that they are in need. It is part of the problem."

Dr. Blackburn set a hand on Father's shoulder, a gesture of support that Miriam didn't believe for one moment to be sincere. The doctor could be whatever the situation called for. He could convince almost anyone of almost anything. He lied as easily as most people breathed.

"We won't disrupt your meal," Dr. Blackburn said. "Carlton and I have a few things to discuss." He motioned Father to the opposite side of the room. Before walking away, he met Miriam's eye. "I expect to receive word from the judge in Laramie soon."

She kept her expression neutral. Even when the men were settled at a different table, she didn't let her posture slip. They would be watching. She would not allow them to see her as anything but strong.

"Do not give up hope, sweetheart," Mr. MacNamara said. "We knew this would not be fixed in a single evening. We have planted seeds, just as we wished to."

Mrs. MacNamara smiled. "Indeed. I am entirely hopeful."

Miriam tried to smile. They were hopeful, which was good, but she was not. They were up against two men Miriam knew far better than they did. Her father was both vain and easily persuadable, and Dr. Blackburn knew precisely how to manipulate people like her father.

Only one thing had grown more certain over the course of the evening: she was running out of time.

Chapter 34

Only four children remained at Gideon's house by noon the next day.

"It is admirable that you are so willing to work," Dr. Blackburn said as Miriam stripped bedding from one of the now-empty sickbeds. "But the crisis has past. There is help enough without you."

Gideon accepted the rolled pile of bedsheets Miriam handed to him. "On the contrary, Blackburn, medical training is still very valuable. I am certain you know the dangers of scarlet fever do not disappear the instant the rash does."

Miriam had adopted the strategy of not speaking to Dr. Blackburn, of keeping her head held high and going about her work. She knew he was right, that her assistance was not actually necessary during the final stage of this epidemic. Gideon could easily see to the task of burning linens and rags and scrubbing furniture without her. But the chores granted her time to formulate a strategy.

She had spent much of the night pondering, lying in the quiet stillness of the recovery room, where she'd been staying, knowing Dr. Blackburn and her father were at the hotel. She would not have been safe there.

In those long hours of darkness, she had accepted the reality of her situation. She had no choice but to run again. But she needed to be smart about it this time.

She would not keep her same name or profession or credentials. Anonymity was her only hope. Disappearing was the only way she could protect Cade and Hawk and Paisley and, most of all, Gideon from the consequences of her refusal to return to the asylum. It was the only way to save her own life.

"Are you here, Doc?"

Andrew. Thus far they'd managed to shield him from Dr. Blackburn's attention. How would they now with both men in the same house?

"I'll speak with Andrew," Gideon said. He gave Miriam back the armful of linens. "Will you add this to the pile downstairs?"

She walked alongside him, grateful for the buffer he provided. Were she alone with Dr. Blackburn, the haranguing would be ceaseless, provided he didn't physically restrain her and drag her away. Though he maintained an almost impeccably civil demeanor around everyone else, she knew it would disappear if they were alone.

Andrew hurried past the foot of the stairs, toward the kitchen. "Barney, you have to stay here so Doc can talk to you."

Mr. Bell was there as well? What had happened?

Gideon asked the question before she could. "Has something happened to Mr. Bell?"

"He keeps saying he needs to find his dog. He's wandering all over, and I can't stop him." Andrew wrung his hands, his neck craning to watch the kitchen door, then back to Gideon, then back at the door. "He keeps calling me 'Mister,' like he doesn't know me at all."

He likely didn't. Mr. Bell's mind was slipping away faster and faster all the time.

Dr. Blackburn pushed past them all. "Allow me to be of assistance, MacNamara. This is my area of expertise."

"Be that as it may, I am this man's doctor," Gideon said. "I will see to his care."

Dr. Blackburn dipped his head in acknowledgment, though the movement was stiff. The veneer was growing thin. "I am at your disposal should either of these men need someone versed in the care of lunatics."

Andrew swallowed hard. "I am not a lunatic."

"Those who are seldom realize it." Dr. Blackburn's eyes hardened the way they did when a patient was inconveniencing him. "You would do well to track down the other one before he lands himself in trouble."

"'The other one' has a name." Miriam ought to have bit her tongue, but she'd kept quiet for two long years. Hearing him dismiss the struggles of yet another human being was too much. "His name is Barney Bell. He founded this branch of the Omaha National Bank. He held the respect and good opinion of a great many people. And while he has grown confused and lost, he has never caused anyone any trouble."

"As always, you twist my words." Dr. Blackburn produced a look of empathetic discontent. "Lashing out at me because your life has not played out as you wish has never accomplished what you seem to think it will."

"I do not do that," she insisted.

He lowered his voice along with his brows. "Do try to stay calm. A fevered mind will never function correctly. Once you are back at the asylum, you will benefit from the calm I have created there."

He demanded calm at all costs, and his patients paid the price. Most he broke with neglect, but those who truly upset his ordered world, those like poor George, he medicated into unnatural silence. Miriam was well aware that she had toppled his haven more than anyone else had, having proven that he did not have ultimate control over her, and he meant to break her for it.

Andrew, who normally avoided speaking to strangers, especially combative ones, stepped directly between Dr. Blackburn and Miriam. "She doesn't have to go with you. We'll not let you take her."

Miriam felt a wave of warmth at his show of courage. If not for Dr. Blackburn's presence and her doubt that Andrew would appreciate it, she would have hugged him.

"She needs the help I offer," Dr. Blackburn said. "You and your friend—Mr. Bell, was it?—could likely benefit as well. We could make room for you."

"No." Miriam spoke quickly, sternly. "They do not need anything you have to offer. Their doctor will not certify them in need of it, and their families will not sign them over."

Dr. Blackburn turned to her. With his back to the others, his façade slipped entirely. The sheer, unmitigated hatred in his gaze sent her back a step.

Gideon slapped Andrew on the shoulder. "Let's go find Mr. Bell."

"What about *him*?" Andrew nodded toward Dr. Blackburn.

All manners once more, the horrid doctor turned back to the others. "Do not worry over me. I have arranged to take my midday meal with Mr. Bricks. We have become good friends."

With that pronouncement, Dr. Blackburn strode to the front door, stepping out without a backward glance.

To the closed door, Andrew said, "I am *not* a lunatic."

"He is a terrible person, Andrew," she said. "Please do not put any store by the things he says."

Andrew shoved his hands into his trouser pockets. His head stayed down as he moved toward the kitchen himself. "I'm going to help Doc find Barney."

"I am sorry about Dr. Blackburn."

He didn't reply but simply shuffled out. Dr. Blackburn's vitriol had wounded such a sweet-tempered man. Inflicting agony was second nature to the doctor.

She dropped her armful of linens out of the open parlor window onto the pile below, returning a few times to repeat the task with more sheets and rags. Once all the linens were burned and the furniture scrubbed to a blinding shine, they could no longer argue that she was still needed.

She pulled the window closed, wincing at the pain the motion sent through her shoulder. It had healed enough to be out of its sling, but it was still tender. She moved toward the kitchen, meaning to slip out around the back, but the sound of Gideon's voice in the dining room stopped her.

"We can put off Blackburn for a while, but only if we push the boundaries on a few things."

"We can only do that for so long," Cade said. "There are consequences for flouting the law. Pais and I, Hawk, you, Andrew, likely your parents—we'll all quickly find ourselves in hot water."

"I won't abandon her," Gideon said firmly.

"I wasn't suggesting that you should, only warning you of the battle we're facing."

"And the cost," Gideon added.

The cost. Miriam would not allow them to pay for her freedom with their own. She would not.

Fleeing truly was her best and only option. She would escape Dr. Blackburn's clutches, and he would leave Savage Wells and stop harassing the people she cared for so deeply. She would prefer not to be on her own while her arm was still healing, but hers was not the only life at stake. She would do what she had to.

She hurried up the stairs, meaning to fetch a scarf she'd seen in a bureau drawer. The nights were chilly; the scarf would be helpful. What else could she gather quickly? A bit of food. If she was very quick and very careful, she could grab some clothes from her hotel room. She'd have to make do with what she could easily carry. At least the weather was being cooperative; making this flight in the winter would have been catastrophic.

Rupert was awake in the room when she walked in. "Howdy, Miss Bricks."

"Howdy to you, Rupert. How are you?" She tried to hide the franticness she felt.

"Why couldn't I go home today?" he asked. "The others did."

"You're not well enough yet."

He was more alert, though. Had more life. "Can I send my parents another drawing?"

"I think they would like that." She pulled her sketchbook from her apron pocket along with her last remaining pencil. "Find an empty page and draw your picture. Give the sketchbook to Dr. MacNamara when you are done, and he will give your drawing to your parents."

"You don't want to keep your book?"

She shook her head. "No. Give it to him, only to him. There are things in there he needs to see." Bits of herself, her past, the people she had known. So much of their time together had been marred by the secrets she carried with her. He deserved to see the truth. "Will you make certain he gets it?"

"'Course I will." He was already bent over it, flipping for a blank page.

Miriam kissed the top of his bare head. "I love you, sweet Rupert."

He just laughed.

She slipped the scarf from the bureau, made a quick check of the Clark children, who were engaged in a game of Jacob's ladder. They were all improving quickly. She could leave with a clear conscience where they were concerned.

She hurried back downstairs and strode into the dining room where Cade and Gideon were. "Sorry to interrupt. Did you ever find Barney?" she asked Gideon.

He nodded. "Paisley and Andrew took him home. It seemed best."

That was a relief. "Would it cause you trouble if I rested in the recovery room for a while? I'm so tired I could sleep for days."

"Of course," Gideon said. "Rest as much as you need to."

It was the answer she'd hoped for. No one would think twice if they didn't see her for the rest of the day. It'd likely be mid-morning tomorrow before anyone began to wonder.

"Thank you for all your help today," Gideon added, taking her hand as he'd done so often. "Rest well."

"I will do my best." Oh, how she wanted to throw herself into his arms, to cry out all the fear and uncertainty she felt, to kiss him one last time. But doing any of those things would tip her hand, and she didn't dare risk it.

She slipped from the room. She snatched up a basket in the kitchen and filled it with every bit of portable food she could find. Knowing Cade always watched the street when he was at

Gideon's house, she slipped out the back door. She would take a longer route, but avoid detection.

She moved carefully up the hotel stairs to the room she'd avoided while Dr. Blackburn and her father were in town. With effort, she kept her mind clear of even a thought of what she was about to do. She would fall to pieces if she wasn't careful.

An extra dress, her one nightgown, and a few underthings went into her small carpetbag. Bringing her trunk and other belongings would only slow her down. A carpetbag and a basket of food. She could move quickly with only those two things.

She counted out the remainder of what she owed for her room and left it on the bureau.

There was little else to be done. She could make no goodbyes. Neither could she delay any longer. She hurried down the empty stairs and out the back door of the hotel. If she kept moving, kept going, she would be far away before anyone noticed she was gone.

She carefully made her way toward the east of the building and behind the hotel, making her journey in the opposite direction.

Savage Wells had begun to feel like home these past weeks. If only she'd had more time to prove herself to the rest of the townspeople, she felt certain she could have built here the new life she'd dreamed of in the dark confines of Blackburn Asylum. She could have been free.

There was nothing to be done now but escape. Again.

She'd left people behind before, people she'd cared about, but running had never hurt this much or this deeply. Life, in all its cruelty, had left her no choice.

Chapter 35

"I have arranged for Miriam and me to take tea with Mrs. Endecott," Mother said. "She speaks very highly of Miriam and, when I told her Mr. Bricks was in town, she was eager to meet him and tell him what a wonderful daughter he has."

Gideon didn't know whether to be encouraged or worried. A preacher's wife speaking well of Miriam couldn't hurt, but Miriam's father speaking ill of her to Mrs. Endecott would only hurt Miriam further. She had endured so much. She had looked entirely exhausted when she'd gone to lie down the afternoon before. She likely wasn't still sleeping—twenty-four hours had passed—but Gideon suspected she needed the peace and quiet. He didn't mean to disturb her.

Father stood at the front window, watching the street outside. He'd taken to doing that during the day, not with the ominous air Cade and Hawk assumed when keeping an eye on the town. Father's was a mien of pure curiosity. He enjoyed Savage Wells.

"William, are you listening at all?" Mother pressed.

He turned around. "I think your tea idea is genius. I've talked with the men of the town council, and they mean to invite Mr. Bricks to join them for their weekly game of horseshoes."

"Horseshoes?" Mother scoffed. "How is that going to impress him?"

Father shook his head. "The purpose of the invitation is not to make him think Savage Wells is a bastion of high society, but that his connection to Miriam has benefits, even this far from home."

Gideon held up his hand, stepping between them. Chances were high that they'd descend into their usual bickering, and he hadn't the patience for it.

"There is an aspect of this I don't think either of you have considered," he said. "Spending this much time with the people of this town—who will most certainly discuss Miriam—increases the chances that something Mr. Bricks says will reveal to them her health issues and her recent institutionalization. At this point, the town is not aware of either."

"I hadn't thought of that," Mother said.

"Neither had I." Father rubbed his chin with the pad of his thumb. "Do you think they would turn on her if they knew?"

"They might have two weeks ago," Gideon said. "But she saved the lives of their children. I wouldn't be surprised if they renamed the town after her."

Mother nodded slowly. "They love her, which means they would not only want to help her but would believe you, Gideon, if you explained her situation and her need for their help."

"It would be best if they hear it from you first and not from Mr. Bricks or Dr. Blackburn," Father said. "That man could convince a mother to turn on her child."

"Or a father on his," Mother pointed out.

"I need to make certain Miriam is comfortable with this

plan," Gideon said. "She should get to decide what people know of her private concerns and how and when they find out. It is a courtesy she has been denied too many times."

"There are far too many people in this world who would not be nearly so considerate," Mother said. "I cannot tell you how pleased I am that you are not one of those."

It was a rare moment of feeling something like pride from his mother. Gideon wasn't entirely certain how to respond.

"Is Miriam still resting?" Father asked.

He nodded. "She seemed extremely worn down yesterday when she left. I wouldn't be the least bit surprised to hear she was feeling poorly."

As if to contradict his declaration, footsteps sounded from the entryway. It seemed Miriam was awake after all. Perhaps she would let him hold her, comfort her, and, by so doing, he could regain some measure of peace himself.

It was not, however, Miriam who stepped into the parlor. It was Tansy.

"I've a cow that's sick," she said in her usual abrupt way. "Seems to have a touch of that hoofrot you found in another one last year."

"Are you certain it's rot?"

"Can't say for sure. I ain't a doctor." Tansy eyed Mother and Father, then said, "I've left a jar of moonshine on your porch as payment."

She always did that: paying him *before* he rendered services. Life had taught her not to trust people, so putting him in her debt was her way of making certain he didn't brush her aside. He also knew better than to insist he was still in her debt for all she'd done to see the town through the scarlet fever outbreak. Tansy was both proud and prickly. If she declared that doctoring her cow warranted a jar of sweet tea, then it did.

He nodded. "I'll come have a look. It might not be until tomorrow, though."

"When you can, but don't drag your feet." Tansy spun back around and left.

Mother had moved to Gideon's desk and began writing on a sheet of paper. "Besides the preacher and the town council, who else ought we to have over to make this appeal and explanation? Assuming, of course, Miriam agrees."

Gideon returned his mind to the issue at hand. "Mrs. Wilhite and Mrs. Carol. Mr. and Mrs. Fletcher. Mr. and Mrs. Clark. They have all grown very close to her. They will wish to help."

"Gideon?" Father's tone was calm, but something in it instantly set Gideon on alert.

Father motioned to the parlor doorway, where Rupert stood, barefoot, bareheaded, eyes filled with worry.

Gideon knelt in front of the boy. "Is something the matter?"

"I forgot." Tears threatened beneath the surface of his words. He held up Miriam's sketchbook.

"Where did you get this?" Gideon had never known Miriam to let it out of her possession.

"I forgot. She said I could make a picture for my ma, but that I should give it to you when I was done. I forgot."

That made no sense. Not the bit about letting him draw a picture—she'd done that before—but instructing Rupert to give the book to him. She guarded it very closely. It was important to her, invaluable.

"Are you certain she wanted you to give it to *me*?"

He nodded. "She said that she wanted you to see what was in it, or that you would want to see it. Something like that. I should have given it to you when I finished my drawing, but I forgot. I'm sorry, Doc."

The poor boy looked so disappointed in himself. Gideon pulled him into a hug. "I'm not upset with you. And I know Miss Bricks isn't either."

"She was sad when she gave me the book yesterday."

Yesterday? Rupert might have forgotten about the book for an entire day, but Miriam wouldn't have. Something wasn't right.

He offered Rupert a smile. "Go back on upstairs and rest. If you do, you can go home that much faster."

"You'll give Miss Bricks her book?"

"I promise," he said.

Father stepped up beside them. "I'll walk Rupert back to his room. I want to hear more about the chicken he told me of a few days ago."

"Her name is Annabelle," Rupert said. "Mr. Clark says she's the prettiest chicken in the world."

Father scooped Rupert into his arms and carried him up the stairs.

Gideon stood, holding tight to Miriam's sketchbook. He had a terrible feeling, one he couldn't shake.

For a moment, he stood outside the door to the recovery room, willing himself to knock. He couldn't convince himself his suspicions were wrong. She wouldn't have left her sketchbook for him if nothing was amiss.

He rapped his knuckles against the door. "Miriam?"

There was no answer.

He tried again. "Miriam?" Then again, more urgently. "Miriam."

Please answer. But he knew she wasn't going to.

"Mother," he called back to the parlor.

A moment later, she stepped into the entryway, a look of inquiry on her face.

"Miriam isn't answering, and it would feel less like an invasion of her privacy if you checked rather than me."

She switched places with him. "I'm opening the door, Miriam," she said as she turned the handle. She inched the door open. After a quick look around the small room, she turned back to Gideon. "She's not here."

He stepped past her and into the room. Empty. The bed was pristinely made, everything in perfect order.

"I thought you said she was sleeping," Mother said.

"She said she was." *Where are you, Miriam?* "It's possible she went back to the hotel, hoping to get more rest than she would here."

"With her father and Dr. Blackburn staying there?" Mother asked doubtfully.

Gideon knew it was far-fetched, but he didn't have any other explanation. He made the very short walk faster than he ever had before.

"Has Miss Bricks been here lately?" he asked Mr. Cooper once he reached the desk of the hotel.

"I haven't seen her here in weeks—other than the supper your family had here two nights ago."

Still, it wasn't a guarantee she hadn't been by. "I'm going to knock at her door."

Mr. Cooper's expression grew concerned. "Is she ill? In some kind of trouble?"

"Stars, I hope not," he muttered.

"I'll go with you," Mr. Cooper said. "If she's in need of anything, I want to help."

"Have Dr. Blackburn or Mr. Bricks been here the last twenty-four hours?" Gideon asked as they climbed the stairs.

"They had breakfast in the restaurant this morning."

"Did they talk about Miriam?"

Mr. Cooper thought a moment. "Yes. They said the epidemic was all but over and she wouldn't be staying at your house for more than a couple days longer."

Which meant, as of breakfast this morning, she wasn't with them.

When Mr. Cooper knocked at the door of her room, it slipped open. The bed was neatly made, the room left in perfect order, just like the recovery room. Her traveling trunk sat in the corner. Surely she would not have left without her belongings.

Except, if she was on the run, she would be on foot. A trunk that large would be too cumbersome to carry. He opened the armoire doors. Empty. Her carpetbag was nowhere to be seen. He didn't spot it in any drawers, on top or underneath any furniture.

Mr. Cooper counted out the money on the bureau. "It's exactly what she owes for the room."

She'd paid her bill in its entirety and packed essentials. She really was gone.

"Is she in trouble?" Mr. Cooper asked again.

"I'm afraid she might be." He needed to think, decide what to do next. "Can I rely on your discretion?"

Mr. Cooper agreed without hesitation.

"Thank you." Gideon left as quickly as he'd come. He tamped down his growing panic.

He needed to talk to Cade and Paisley. Miriam must have been desperate to run like this. She had nowhere to go, no means of supporting herself that wouldn't give away her identity.

The fight they were waging against Blackburn and Miriam's

father and the law itself was an uphill climb on its own. This new complication was more than merely that. He was genuinely terrified for her.

There was a reason the women of the West needed their own deputy marshal looking out for them. The wild, untamed world around them was anything but kind and gentle. And it was never forgiving.

The shed at the edge of the Faulkners' pasture was empty, as were all the sheds and shacks and abandoned homes and outcroppings Gideon and Cade had searched. And, just as the others, this location didn't show any signs of recent use.

Gideon kicked at the wall. His worry for Miriam alternated between panic and anger. "Where is she?"

"I'd wager either Pais or Andrew have come across her walking the road. She likely wants to put as much space between her and the town as possible."

It was sensible and logical, but Gideon felt in his gut it wasn't accurate. She must have realized she would have been discovered missing by now and that they would go looking for her. She would be more likely to hide this first day or two so she wouldn't be found. She likely thought that was all it would take for him to give up on her.

"I don't know where else to look." He hoped Cade wasn't equally bereft of ideas.

"We can't check everything; there are too many places she could be hiding."

"You aren't helping," Gideon muttered.

Cade pulled himself up into the saddle. "She's bright, Gid, no matter the foolhardiness of her plan. I'd wager she's found shelter and something to eat. She's likely as safe as she can be."

Gideon climbed into his saddle as well. "We need to find her before she moves on, or we never will."

Cade nudged his horse forward. Gideon followed suit. They moved at a quick clip, both scanning the area as they went, looking for some kind of clue. Miriam was somewhere nearby. She had to be.

Yet they reached Savage Wells without any sign of her. They tied their reins to the hitching post in front of Gideon's house, then made their way onto the front porch and through the door. Voices sounded inside.

"Seems you're to do a bit of doctoring," Cade said.

Terrible timing. But no one in his parlor—and there were a number of people—looked injured or ill. Paisley stood near his desk. She waved him over.

He passed the Clarks, the Fletchers, Mrs. Wilhite and Mrs. Carol, the Endecotts, Mr. Cooper, and Miss Dunkle. It was an odd assortment of people.

"You didn't find her?" he quietly asked Paisley once he reached her side.

She shook her head. "We need help, Gideon. We won't find her alone, and it won't be long before Blackburn and Bricks realize she's gone. They'll go looking for her."

Cade nodded. "And if they find her first—"

"Understood." Gideon looked out over the crowd. Miriam mattered to these people. They would help; he knew they would.

"Andrew's guarding the kitchen door," Paisley said. "Your father will keep an eye on the front. Rally the troops while you can."

Gideon faced the gathering. Concerned, anxious faces looked

back at him. He needed their help. *Miriam* needed their help. And here they were, ready. "Thank you for coming."

Mr. Fletcher chimed in. "Paisley said Miss Bricks is in some kind of trouble. You tell us what to do, Doc, and we'll do it."

Though he would have preferred letting Miriam decide what and when to reveal her secrets, he no longer had that luxury.

"Miriam is ill," he said. "Not an illness like a fever or a cold, or anything short-term like that. And it isn't anything catching."

The confusion on their faces only grew. He would have to provide more details.

"On rare occasions, her body experiences unexpected tremors, strong shaking that she cannot control and which doesn't have an identifiable cause. The episodes do not last long, and, other than rendering her quite tired and temporarily disoriented, they have no lasting consequences." That was an oversimplification, but he needed Miriam's allies to know that Blackburn's portrayal of her condition was wrong. "These tremors cannot be prevented, neither can they be cured—not unlike the coughing fits you are prone to, Mrs. Carol, or the stiffness you experience in your knee now and then, Mr. Clark."

"Or like the headaches I have now and then?" Mrs. Fletcher suggested.

"Yes, exactly." They were accepting this far easier than he had feared. "As we have all seen, they in no way diminish her ability to be a good nurse or a good neighbor or a good friend." The nods of agreement he received put the last of his worries to rest. "But there are people who use these bouts of illness to justify hurting her. They are in this town with the intention of forcing her to leave and locking her away."

"They'd put her in prison?" Mrs. Clark asked in horror. "Just because she's ill?"

Gideon nodded. "And I am afraid the laws of this land allow them to do so."

A rush of earnest, adamant voices denounced that revelation.

"It's Dr. Blackburn, isn't it?" Mr. Cooper asked, not bothering with his usual faux-accent. He looked genuinely worried.

Gideon nodded. "Yes. His arrival here was not the coincidence he made it out to be. He came for her."

"But her father is with him," Mrs. Endecott said. "Surely her own father would stop him."

"Blackburn has convinced Mr. Bricks that locking Miriam away is for the best. We are working on convincing him otherwise."

The crowd muttered and murmured. Gideon held a hand up for silence.

"As I said, we have people working tirelessly to try to untangle the legal web connected to this, but I need your help on another aspect of Miriam's situation." He took the length of a breath to will himself to talk about her current danger, about his inability to find her. "Her life is in danger. I have every reason to believe that if she is taken away, she will suffer horrifically, perhaps even die. And I firmly suspect she worried as much, if not more, about the consequences that may fall upon those she cares for were she to remain. Considering those two dire difficulties, she did the only thing she felt would secure her safety and ours. She ran."

Shocked silence descended on the room. Worry, concern, and surprise filled each face.

"We don't know where she is," he admitted, even as a new surge of worry clawed at his mind. "We can't find her. Cade, who has more expertise in this kind of thing, believes she is hiding somewhere relatively nearby to avoid the risk of being caught walking the roads.

"Dr. Blackburn and Mr. Bricks will realize soon enough that she is gone; we cannot prevent that. So I am asking you, please, keep an eye out for her, look for her if you can do so without drawing notice. And, I beg you, if you find her, help her hide. Keep her safe. And, please, find a way to tell me."

Mrs. Wilhite rose and crossed to him, giving him a gentle, reassuring hug. Mrs. Carol joined her a moment later.

"Don't you worry, Doc," Mr. Fletcher said. "We'll look out for her. Not one of us will let anyone hurt her."

How he hoped that was a promise they were able to keep.

Chapter 36

Night was coming on fast. Their search south of town had come up empty. Gideon couldn't keep still, couldn't calm his thoughts. What if she'd wandered too far afield and was lost? What if she'd had a seizure and injured herself? Anything might have happened, and no one would ever know.

And, to add to his worry, Blackburn and Bricks now knew she was gone.

"What else is being done to recover her?" Dr. Blackburn's question, on the surface, sounded like concern for Miriam. Gideon didn't believe it for a moment. "She is ill and without a doctor's care, yet you are not the least bothered."

Cade leaned back in his chair, his booted feet up on the desk, crossed at the ankles. "Oh, I'm feeling plenty bothered, I promise you that."

"The judge in Laramie is scheduled to arrive in only a few days' time. You will be required to hand her over to me."

Cade set a toothpick between his front teeth. "Can't do that. I don't know where she is."

"But he does." Blackburn pointed at Gideon. "Require him to tell you. Force him to. It is your job."

Cade rolled the toothpick to one side of his mouth. "Are you telling me how to run my town?"

Blackburn seemed to understand the tenuous nature of his situation. He pushed away from the desk and paced away.

Gideon hadn't left the doorway all evening. Andrew was still out searching, having agreed to ride all the way to the Bentley place—a ninety-minute ride—and back. He was the last hope Gideon had of finding Miriam before nightfall. He hated the thought of her out there, on her own, in the dark.

"Her father is beside himself," Dr. Blackburn said. "I don't know how you intend to explain this to him."

"I would love the opportunity to 'explain this to him,'" Gideon said tightly. "I think he ought to know a little more about you, Blackburn."

The façade of care and concern slipped quickly. "How dare you threaten me."

"Didn't sound like a threat to my ears," Cade tossed out.

"Mark my words, both of you. She will be returned to where she belongs," Dr. Blackburn said firmly. "And this time, she will not escape. I will make certain of it."

Tansy stepped inside at the tail end of Dr. Blackburn's speech. "I still have an ailing cow," she said abruptly, skewering Gideon with a look.

"We have something of a crisis on our hands, Tansy. I will come tomorrow if I can, but—"

"I already paid you, Doc." She looked downright livid. "M' cow needs looking after, and you're the only doctor nearby." Her eyes darted to Blackburn. "This'n ain't worth nothin'."

As much as he appreciated the sentiment, Gideon wasn't about to leave while Miriam was still missing. "I can come tomorrow."

"I can't wait until tomorrow."

It wasn't like Tansy to be so irate, not over something as inconsequential as a cow with a sore hoof. "Are you feeling unwell?"

Her mouth pulled inward, and her eyes snapped. "I only think a person who helped out another person as much as I helped you with that fever shouldn't have to argue with that person to get a little help."

"Are you truly this worried about your cow?" It was an overreaction by anyone's estimation.

"I am. Now, what're you going to do about it?"

Blackburn wandered to the window. "This entire town is in chaos."

"You'd best go with her, Gid." Cade hadn't moved from his casual position, though Gideon didn't doubt he was as concerned as anyone. "I'll send word if Andrew finds anything."

"This is not how it's done," Blackburn shot back. "If your imbecile finds mine, I had best be the first person he tells."

"Keep shooting your mouth off like that, and I'll see to it you experience a bit of 'chaos.'" No one hearing Cade could interpret that as anything but a threat.

Gideon snatched up his bag from near the door. He hadn't been without it since learning of Miriam's disappearance. "Let's go look at your cow," he muttered to Tansy.

She'd come in her wagon and motioned for him to climb in. He didn't want to waste time arguing with her that it'd be more convenient if he rode out on his own. The sooner he saw to this, the sooner he could return to town and rejoin the efforts to find Miriam.

The moment they left town, she urged the horses to a much faster speed.

"You must be really worried about your cow."

"I am."

What in heaven's name was wrong with the animal that she was this upset? Perhaps it had a wounded leg that had taken an infection or had fallen ill in another way. Tansy was not well-off by any stretch of the imagination. Replacing a cow would be a tremendous financial burden. That would be reason enough for her to worry a great deal.

"I'm sorry I've been short with you," he said.

She shook her head. "You're worried about Miriam. I understand."

"Tell me about your cow's hoof."

"You'll have to see it for yourself." She turned the wagon off the road and along the path to her barn.

This didn't sound like a simple case of hoofrot.

Tansy hopped down and wrapped the horse's reins around a hitching post. "In here." She led the way to the barn.

Sunset had come, and the barn interior was dim. Tansy was a step ahead of him, lighting a lantern.

Now able to see, Gideon stepped over to the cow quietly chewing on a bit of hay. Tansy, however, walked right past the animal.

"I'll need the lantern," he reminded her.

"This way." She spoke too firmly to be dismissed.

Gideon followed her to the back of the barn. "Is there another cow? I thought you only had one."

"Had to say something to get you to come without that blowhard figuring things out." She reached down and pulled open a door in the floor. "Come on."

What was going on? He followed her down a ladder into a

root cellar. Gideon blinked a few times and squinted to help his eyes adjust.

"She'll either be hiding or sleeping," Tansy said. She hung her lantern on a peg on the wall, illuminating a cot tucked into the corner of the cellar. There, fast asleep and pale as a ghost, lay Miriam.

"Thank heavens." Gideon knelt beside the cot and carefully took Miriam's hand in his. She didn't awaken. "Where did you find her? How did you convince her to stay with you?"

"She had another of her episodes," Tansy said. "Dragged herself here afterward. She knew I wouldn't turn her over to that brute who's chasing her."

His heart dropped. "How bad was it? Has she had more since?"

"She hasn't said there've been any more, but the one she had roughed her up bad."

He pulled open his doctoring bag. "Is anything broken or out of joint?"

"A lot of bruising and a deep cut on her leg. It don't seem putrid or nothing, but I thought you'd like to see it." There was something conspiratorial in Tansy's tone.

"You mean, you thought I would like to see *her*."

Tansy nodded. "I ain't blind."

"Thank you," he said. "For keeping her safe, for bringing me down here, for not even hinting at any of this while Blackburn was listening."

"She's good people," Tansy said. "And I've been where she is, when the most dangerous path is the only safe one. Patch her up, Doc. Say your piece if she'll let you. But if you all can't thwart that horrid doctor who's waiting for her, she'll run again, and I won't stop her. At least out on her own she has a chance."

"We're going to beat him, Tansy. One way or another, we'll

beat him." The declaration was overly confident, he knew that. But he wasn't ready to admit defeat.

"I don't think he suspected nothin' with you coming out here tonight, but I'll plop myself on the stool by the barn door and keep an eye out, just in case." Tansy watched Miriam a moment. "She was kind to me right from the first. Never looked down on me for not being cultured."

"Like you said, she is good people."

Tansy climbed the ladder back out of the cellar. The trapdoor closed with a thud. He had only the light of the lantern they'd brought down. Examining a wound would be far easier if it weren't so dark.

Gideon found an unlit candle in a dinged and battered candlestick holder. He lit it with the lantern and set both carefully on a makeshift table close to the cot. The small flicker of additional light helped.

"Miriam," he said quietly. He knelt beside her cot and ran his hand over her mess of copper curls. "Miriam, dear. I need you to wake up."

She stirred but didn't fully awaken. She had a few cuts on her face. Bruises. Even asleep, her features wore a look of distress and pain. He didn't rush her. Blackburn wasn't likely to grow suspicious unless Gideon was gone for hours. He had time to hold her and convince himself she truly was there with him, relatively whole and temporarily safe.

He slipped his hands around hers, warming her cold fingers. Cellars were perfect for keeping food from spoiling, but not such a comfortable hideout for a person.

"Miriam."

Her eyelids flickered. Was she sleeping so deeply because she was tired, or had she taken ill?

He kept her hand in one of his and used his other to check her forehead. She didn't feel overly warm. She certainly wasn't flushed. Indeed, her coloring was worryingly pale.

Her eyes opened at last, though they were unfocused. In the next moment, she sat up. "Gideon?"

Oh, to hear his name on her lips. He would never again take that sound for granted. "You are a difficult woman to find, Miriam Bricks."

"How did you—?" She dropped back to the cot. "Tansy. I told her not to worry you about this."

"You've been hurt, love. She had certainly better 'worry me about this.'"

"Nothing severe," she said. "And there are no signs of infection. I wouldn't even still be here, except I felt certain the lot of you were out looking for me, and I didn't want any of you breaking even more laws or taking even more risks."

"If we didn't know where you were, we couldn't be faulted for not turning you in, is that it?"

"I won't let you ruin your life."

"You've opted, instead, to ruin it for me."

She looked genuinely confused. Did she have no idea of his feelings?

He took up her hands again. "We may have begun under less than ideal circumstances, but I count the day you stepped off that stage as the best and most important day of my life. If I were to lose you, there would be little point in continuing on."

"But with this ax hanging over my head, there *is* little point in continuing on."

He would not allow her to live with such despair a moment longer. "Tell me which leg is injured, and while I examine it, I will tell you what we've concocted."

"The left one, just below the knee."

Over the next few minutes, he discovered two things: she was right about the relative insignificance of her wound, and she was even more terrified of Blackburn Asylum than she had admitted. Over and over she kept saying, "I cannot go back there."

"Tansy will let you stay here while we await answers to our telegrams or until Blackburn leaves," Gideon said. "I know it isn't the finest of accommodations, but it's better than wandering the expanse of Wyoming. And decidedly better than returning to Nebraska."

"You underestimate his tenacity." She sat up fully, tucking her legs beside her and pulling the blanket close. "He won't give up."

Gideon set his arms around her. "If we can't stop him, I'll go with you."

She shook her head. "He will find me."

"We'll go north to Canada, if need be. His claims have no hold there."

She shook her head. "But this town. Your practice. You can't simply abandon them."

He kissed her temple, then rested his head against hers. "None of that matters without you. None of it."

She wrapped her arms around him, and he returned the embrace. He was not an easily emotional person, but having her in his arms again, safe and whole, nearly undid him.

"Does Dr. Blackburn know I'm gone?"

"He does. As does your father. Blackburn has been demanding you be returned, even going so far as to threaten Cade."

"He is most dangerous when he is no longer trying to appear harmless." The fear in her words could not be mistaken. "A person with a conscience has limits. Dr. Blackburn has neither."

"I will warn Cade," he promised. "And we will all take care."

"Is my father angry?"

"He has said very little. The one time I have seen him since he learned of your disappearance, he was quiet, contemplative."

She sighed and leaned more heavily against him. "I wish that were more encouraging. If I had the least hope that he loved me, I might feel more confident."

"Know that *I* love you, deeply and fully and truly."

The trapdoor pulled open. Gideon positioned himself in front of Miriam, shielding her as much as he could from view.

"It's me," Tansy called down. "Get your sparkin' out of the way, you two. If Doc's here much longer, someone might suspect something."

"I'll be up in a minute," he called to her. He turned back to Miriam. Her downcast expression tore at him.

"I had fully expected to never see you again," she said. "Now that I have, I can hardly bear for you to leave."

He took her face in his hands and held her gaze with his. "Promise me that you will not run. Not unless you have to."

"I promise."

"I can likely make a reasonable argument to return in a day or so without drawing too much attention." He kissed her forehead first, then the tip of her nose. "Please be careful."

"I will." She leaned forward and kissed his lips.

He slipped his arms around her again, returning her kiss with every bit of desperation he'd felt that day while searching for her. Though he'd never allowed himself to fully think it, there'd been many times over the course of the day when he'd feared he would never find her.

"I love you, Miriam Bricks. Do not ever doubt that."

Chapter 37

Without a window, and with only the meals Tansy brought her to mark the passage of time, Miriam had only the vaguest idea how long she'd been in the cellar. By her estimation, two days had passed since Gideon's visit. She knew he stayed away to keep her location a secret. Loneliness was the price she paid for her safety. But she was growing nervous.

Footsteps sounded overhead at a time she wasn't expecting. She'd eaten a few hours earlier; it wasn't time for another meal. And this footfall was different than Tansy's heavy and determined steps. These were slow, light, furtive. Someone was either looking for something or didn't want to be heard. Or both. Gideon would have come directly to the trapdoor. Unless, of course, he had reason to think someone was watching him.

Miriam took up the candle and slipped into the corner, listening. Whoever was in the barn stepped on the trapdoor, but kept going, only to return and step on it again. Then once more. Testing it, likely listening to the sound, sorting out what it meant.

Gideon knew where the door was. Tansy knew where the door was.

Someone else had found it.

The cellar was small with almost nothing to hide behind. Whoever was coming would find her quickly. She didn't know if the new arrival was friendly but had to assume not.

The trapdoor shook. Someone was hopping on it.

Miriam sat on the floor between the wall and a few barrels. She blew out the candle. It wasn't the best hiding spot, especially if it was daytime—light would come in through the trapdoor once it was opened—but she had no other options.

The door squeaked. No light spilled in. It was nighttime, then. That would help her. She knew the cellar better than anyone other than Tansy, well enough to navigate in the dark. That would give her an advantage.

Footsteps sounded off the rungs of the ladder. Miriam held her breath. Whoever was coming down hadn't brought a lantern. She didn't hear the swish of a skirt. A man, then. Who would be looking for her in such a secretive way other than Dr. Blackburn? She didn't allow the thought to take root; she couldn't afford to panic.

The new arrival stepped onto the dirt floor with the same light step he'd used in navigating the barn above. Miriam had spent enough time in the dark that she could likely see better than he could, but even her vision was dim.

Should she stay hidden and hope he didn't make a thorough search, or should she try to climb out while he wasn't looking? She likely wouldn't be fast enough, but it might be her only chance.

She inched closer to the ladder, praying the darkness would keep her hidden long enough to make her escape. Her shoulder was still unreliable and tender. The wound in her leg, while not debilitating, made her less steady on her feet. The Fates seemed determined to undermine her.

"Miriam?"

She froze. That wasn't Dr. Blackburn.

"Doc said you was down here." It was Andrew. "Blackburn has sorted it out. He knows you're hiding on this end of town. Won't be long 'til he starts searching here."

Miriam could see enough to make out Andrew's silhouette. "How much time do I have?"

"He's just finished at the Clarks' house. I'm gonna sneak you there, and Mr. Clark will take you to town."

"To town?" She shook her head. "Dr. Blackburn will return there. My father *is* there."

"And they've both combed the place," Andrew said. "They won't be looking for you there." Andrew knocked into a barrel on his way back to the ladder. "Mrs. Wilhite and Mrs. Carol have an empty room above their shop."

"I won't expose them to Dr. Blackburn's viciousness." Still, she climbed out of the cellar, Andrew right behind her.

He dropped the door back into place. "There's not a soul in this town who wouldn't do everything they could for you. We won't let Blackburn hurt you. We won't let your pa hurt you, either."

"And *I* can't let them hurt *you*, any of you. If you break the law to thwart him, there will be consequences."

Andrew squared his shoulders and stood firm. "We need you here, Miriam, and we're tucking you away until we are sure we can keep you."

"Andrew—"

"I'm deputy sheriff of this town. It's my job to look after the people here. Let me do my job."

She had never seen him so resolute. He was bravely and willingly undermining the very man who had labeled him a lunatic. He was thwarting that man's cruelty despite the danger. There was firmness and confidence and surety in his words and bearing. Perhaps some of his wounds were finally beginning to heal.

"I am sorry, Andrew," she said. "You are right. I'm being stubborn."

"We need to hurry." He led her from the barn and into the fields behind Tansy's house, away from the road. "I know a back way to the Clarks'. We'll not be seen."

Not another word was spoken as they traversed the dark fields. She kept close to his side, and he checked for her at regular intervals. Mr. Clark was waiting for them when they arrived.

"Blackburn's already gone up the road to Tansy's. Now's our best chance for getting you to town without him noticing."

"This is such a risk," Miriam said.

"My wife's kept the children in the back. They'll not know you were ever here, so there's no chance of them giving you away."

That was at least comforting. "What do you need me to do?"

"Though I hate to ask it of you, I need you to climb in the wagon bed under the canvas and tuck yourself among the barrels and crates." He pulled back the cloth. "I don't think we'll run into Blackburn, but it'd be best not to have you sitting out in the open."

She didn't argue. If they were willing to break the law for her, risk imprisonment, she would not increase the danger by hesitating. Mr. Clark climbed onto the wagon seat.

Andrew gripped the canvas. "I'm going home for the rest of the night. Blackburn might get suspicious if he sees me in town."

"I know you've suffered because he's been here. I am so sorry for that."

He shook his head. "He's nasty, but I learned something from his being here. I have my troubles, but I know who I am, and I know what I'm capable of. Wretches like him don't get to decide that for me."

He'd found strength in the face of misery. Her heart swelled for him. With that newfound determination, he would conquer his demons in time.

"Tuck down, Miriam," Andrew said. "You've a bit of a ride ahead of you."

She all but held her breath as the wagon rolled along the road. Returning to town was a risk, but she understood the wisdom of it. Everyone was looking for her on the outskirts and along the stage route. Hiding directly under the noses of those who were hunting her might just be the key.

After a long stretch of rough and bumpy roads, the wagon came to a halt. Miriam held still, waiting. She wouldn't move until Mr. Clark told her it was safe.

"Oh, Mr. Clark," Mrs. Carol called out. "Have you come with my feathers? I'm running terribly low."

"I have," he answered. "In a crate in the wagon bed. Where do you want them?"

"I'll walk with you around front. We can take them in there."

A moment later, the canvas inched back. Mr. Clark didn't look in her direction but spoke in a whisper. "We'll make a show of taking this around front to explain my wagon being here in case anyone saw me pull up. Wait just a minute, then climb out. You're behind the millinery. Mrs. Wilhite is watching for you."

He climbed back down, carrying a crate. "Lead the way, Mrs. Carol."

A moment later, Miriam carefully climbed out of the wagon bed. As promised, Mrs. Wilhite stood nearby.

"Quickly, dear," she said.

They rushed inside the back door and up a narrow stairwell. At the top was the older ladies' living quarters.

"This room here is empty," Mrs. Wilhite motioned to a door

at the far end of the parlor. "We've put up thick drapes. You'll not be seen, but you will have to go without a candle or lantern in the evening."

"I understand." She met the woman's eye. "Thank you."

"You have an entire town determined to keep you safe. You simply need to let us."

She received a hug so maternal, so comforting, that she felt tears spring to her eyes. Thank the heavens for this town and for the twists in her path that had brought her here.

Gideon watched out his front window, waiting for the predetermined signal that Miriam was safe with Mrs. Carol and Mrs. Wilhite. He'd seen Mr. Clark step inside the millinery, but knew it was no guarantee Miriam had arrived as well. Any number of things could have gone wrong.

But then it appeared: a candle in an upper window. He pushed out a sigh of relief.

"She's arrived," he said to his father, who sat in the parlor.

"Resist the urge to go check on her, son. Blackburn's away from town, but her father is not. Don't risk it."

He stepped away from the window. "Keep reminding me of that."

"Your mother should be back soon. She'll remind you as well."

Gideon dropped into an empty chair by the fireplace, eyeing the low-burning embers. The night had been chilly. "At least I know Miriam's not cold or hungry."

"You can count on those dear ladies to see to her every need and comfort."

Gideon rubbed at his face. How long could they keep this up, moving her from place to place, risking discovery every time?

His gaze shifted to the end table beside his chair and Miriam's sketchbook lying on top of it. He hadn't convinced himself to open it. It was so personal to her. She guarded it closely. The simple act of untying the leather strap felt like admitting she wasn't coming back.

But she was nearby again. She was close. And he was not alone in his efforts to protect her.

"She wanted you to see what was in it," Rupert had said. The recollection of a six-year-old was not always entirely reliable, but he didn't doubt Miriam had told the boy to give Gideon the book. Why would she insist it be given to him if she didn't want him to open it?

He pulled the sketchbook onto his lap and carefully pulled at the leather strap. Some loose sheets sat inside. He was careful not to allow any of them to fall out as he turned to the very first page.

He didn't recognize the people there, young people who bore a resemblance to one another. Siblings, perhaps. Maybe *her* siblings. The next page must have been her parents; Gideon recognized a younger, happier version of Mr. Bricks.

A few more pleasant and idyllic scenes gave way suddenly to rougher, darker sketches. A barren room with a barred window. A surgical room with edged instruments. Pale and languid figures with worried expressions and heavy eyes. This was the asylum; he knew it.

The next sketch was of Miriam. He recognized her in an instant, though he could not at first identify what was different about her. She was younger, that was clear. But the drawing was labeled "1874," only two years earlier. She looked more than two years younger than she was now. There was a rosiness to her cheeks, a roundedness to her face that spoke of youth and health. Miriam didn't exactly look sickly now, but there was an extra measure of health in this depiction.

He paused on the image for a long time before turning the page.

He reached the sketch of George she had shown him so many weeks earlier. Empty eyes and languid mouth. He flipped back a few pages, certain he'd seen a sketch of George before. Sure enough, there he was, but different. His expression, though worried, was lucid in a way it wasn't in the second sketch. There had been life in him once, life that was utterly missing in the later portrayal.

She had said Blackburn plied his patients with concoctions that rendered them essentially empty. Seeing it for himself pierced his conscience. He reluctantly turned the pages, bracing himself for what he would see.

More empty eyes. More sagging features. He found sketches of what looked like prison cells, filth and squalor apparent in every image. She had drawn in tremendous detail shelves of tinctures, powders, and tisanes. She also included a sketch of a graveyard. Headstones overlapped bushes, an indication that the stones had been added after the sketch was first finished. Several more scenes depicted appalling conditions: patients crowded into small spaces, their clothing dirty and ragged. No one had shoes or stockings. Their features were pulled and gaunt.

He reached another drawing of Miriam, herself. In the bottom corner of this one she had noted the year "1876." Her face was too thin for health, with dark circles beneath hopeless eyes. She had aged. She was desperate. The difference between this image and the first was jarring. Horrifying. She had documented the impact of her imprisonment.

Gideon swallowed back the emotion that surged inside.

Blackburn Asylum had been slowly killing her. It had eaten away at her as surely as it had changed George, only more gradually. How long had she been away from the asylum before coming to Savage Wells? Had she arrived looking like this, Gideon would have been genuinely worried for her very life.

"Is something the matter, Gideon?"

He glanced at his father, but returned his attention almost immediately to the book. "Miriam's sketches. She has drawn in detail the conditions at Blackburn's asylum. It's horrifying."

Father crossed to him, looking over his shoulder. Gideon flipped to a few different depictions. He showed him the change in Miriam during her two years there, and the heartbreaking transformation in George. He showed him the squalor, the cemetery.

"Mercy," Father whispered. "How has this been so well hidden? I don't know a soul who would condone this."

"Nebraska is a bit far from the beaten path, easily overlooked. And people are often institutionalized specifically so they can be forgotten."

Father motioned to the notepad. "These sketches, if run with a well-written, meticulously accurate article, would raise a tremendous ruckus in Washington."

People would likely disapprove of the inhumanity of the arrangement, but who was to say it would be enough to close down the asylum altogether? It certainly wouldn't happen fast enough to save Miriam.

"Have you shown these to Mr. Bricks?" Father asked.

Gideon met his eye. "Does he care enough to be moved by them?"

"He is not the monster Blackburn is, though that is faint praise."

It was worth considering.

Gideon flipped back to the shelves of medicines. It was an odd thing for her to draw. Every other sketch was of people or entire rooms. Only these shelves and the cemetery fell outside of those two categories. The graveyard was, no doubt, meant to be an accounting of the people who hadn't survived their time at the asylum. There had to be a similar reason for the shelves.

"I don't recognize any of those bottles," Father said.

"We used a few at St. Elizabeth's, but others I can't immediately give a purpose to."

Father leaned a bit closer, eyeing the sketch. "Is that a bottle of strychnine?" He pointed at the bottom-most shelf.

Heavens, it was.

"What medicinal use does strychnine have?"

"None," Gideon said. "It's poison."

Yet Blackburn kept it on his shelves of medicines he gave his patients. This was the reason Miriam had included it.

"Blackburn is poisoning his patients," Gideon said quietly.

"Have you any proof beyond this sketchbook?" Father pressed.

Gideon shook his head. "But it's a direction to take." Anxious, hopeful, horrified, he flipped quickly ahead in the book. Doing so knocked a loose paper free. It floated down to his feet. He picked it up, and curiosity led him to unfold it.

A hand-drawn chart filled the page. The first column contained names. The second was labeled "Private Funding" and the third "Public Funding." Tick marks sat next to the names, nearly all of which were followed by two checks.

"Is he receiving payments from both families and the state?" Father asked, even as his eyes darted over the page.

"It certainly seems that way."

"This is very specific information," Father said. "It would

have to be verified, of course. This is not the original ledger, and she is not a disinterested party."

The fourth column was labeled "Passed." Perhaps a quarter of the rows had a check.

Passed. Passed what?

Father pointed to a line. "That name was on one of the headstones in her cemetery sketch." He pointed to another. "That one, as well."

Passed away. She had documented their deaths.

Column five was labeled "Death Reported." Not a single check.

"Blackburn isn't reporting their passing. Their families likely don't know, and neither does the state. He is still being paid double for all of them, even the ones who have died. The ones he has killed."

Father met his eye. "Fraud, on this large scale, must certainly warrant jail time. And if you can prove poisoning, he would likely face charges of murder as well."

"Proof is the issue, though." Gideon felt painfully close to the answers they needed to pry open Blackburn's grip, yet so far away at the same time. "Her word alone, even coupled with these images and information, isn't likely to be enough."

Father nodded. "Especially since Blackburn has worked so hard to discredit her."

"Which is doubly frustrating. Insisting she cannot be believed *before* she has a chance to speak the truth about him means that once she does, she is far less likely to be listened to."

Father paced away. "This must be why she hasn't told anyone about this yet. She knew if she revealed his perfidy, he would simply cry 'false accusation from a madwoman,' and she wouldn't be heard."

"I would have heard her," Gideon insisted.

"But you haven't the authority to do anything about it," Father countered.

There was truth in that. "Surely this is enough to at least delay Blackburn."

"I think it could be."

Gideon slipped the paper back inside the sketchbook. He took it carefully to his desk and set it in a drawer where it would be safe. "I will talk to Mr. Larsen in the morning."

"I'll wire a few of my associates in Washington, as well. We can start the process of an investigation."

The brief bit of hope he felt ebbed. "Miriam said she helped tend patients, that her nursing abilities were put to use."

"Yes?"

"Blackburn has to know that she is aware that he intentionally poisoned his patients. He knows she can incriminate him." Gideon rubbed at his face. "I'm certain this is why he was so eager to see her diagnosis stand. He would be far safer if she were back at the asylum where he could silence her without drawing attention."

"I very much fear you are correct, son."

"If we can't stop him," Gideon said, "Miriam and I will run for Canada. I don't mean to make that common knowledge, but I need you to know, you and Mother."

He nodded. "If fleeing proves necessary, we'll help you in any way we can, but don't give up hope. She has given us enough to turn the tables. Blackburn will soon be the one being hunted, and we will have more powerful weapons than he."

Chapter 38

"Judge Irwin is set to arrive today." Paisley stood in the storage room of the millinery, where Miriam had been brought. "It is imperative that you have a chance to speak to him without Blackburn there. We're going to sneak you around to the jailhouse. Blackburn is in town, though, so it'll be tricky."

"Can we manage it?" Evading capture had been far easier while she'd been hiding at Tansy's. Being so close to the man searching for her was riskier.

"Mrs. Fletcher, Mrs. Abbott, and Mrs. Clark are going to undertake a distraction by the hotel, where Blackburn and your father are. That should grant us enough cover to sneak you across the street and behind the buildings. Taking the back way to the jailhouse will be a simple enough thing after that."

Miriam took a fortifying breath and nodded. "How soon do we need to leave?"

Paisley peeked out of the room for a moment. "Only a minute more. Are you ready?"

"As ready as I can be."

Paisley motioned her out into the shop. Miriam followed close on her heels. Her heart pounded hard in her throat.

We have only to get across the street. Only that far. Surely they could manage that.

Paisley held a hand up to stop her a step away from door. Miriam held her breath as Paisley checked the street outside. With one hand hovering over her gun, Paisley waved her forward. The group of women stood outside the hotel, chattering loudly and animatedly. It wasn't much cover, but it would help.

Miriam and Paisley stepped off the boardwalk. Someone was running down the road toward them, waving his arms.

"Behind me," Paisley barked.

Miriam obeyed without hesitation.

The man proved to be Mr. Cooper. "He's not in there," he called out. "He's not there."

"What does—?" Miriam started.

Paisley cut off her question. "Blackburn. He isn't in the hotel."

Panic gripped Miriam as she searched every window, every front overhang. "Then where—?"

"Quick," Paisley said. "We need to get you out of sight."

They rushed off the road and behind Gideon's house, making their way toward the jailhouse. They were nearly there, nearly clear.

Dr. Blackburn stepped away from the back wall of the jailhouse. "Abetting a fugitive. You'll lose your badge for that."

"How do you know I haven't just apprehended her?" Paisley answered coolly.

"If that's true, then turn her over." Dr. Blackburn moved closer.

"You aren't the law," Paisley said. "I don't turn prisoners over to civilians."

His jaw tightened, and his eyes narrowed. "I have authority over all the inmates of my asylum, especially this one."

"I am a US deputy marshal," Paisley said. "You have no authority over me."

"Hand her over, or I will force you to."

Paisley actually smiled. "Try."

Quick as lightning, Dr. Blackburn pulled a gun and pointed it directly at Miriam. "Hold your hands up, *deputy*, or I'll drop her. I've the right to."

"Behind me, Miriam," Paisley said as she raised her arms.

"I won't make you my shield," Miriam said. "Your life is not worth mine."

"Come with me, Miss Bricks," Dr. Blackburn said. "We'll return you where you belong, without bloodshed—if you are cooperative."

"You cannot shoot an officer of the law," Miriam said. "You would never get away with it."

Dr. Blackburn shook his head in a show of pity. "There are no witnesses here but you and me, and only one of us is known to be mad. Afraid of being turned over, you shot Deputy O'Brien. I managed to apprehend you. A neat bow tied around an unfortunate package."

"She's not the only witness." Mr. Cooper had followed them off the road. "I'll speak for her."

"I have bullets enough for you, too," Dr. Blackburn spat.

"For me, too?" Mrs. Fletcher stepped up, surrounded by the other women who'd been outside the hotel.

"And me?" Andrew came around the far corner of the building, his gun drawn and pointed at Dr. Blackburn.

"No matter the number of bullets, you'll not be fast enough for me." Cade stood not far distant, his gun drawn as well.

"You cannot aid a fugitive," Dr. Blackburn insisted. "It is against the law."

"Too bad you ain't the law," Cade said.

Someone took Miriam's hand. Her first instinct was to yank free, but then she saw it was Gideon. He pulled her into the growing crowd. Before she could say a word, she was enveloped by a rush of townspeople and tucked out of sight.

"Hand her over," Dr. Blackburn growled.

"Lower your weapon," Cade instructed. "I've shot men for far less than this."

"All I need to do is tell the judge I was attempting to apprehend her because none of you would. No charge will ever stick."

"But a bullet will." Cade could be terrifying when he needed to be. "Hard to tell a judge anything when you're dead."

Through gaps in her wall of protectors, Miriam saw Dr. Blackburn shoved against the wall. Paisley took his gun. Cade handcuffed him.

"You'll lose your badges over this," Dr. Blackburn hissed. "And she'll still be coming with me. You can't stop that."

"A man who threatened the life of a deputy marshal is hardly in a position to simply waltz away from town." Cade yanked him away from the wall. "That'll have to be sorted out before anyone goes anywhere."

Dr. Blackburn turned his threatening glare on Miriam as he was dragged past. Gideon set his arms around her, a gesture of protection she needed in that moment. That had been too near a thing. If the townsfolk had not stepped up, the doctor would have killed Paisley. And then he likely would have killed her.

"If we'd known he was waiting for you, we never would have risked moving you," Gideon said.

"He was going to kill her," she whispered.

"He was going to kill *you*," Paisley said, having made her way through the crowd to where they stood. "None of us would have let him. Not without a fight."

Gideon kissed Miriam's temple, keeping her in his arms. "Your father's waiting in the jailhouse."

She looked up at him, fear flooding through her. "He's going to send me away?"

"I doubt that." He kept his arm around her back and led her toward the narrow alleyway between his house and the jail.

She received looks of encouragement from the people she passed. She hoped they could see her gratitude despite the worry she felt.

Dr. Blackburn was in the jailhouse, still roundly denouncing Cade, Paisley, and the town. When Miriam stepped inside, he turned his venom on her. "You will be coming with me, and you will answer for this. Mark my words."

Gideon led her to the desk, but his gaze focused in the other direction. "Does that sound like someone who has only her well-being in mind?"

Miriam followed his gaze. Her father sat at a round table, watching the events with wide eyes. Mr. and Mrs. MacNamara sat at the table, along with Mr. Larsen. Miriam's sketchbook lay open on the table in front of them.

"How did they get that?" she asked.

"You created quite a case against Blackburn in the pages of that book, Miriam," Gideon said. "Your father is hearing the details."

"The word of an imbecile cannot be trusted," Blackburn spat from his cell.

"Another outburst, and I'll cuff you to the banister outside," Cade said. "The town's still out there, and they're spittin' mad.

It'd be a shame if there were too many of them for me to stop them from . . . expressing their disapproval."

Mrs. MacNamara stood and crossed to them, looking them both over. "We heard this monster pulled a gun on you, my dear Miriam."

"He did," Gideon said. "Murder, it seems, is well within his wheelhouse." He looked over at Miriam. "But, then, you've known that for a while, haven't you?"

Her father held up the sketchbook. "Is all of this true, Miriam?"

"Does it matter?"

The answer clearly surprised him. "This indicates he was killing people."

"People sent to him to be forgotten," she countered. "We all knew why we were there. No one wanted us. What did it matter if he killed people whose own families wanted them to disappear?"

"I never—You needed help." It was the same argument Dr. Blackburn had used again and again.

"I needed someone to care what happened to me. I needed someone to recognize that a mind is like nearly any other part of the body. It doesn't have to be perfect to be good."

Gideon slipped his hand around hers.

"I needed you to see that I was more than this illness. That there was ample reason to be proud of me instead of ashamed. But you never saw any of that. You locked me up with a murderer, and even now that you know, I still have no confidence you won't insist upon returning me there."

Gideon, still holding her hand, stepped over to the table, bringing her with him.

"Miriam is a gifted nurse, quick to identify and address

issues, able to look at illnesses from multiple angles, and devoted to finding the *right* answer, not just an *easy* answer." Gideon faced her father directly. "The fact that she recorded in that book exactly the information needed to begin building a firm case against the man who was terrorizing her speaks to a whole and fully functioning mind. She could not do all she has done, nor survive all she has survived, if she were truly as mad as Dr. Blackburn has claimed."

Her father's eyes returned to the sketchbook. He didn't speak. He steepled his hands in front of him. His mouth pressed in a tight line.

"My other son, Ian, has already spoken with several people at the government agency that oversees asylums," Mr. Mac-Namara said. "An investigation into Blackburn Asylum will likely begin immediately. This information will, I am certain, be confirmed."

Dr. Blackburn grabbed the bars of his cell. "You can't do that."

Cade held up the handcuffs. "Are you wanting to be cuffed outside?"

Dr. Blackburn stepped back into his cell, pacing around the small space.

Mr. Larsen spoke next. "As Miss Bricks's legal counsel, I have drafted a very detailed letter, arguing that her diagnosis was made in error and with prejudice. Dr. MacNamara has assembled testimony from multiple colleagues denouncing that same diagnosis. That, coupled with the soon-to-be verified evidence that Dr. Blackburn is far from unbiased in this situation, might be enough to have her legal status reinstated."

Was that true? She looked to Gideon, but his attention was solely focused on her father.

"She doesn't belong in an institution," he said quietly. "You know she doesn't."

"But the seizures," Father said. "They're unpredictable. They can't be cured."

"There is a woman here in town who has a persistent cough, a man whose knee aches him at unpredictable intervals," Gideon said. "I have a brother whose reliance on spectacles 'can't be cured.' None of those things negates who they are or what they can accomplish."

Miriam pulled her hand from Gideon's and took the chair Mrs. MacNamara had vacated.

"I know that you worry what people will say and think and do if they ever witnessed one of my episodes," she said. "But I have no intention of ever returning to New York. No one there, no one who matters to you, will ever know of my condition. If you choose, no one need ever know of my existence. I can change my name, not speak of my early years to anyone, not even hint at having ever lived east of the Mississippi."

He met her eyes. "You would hide your identity?"

"To avoid returning to an asylum or dying in that man's custody"—she motioned to Dr. Blackburn—"I was ready to face the cruelty of the world alone, to abandon my nursing skills and the respectable employment it offered me. Pretending that I have no family would hurt, but I am ready for that."

"I saw your drawings of your brothers and sisters, of your mother and me," Father said. "You never drew yourself with us."

"I knew I wasn't considered part of the family after your first attempt to have me institutionalized," she said. "That didn't mean I didn't miss all of you, that I didn't wish things were different, that I didn't wish you weren't ashamed of me."

"It wasn't just about embarrassment," he said quietly. "I didn't know how to help you."

"But you *can* help me now." How she prayed he would. "Let me stay here in this town where the people love me and care about me. Let me be free."

Chapter 39

"We have testimonials from twelve different doctors who are in complete agreement with Dr. MacNamara's opinion that Miss Bricks's diagnosis of madness is unjustified," Mr. Larsen told Judge Irwin. "Three of the testimonials denouncing the diagnosis outright are from doctors for whom Miss Bricks previously worked."

Miriam wasn't sure she would ever grow accustomed to hearing herself discussed so impersonally. But, if the day went well, this would be the last time she would endure this.

Mr. Larsen held up the written testimonials, emphasizing his words with flicks of the papers. "These men of medicine who know her personally, who are aware of her medical condition, do not, as a matter of professional opinion, believe she is mad."

"But Dr. Parnell, as a matter of professional opinion, believed she *was*." Judge Irwin had shown himself hard-nosed. But he had opened the hearing with the promise that, if they presented sound arguments, he would listen with an open mind.

Mr. Larsen was unshaken by Judge Irwin's rejoinder. "Dr. Parnell sent four different patients to Dr. Blackburn. That is a higher number than any other admitting physician. The same investigators who are looking into the possibility that Dr. Blackburn was involved in both fraud and murder are also investigating Dr. Parnell."

Miriam hadn't heard that. Could Dr. Parnell have been part of the scheme from the beginning?

"The only physician corroborating Dr. Parnell's diagnosis is Dr. Blackburn himself, who is currently in the custody of the US marshal over Wyoming Territory on account of his having held two law enforcement officers and several people in town at gunpoint while repeatedly threatening lives. Is his word to be given equal weight in this matter as those of physicians without his very questionable history?"

The judge didn't have a ready response.

"We must, Your Honor, bear in mind that the case against Dr. Blackburn relies heavily upon evidence Miss Bricks uncovered, casting further doubt about his motivation in keeping her in his asylum."

Judge Irwin nodded ponderously.

Mr. Larsen was quiet as a rule, withdrawn, and more than a little mysterious, but he was inarguably good at what he did. Miriam couldn't account for his decision to settle in a place where he couldn't possibly make a living, when he might have worked for any number of prestigious firms back East, but she was deeply grateful that he'd chosen the life he had.

"Sheriff Cade O'Brien and Deputy Andrew Gilbert, along with US Deputy Marshal Paisley O'Brien, have all testified that Miss Bricks is an invaluable and contributing member of this town. US Marshal John Hawking, who has interacted with a good number of criminals who were violently unstable by *anyone's* estimation, has testified that Miss Bricks in no way resembles those individuals, and has staked his reputation on his belief that she is not a threat to anyone, including herself."

Miriam sat at the table with Mr. Larsen, facing the judge. Her friends and supporters were behind her. Gideon sat among them. She wished she could see them all, gauge their reaction to this final argument. As it was, her only barometer was Judge Irwin's reaction, and he played his cards too close to the chest for any reliable evaluation.

"You set us a difficult task," Mr. Larsen said, "and for good reason. This is not a decision which ought to be made in haste, as the consequences of making a mistake are enormous. Your Honor, Miss Bricks has already spent two years paying the price of an incorrect diagnosis, an unwarranted incarceration, and an unjustified stripping away of her legal rights. It is time she was given back her life."

What would that be like? Her illness and its subsequent complications had controlled every aspect of her life for years.

"Marshal Hawking." Judge Irwin eyed Hawk over his spectacles. "You are certain Miss Bricks presents no safety concerns?"

"I've not a single doubt," he answered.

"Dr. MacNamara." Judge Irwin's gaze shifted. "You are certain Miss Bricks is in full possession of her faculties?"

"I am certain," Gideon answered.

"Mr. Larsen, I am charging you with providing a detailed accounting of all the evidence you provided today. I do not wish for this day's decision to ever be called into question."

"Of course, Your Honor," Mr. Larsen said.

"Miss Bricks, would you please approach?"

Miriam took in a deep breath and rose. She moved with slow, slightly unsteady steps around the table and to the space directly in front of Judge Irwin.

"You have some fierce champions, Miss Bricks." The judge took off his spectacles and laid them on the desk. "The law is not kind in matters of lunacy, which makes this a difficult case."

Was this his way of telling her the appeal had not been successful?

"I will confess, I came here having already heard testimony on your behalf," Judge Irwin said.

"I don't believe I know anyone in Laramie."

Judge Irwin shook his head. "From a stage driver, who, upon hearing that Savage Wells was my final destination, praised to the heavens a Nurse Bricks who had helped save his wife's life. Apparently, he now has enough money to take her for a surgery you discovered she needed."

"Mrs. Driessen." She breathed out the name. "They are going for the surgery?" She spun around to look at Gideon with a happy smile. "The Driessens are going to get the surgery."

"Oh, hallelujah," Gideon answered with a matching smile.

"Miss Bricks." The judge's tone was both impatient and amused.

She turned back to him. "My apologies, Your Honor."

He nodded. "Mr. Driessen spoke at length of your thoroughness, your competency, the depth of your understanding and effort. I found myself wondering how someone with the degree of your supposed madness could manage all of that."

Gruff and difficult Mr. Driessen had helped her without even realizing it.

"Then I arrived, only to be accosted by an almost constant stream of people pleading your case, telling me how much you are valued and needed here." Judge Irwin tapped his fingertips together. "I was particularly moved by the pleadings of one Rupert

Fletcher. None of their arguments are legally binding, of course, but they do paint a very vivid picture of you."

"This is a wonderful town," she said. "And these are wonderful people."

"And Mr. Larsen, as it turns out, is wonderfully thorough," the judge said. "He's made an excellent argument, one that even the disproportionate leanings of the law cannot dismiss out of hand, both in the matter of your particular circumstances and the situation at Blackburn Asylum, which is already being addressed in Nebraska."

"The other patients at Blackburn Asylum," she said. "What will happen to them while the matter of Dr. Blackburn's behavior and violations is decided? I am worried for them."

An unexpected softness entered the judge's expression.

"I realize that matter is not in your hands," she continued, "but do you have any indication that their welfare is being considered, that someone reliable and compassionate and capable is looking after them?" She had fought for those poor souls for two years; she would not abandon them.

"It is my understanding, Miss Bricks, that the state, now made aware of the ongoing abuses there, has appointed a new doctor. In addition, someone from the state and an observer from Washington will take over the supervision of the asylum."

She took a shaky breath. "They will be cared for? Someone will advocate for them?"

"I have every confidence they will be," Judge Irwin said.

Relief rushed over her.

"Likewise," the judge said, "based on the testimony I have heard and the sound legal arguments made by Mr. Larsen, I can, with confidence, revoke the legalities connected to your diagnosis and return to you the rights stripped from you because of it."

He was overturning her diagnosis. Shock made it almost impossible to even comprehend.

"I spoke with Mr. Bricks before this trial," Judge Irwin continued. "He said that if I were presented with enough evidence to revoke your diagnosis, then he would revoke his authorization."

Father would release her if the judge deemed her not mad? Was that what had just happened? Had she just been given her freedom? She did not dare believe it.

"Your Honor?" Mr. Larsen pressed.

"Miss Bricks's legal status is returned to what it was before her diagnosis. And Mr. Bricks's agreement to withdraw his confinement authorization means she is free to go."

Her heart leapt to her throat. "Truly?" She nearly choked on the word.

Judge Irwin smiled, the first time she'd seen him do that. "Truly."

"Thank you, Your Honor."

He nodded once, then looked over at Mr. Larsen. "We're done here."

Miriam's sigh of relief was drowned out by the chorus of hoorahs and shouts of triumph from the people gathered behind her. She returned to Mr. Larsen's table. He was sitting down, gathering papers.

"Thank you," Miriam said. "I could not have hoped to succeed in this matter without you."

He silently nodded, not meeting her eye, not looking up from his papers. Gone was the eloquent man who'd so expertly pleaded her case.

In another moment, Gideon was at her side.

"We did it, Miriam," he said, throwing his arms around her and spinning her about. "We did it!"

She could not hold back a triumphant grin. "I never thought this day would come. I've been hiding from this for so many years."

"No more hiding, dear." Excitement pulsed through his words and lit his expression. "You are free."

She clung to him, unsure if she was more likely to grow weak with relief or begin trembling with excitement. "Free," she whispered.

He kissed her forehead, holding her close. His parents stood nearby, watching with nearly identical smiles of approval.

"Thank you," she said, knowing they'd played a role in her deliverance.

"Our pleasure, sweetheart," Mr. MacNamara said.

Miriam, still wrapped in Gideon's arms, turned to Paisley and Cade. "And thank you."

Paisley smiled. Cade nodded.

She turned her gaze to Hawk, but he held up a hand to forestall her. "Helping people is why I took this job."

"But you went above and beyond for me. That deserves an expression of gratitude."

The tiniest hint of a smile crossed his features. "You're the first person in a long time who hasn't firmly decided I'm hard-hearted."

"I would wager I won't be the last," she said.

Hawk popped his black hat on his head. "Well, I've a territory to protect. I'll leave Doc, there, to plan your celebration."

She looked at Gideon. "Are you planning a celebration?"

"Oh, my dear, I am planning a great many things."

"Dearly beloved . . ."

Gideon remembered all too well that the last time those words had been spoken in Savage Wells, Miriam had fled the building at a dead run. This time, she stood serenely beside him, holding a bouquet in her hands. Her family had not chosen to attend the ceremony, but Gideon's brothers had both arrived in the last twenty-four hours, joining his parents, who meant to make their long-delayed return to Washington after the ceremony.

Gideon's brothers were happy for him, and they had fallen instantly in love with Miriam. They insisted on calling her their sister.

"I have a family again," she had said in a tone of awe the evening before. "I have a family."

The ceremony flew by in a blur. The hoots and hollers that followed the pronouncement of "Man and Wife" brought grins to his brothers' faces. They were used to the decorum and fine manners of the East Coast. The rough-and-tumble West was utterly foreign to them.

The weather was fine, likely one of the last truly nice days left before winter would arrive, so the town and guests spilled out onto the grassy area surrounding the building with every intention of enjoying a wide assortment of cakes, punch, pies, and cookies.

Miriam saw to it that Mr. Bell had a comfortable seat, a plate heaped with goodies, and Andrew sitting nearby, before rejoining Gideon, who stood next to Mother and Father. Gideon slipped his arm around Miriam's waist, holding her to his side. She fit so perfectly there.

"Always a nurse, aren't you, my dear?"

"He is growing more distant and more easily confused," she

said. "I want him to pass the remainder of his time comforted and happy."

"I want you to be happy as well," Gideon said.

"I am, my sweet Gideon. I am."

He kissed her, unabashedly and in full view of the gathering. It was their wedding day, after all. Affection was definitely permitted, if not encouraged.

The townspeople passed by to offer their love and congratulations. What a change from her initial arrival in Savage Wells: she had been afraid, and the town had been suspicious. His feelings were entirely changed as well. He'd intended her to be nothing more than a work associate, a convenient wife to help with his patients and offer some conversation and companionship.

He hadn't anticipated loving her so entirely.

She slipped from his side to embrace Paisley. Gideon shook Cade's hand.

"Congratulations, my friend. I'm happy for you," Cade said.

"I'm happy for myself." Gideon couldn't keep his gaze away from his new bride. *Bride.* It was almost too good to be true.

"Ladies and gentlemen, your attention please." Father's voice boomed out over the gathering. "If you'll indulge us, the MacNamara family has an offering to make."

"I like that," James, Gideon's middle brother, called out. "*The family* has an offering that only Ian and I are required to make."

What were his brothers up to? Ian emerged with his violin, James with his clarinet.

"We understand this is a favorite," Ian said, with a wink in Miriam's direction.

"I suspect your brothers are a handful." Miriam spoke with clear amusement.

"They are trouble, is what they are."

But a moment later, they struck up the strains of "Gentle Annie," and he pulled her into a dancing position. "Will you dance with me, my darling?"

"Always," she answered.

Around and around they danced, as the town watched with smiles and tenderness. His parents could not have looked more pleased. Mr. Bell paid them no heed, his attention focused on his plate, distracted but no longer frightened and desperate. Andrew, however, watched them with a smile, openly happy. He, who had hidden so much of himself these past years, was slowly finding himself once more.

Miriam had played a vital role in the transformations around them. He would spend the rest of his life thanking the heavens for her and doing all he could to ensure her contentment and joy.

The festivities continued for hours, with no end in sight. Dancing became more general. Others took up the task of providing music. Miriam sat in Gideon's arms, watching as the town celebrated. Though she was clearly happy, she also looked tired.

"We should go home, my dear."

She sighed. "Home. I love the sound of that. I've been without one for so long."

"You never will be again." He kissed her quickly as they rose. Goodbyes were made, and expressions of appreciation for the party in their honor.

As they passed the jailhouse, he kissed the top of her head. "I think I need to write a letter thanking the Western Women's Bureau."

"*Thank* them?"

"Profusely," he said. "If they hadn't sent you here, I never would have met you. And if I'd never met you, I never would have fallen in love with you."

"I, for one, am glad you did."

They reached the front porch of their home. *Their home.* Gideon paused at the door. "And I am *beyond* glad." He faced her, his heart swelling with gratitude and hope and love. "I am deliriously happy."

She brushed the pads of her fingers along his jaw. "So am I."

He wrapped his hand around hers, sliding it to his lips, and kissing her fingers. "Have I told you often enough that I love you?"

Her gaze was soft, tender. "I would not object to hearing it again."

He closed the small gap between them, holding her close to him. With his forehead pressed to hers, he whispered, "I love you, Miriam MacNamara. I love you with every breath I take."

She tipped her head and kissed him lightly. "And I love you."

Gideon bent, pressing his lips to hers, warm and inviting. Her hands slid over his shoulders. Her arms folded around his neck. The chill of late fall disappeared as he held her, kissed her, cherished her. Years of loneliness faded away, replaced with the abiding promise of forever.

"May I carry you across the threshold, Mrs. MacNamara?"

"I would have to refuse to go inside, otherwise."

How he loved seeing her so joyous and lighthearted.

He lifted her into his arms. "Welcome home, my love. Welcome home."

Home. At last.

Acknowledgments

My sincerest thanks to the following—

Joan, Dave, and a contributor who wished to remain anonymous for offering insights, discussions, and feedback to help me write Miriam's health-related experiences more accurately and sensitively. You were invaluable.

Pam Victorio and Bob Diforio for being the greatest team an author could hope for. Your support, insights, and encouragement make all the difference.

The team at Shadow Mountain for getting this story polished up and out into the world. I couldn't be happier to be returning to the town of Savage Wells, and I am grateful to have the chance.

My family, for being endlessly supportive, reminding me to go to bed, accepting frozen dinners, cleaning up, and loving me in the midst of the chaos.

Discussion Questions

1. After experiencing the pain of two rejections, Gideon decides he won't gamble his heart again and instead will choose a loveless but, he hopes, respectful marriage. In what ways do we sometimes make poor decisions in the hope of avoiding disappointment or heartache?
2. Miriam waits until Dr. Blackburn's arrival to tell Gideon the entirety of her history and the true danger of her situation. Why do you think she didn't reveal it sooner? Should she have? What might have helped her feel safe enough to do so?
3. Gideon's parents have a less-than-happy marriage. In what ways do you think this influenced Gideon's feelings toward matrimony and his journey to find his own happiness?
4. The town struggles to warm up to Miriam, feeling they are being loyal to Gideon by rejecting her. Can you think of instances in your own life when you struggled to change someone's first impression of you or when you changed your initial feelings about someone else?
5. Miriam's skill as a nurse is helpful not only to Gideon but also to Andrew and Mr. Bell. What difference do you think

her continued presence in their lives will make for them and their families?

6. Gideon has kept his talent for and love of the cello hidden from the town, fearing they will ridicule him for something he cherishes. What does his willingness to share this part of his life with the people around him reveal about how he has grown and changed? What does it tell us about his feelings for Miriam?

7. Andrew makes tremendous strides in this book in healing from and dealing with what would today be diagnosed as PTSD. Do you think he will continue to do so? What do you think his future will be?

8. Mental institutions in the mid-nineteenth century were little better than prisons. The treatment of those committed to asylums was often horrendous and inhumane. In what ways do we, today, still allow the stigma of mental illness to justify mistreating those who experience it?

9. At this time, women had very few rights. This was especially true in the area of mental health. Women could, as Miriam explains, be institutionalized for almost any reason, even without an official medical diagnosis. How do you think this powerlessness impacted Miriam's willingness to open up about her past and trust the people around her? What impact do you think it had on her decision to run from town even though her loved ones had promised to help her?

10. What do you imagine for the future of the people of Savage Wells? How will life change for them in the years to come? What do you hope will stay the same?

About the Author

SARAH M. EDEN is the author of several well-received historical romances. Her previous Proper Romance novel *Longing for Home* won the Foreword Reviews 2013 IndieFab Book of the Year award for romance. *Hope Springs* won the 2014 Whitney Award for "Best Novel of the Year" and *The Sheriffs of Savage Wells* was a Foreword Reviews 2016 Book of the Year finalist for romance.

Combining her obsession with history and an affinity for tender love stories, Sarah loves crafting witty characters and heartfelt romances. She happily spends hours perusing the reference shelves of her local library and dreams of one day traveling to all the places she reads about. Sarah is represented by Pam Victorio at D4EO Literary Agency.

Visit Sarah at www.sarahmeden.com.

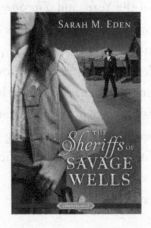